The Hendersons

The Hendersons

Daphne Glazer

**TOP HAT
BOOKS**

Winchester, UK
Washington, USA

First published by Top Hat Books, 2016
Top Hat Books is an imprint of John Hunt Publishing Ltd., Laurel House, Station Approach,
Alresford, Hants, SO24 9JH, UK
office1@jhpbooks.net
www.johnhuntpublishing.com
www.tophat-books.com

For distributor details and how to order please visit the 'Ordering' section on our website.

Text copyright: Daphne Glazer 2015

ISBN: 978 1 78535 404 5
Library of Congress Control Number: 2015960689

A CIP catalogue record for this book is available from the British Library.

Design: Stuart Davies

Printed and bound by CPI Group (UK) Ltd, Croydon, CR0 4YY, UK

We operate a distinctive and ethical publishing philosophy in all
areas of our business, from our global network of authors to
production and worldwide distribution.

Part I

Chapter One

William stropped his razor, and with a lovely flourish, made it sing through the planes of black bristle. Its passage cleared a neat pink strip in the hillocks of white lather. Half of him concentrated on the deft strokes of the razor and half on some mighty tumbling words for his sermon.

And shall we build the New Jerusalem? Or shall we simply pretend that the work houses are not crammed with pitifully poor people; that others are starving. Yes, do you know that in this very city, in this your city ... a proud ...

"Heighup!"

"What's the matter then?" William's big dreamer's eyes flipped wide with feigned surprise.

"You nearly had me nose off!"

"Go on with you, Alec! You've been coming here twice a week for years and I've never got you yet." William rumbled with laughter.

Alec, a foundry-man, even had his own shaving mug with his name printed on it. William liked to try out ideas on Alec who'd generally respond with a show of garrulousness.

Wrenched from the passion of building a celestial city, William negotiated the flaps of Alec's nostrils, taking care not to nick them. But he was soon off again.

It is only if we stand together that we shall achieve this ... only if ... No, that wouldn't do, it was too weak, too boring. You had to win them over, make them feel with you—

"Getting a bit thin on top, Alec."

"Aye, it's me worries."

"And what are they?"

"Moving and such like and Bertha's in the family way again."

After William had finished some dexterous snipping, he took an ebony-handled brush, dusted his customer's thick, mottled

2

neck, and whisked the white towel away, another one for Lydia to wash in the basement kitchen below the shop. The whole place smelled of washing. It was a warm suddy odour and it mixed with the dinner smells: Monday's boiled potatoes, cold meat and rice pudding or sago; Tuesday's stew; Wednesday's soup; Thursday's feast. Thursday being half-day closing was jollification day and the joint would sizzle in the baking tin, wafting the savoury scent of roast mutton through the snipping of the scissors and the forays into politics and the sermons.

And greater things than these shall ye do. What challenges are laid down, what possibilities remain unfulfilled? The meek shall inherit the earth, the Lord said ... and yet we would smite our brethren. The meek ... how can we ...? It didn't hang together, wouldn't work out. Anxiety gnawed at his chest. Things weren't moving right. There was an angry ripple under the surface. It seemed very hot and sticky in the shop. Sweat blistered his nose and forehead. Another fly got its feet stuck to the strip of adhesive; that would stop its caper!

"You're a bit quiet today, William," Alec Ford said, settling his cap on his head and handing the barber his money.

"Am I?" William grinned. "You're not used to it, are you?"

William, in his white barber's smock, went to stand on the doorstep and watch his customer dipping and swaying as he made off down the steep grey hill. It was a brilliant day and the lines of stone houses hedged in the heat; August 1st, the eve of the Bank Holiday, always a frantic time. He'd been working since eight that morning and would probably continue until 11pm; Saturdays were always busy anyway. People greeted him and he nodded in recognition. He knew they called him a little Jew boy because of his mass of greying pan-scrubber hair and his sallow skin. They probably wondered about Lydia too. The unsteadiness of the day was causing all manner of pictures to slide into his head: Lydia as he'd first seen her, a tall girl with dense shadowy skin and her jetty hair in a coronet of plaits.

She'd looked foreign, not a local woman at all, and he'd wanted her so that he trembled.

"My belly feels as though its throat's cut," Joe said, appearing at his elbow. William had dispatched his middle son on an errand. Joe had started work as a lather boy but had now graduated to cutting, though William gimleted him whenever the boy's scissors approached a customer's ear. Joe joked his way along. Of course he lacked his elder brother Matthew's blade-like intellect. William had shot down to the headmaster's office, when Matthew turned thirteen. He wasn't going to let the school use Matthew as an unpaid teacher for Standard 8. In the end they'd let him leave, and ever since he'd been employed in the offices of the steel giant, Brown and Unwin.

"Brush round in there, can you, lad?" he instructed Joe. He lingered, staring out. *What if war did break out? What if after all …?* He lurched on the worn step with its proud line of 'Blanco', but then righted himself. *But it wouldn't. Though what if?* You had only to look at Firth Browns and Henshaws and Brown and Unwins and the other steel firms thriving in Attercliffe to know they weren't producing all those armaments for nothing. Sheffield meant steel, but no longer merely steel for cutlery. Now it was steel for bayonets.

"Who's ready for fish and chips?"

It was Amy, the youngest, the only girl, his pet. She'd come through the shop. Turning to look at her, he had to smile. No bigger than three penn'orth of copper and her long dark plait dithered like a fish tail. She'd tied it with a big lilac bow. Enthusiasm sparked from her. She lived life at a gallop. He knew Lydia wished she'd been ladylike and interested in clothes, but she wasn't.

"It's warm," he sighed, "the lull before the storm."

"What sort of storm?"

"Never can tell. Might as well shut shop for half an hour, it is one. Come on lad," he called through to Joe.

The white pot weekday plates stood on the big deal table and the fish and chips steamed. The four of them sat down and were joined presently by Bob. He was little and charming and a couple of years older than Amy. He dropped a kiss behind his mother's ear.

"For this and all thy mercies, we thank thee, Lord, amen," William said. He ate the meal largely in silence as he continued to struggle with his Sunday School sermon for the next day. Reverend Price had been hawking in his throat and aheming plenty of late as though he wanted to tell William something. In the beginning he had been pleased at the idea of William's Sunday evening class but gradually his enthusiasm had diminished in direct proportion to the school's growth in pupils. William had toured all the homes in the area asking young men whether they'd like to attend. *Perhaps I could have a word, er ... William?*

Well, perhaps he could.

"I'll love you and leave you," William said. "Must get back to the shop."

Lydia nodded and smiled, pushing a strand of dark hair behind her ear.

"Me too," Amy said.

"I'll walk part way with you." Bob grinned. He and Amy were best friends.

* * *

"Here's for an afternoon of my exquisite copper-plate – George Johnson Esquire," Amy growled in a throaty voice.

"Miss Penelope Riddler." Bob joined in fruitily.

"I had a good job and I left, I left, I left!" Amy chanted, striding out to the rhythm of the words. Bob brought his foot down hard in time. "I was arguing in the office this morning," Amy said.

"Tut tut."

"About the Suffragettes. Mr Copeland said Emily Davison was a fool and she'd killed King George's colt. At that I'm afraid I flew at him. He looked at me in surprise. You see, he thinks I'm just a quiet little thing, there to put names on envelopes and nothing else. He practically dropped his pince-nez. And what do you know about Suffragettes, Miss Henderson, a nice young lady like you? You'd be surprised, Mr Copeland. I think Emily Davison was a martyr. You know, Bob, I've pondered on it ever since. I mean about Emily Davison's death, and when I do, goose-pimples shoot up on my arms. It was the bravest, noblest thing you can think of."

By this time they'd reached J.G. Graves. "See you tonight," Amy said.

* * *

Bob carried on back to Browns where he had some work to finish off. He looked at the huge brick frontage. On one level, you could have said it was ugly but it had its own allure. There was beauty in the machinery: the firm's private railway-siding, the trucks of pig-iron, the long high shed housing the Siemen's furnace and casting pit, the rolling mills, boiler house and hammers, the crucible furnaces and the file-cutting room. In its entirety it was redolent of power. It was only when he thought of the products being churned out here, that he began to feel uncertain. What if his father was right and a war was threatening? But surely not.

In the office Bob composed letters for firms in France and Germany. "We can quote you for Ultra Super-spring Steel …" He looked out of the window at the sun blazing from a milky sky and catching the mica in the heaps of coal waiting to be carted to the foundry. Down there in the yard it was quiet. They had run to a halt for the Bank Holiday weekend. The pubs would be packed. When you passed their open doors you'd smell the flat yeasty odour that made you think of poverty. A man crossed the yard lugging a handcart, his features obscured by grime. It was tedious, heavy work, very long hours for low pay. No wonder they needed the beer. He thought fleetingly of his mother. She'd worked for a cutlery firm before her marriage. The acid they used on the knives had pitted the skin on her hands permanently. Lots of things like that ... Mother's fine hands with their filbert nails and slender fingers reddened and flawed by factory work and endless hours in the basement kitchen washing towels and preparing big meals. Joe knew 'The Song of a Shirt' by heart and would recite it at Christmas until Matty bellowed at him to shut up. Stitch, stitch ... it was also rub, rub, polish, grind.

All these people bullied and shoved about, it made you sick to the heart. The chap pushing the cart slouched back for another load. The first socialist was Christ, his dad said.

"Henderson, have you done the letters for Goetzen yet?"

"I'm just on with it now, Mr Seebrooke."

He resented being penned in there in the heat when he would have far preferred to be out in the open air, roaming the countryside, but it was Sunday tomorrow and Bank Holiday Monday to follow with all the joys of being free to walk and talk and dream. And yet even in the midst of his satisfaction at the prospect of two whole days' release from Browns, he still felt an ominous sense of foreboding. It was as though they were all waiting for a catastrophe. *There's been such a rush on food*, his mother had said, *I got down to Dingwalls first thing and all the sugar had gone. They're charging 8d and more now for a loaf and you wouldn't believe how they're buying up cheese and bacon – butter as well. Anybody would think we were getting ready for a siege.*

* * *

When he arrived home from work, he found his mother baking for Sunday. The fire roared in the Yorkshire range and her usually sallow cheeks had flushed bright pink. She was kneading dough in the big bread pansion, her flesh vibrating with the effort.

"Here, I'll have a go." Sweating, Bob took off his jacket and rolled up his shirt-sleeves. His mother stood back, smiling. He enjoyed the elasticity of the huge white mushroom. It clung to his fingers and then fell away as he pounded it on the floured table-top. The kitchen was all sepia after the brilliance outside. Lines of baking trays stood ready. She would produce bread-cakes, fat-cakes, tea-cakes, doughnuts, and currant bread – all manner of mouth-watering treats.

"They're very busy in the shop," his mother said, "your dad and Joe. Matty and Amy aren't back yet."

Bob knew he ought to volunteer to help; he'd often worked as lather boy when he was younger, but he didn't want to. They'd be going over the same old ground. *Oh yes, you watch, there'll be a civil war over there in Ireland – got to watch out for them bs—* The customer would dry up. Everyone knew that William Henderson didn't allow swearing in his shop.

And so as the twilight gathered, Bob sat on the back step. The city fell away below their terrace, and he looked at its grey outline which grew mysterious in the dusk. Soon the lamplighter would come. He wondered at the lives in those houses. Most of the men would be out at the pub more than likely and the children would play in the street until it was too dark to see, and then the moon would come up.

In the house with the blue door and window frames Elizabeth Stanley would be sewing or looking after her younger sisters, or just staring out and dreaming. She had a lovely profile, pure and cameo-like and she wore her honey-coloured hair up. Casual curls drifted down her cheeks and caught in the collar of her high-necked blouse.

Only last evening he had seen her, though it seemed an age ago. In the Bach she'd turned to smile at him. He had looked along the line of women repeatedly meeting her gaze. Their glances had been playing games for months, and he knew she was attracted to him. He could tell from the way she lingered after rehearsals, always glad to walk home with him. She was different from every woman in that choir, but he could not have said why. The saunter along with her, the strains of the St. Matthew Passion sounding in his ears, made him overflow with a kind of ecstasy. She had been at his side and he had turned to address a remark to her and seen the swell of her breasts beneath her white cotton blouse. The collar of his shirt had felt choking. He'd had to look away. He could scarcely believe that on Bank Holiday Monday he would be with her again when she and two cousins and he and his mates would go for a walk in Rivelin Valley. He imagined how it would be to wander down a country-lane with her in the dusk, hearing the weird voices of owls and smelling the greenness of fields and hedgerows. At night everything became more poignant. His earlier melancholy mood evaporated and now he was caught up in sweet longing, which deepened as he watched the lights flowering below him in the grey-stone terraces.

Chapter Two

The moment had arrived. William knew it as soon as Reverend Price's hand flapped in his direction. "Er ... William, could you stay behind for a few minutes?" The congregation streamed out at the end of the Sunday morning service.

It was very cool and gloomy in Holy Trinity Church and William walked beside the Reverend down the centre aisle, listening to the rustle and slap of his vestments.

"Er, William, I've been wanting to have an, er, chat with you for some time."

"Oh yes."

"It's your evening school. Now, I'd like you to bring all the young men into my service afterwards."

"I'll certainly mention it to them, but there's just one snag though, Reverend, they may not be willing to come and we can hardly force them. After all we're talking about things of a spiritual nature."

William could see that the Reverend was having trouble with the word 'spiritual' and felt that the ground had grown spongy.

"Well, in which case ..." Reverend Price's cheeks reddened, his gaze vanishing over William's left shoulder.

William waited for him to say it, make a definite complaint, but Reverend P. was too clever. Rumours must have been circulating. They were on a collision course: the parson's traditional views and William's 'New Theology' which questioned the Immaculate Conception. *The letter's not important*, William wanted to say, *it's the spirit that reigns supreme*. The words rang in his head so loudly, he thought he had spoken them. When he had tried before to explain to the Reverend what he felt, the other man had drawn himself up like a chunk of marble. *You have to be careful you are not committing a heresy, William*, he had said, and there the matter had been closed.

"I shall expect to see you this evening, then."

"I will try to get them to come."

"Very well." Reverend Price scratched the patch of eczema near his mouth.

Somewhere at the back of it lay a menace. The parson's eyes flicked away. Where would it end? William heard his stomach growling at the thought of a nasty scene. It would be made worse because the parson invariably side-stepped issues and never approached head on.

The rest of the family had waited outside. Lydia gave him an enquiring look but he contented himself with nodding. "Just about the Sunday School," he said.

They hadn't walked far when they came to a big open air meeting. It had an unusual atmosphere about it. The crowd, men in dark Sunday suits and hats, and with a sprinkling of women, stood in absolute silence to listen. Two young men dominated a make-shift wooden stage. The taller addressed the gathering.

"Comrades," he was saying, "you can be sure that your labour leaders will exhort you to fight to save democracy. Your leaders in the church will exhort you to fight in the names of the Prince of Peace ..."

"It's an ILP meeting," William said.

At that moment some fierce heckling broke out in the crowd. "Save your breath," someone bellowed, "let's talk about Ireland."

"We'd better move on," William pronounced, mindful of Lydia and Amy, and so they left the scene.

"I wanted to hear more," Amy wheedled, "can't we stay?"

"No, Bits, it could get nasty and I don't want you and your mother involved."

* * *

Sunday tea was the nicest meal of the week. It was set out in the parlour on the dark red chenille cloth, partially covered by a white lace square. Crusty bread and yellow margarine to begin, followed by orange jelly and custard. After these they fell upon the doily-covered glass cake-stands where jam tarts, butterfly buns, currant buns, fruit loaf and a Victoria sandwich dusted with icing sugar waited. Their hands swooped and tried not to appear too eager. They could have finished the lot.

"Oh what a grub-shift!" Joe said, patting his belly.

* * *

Amy still dawdled over her bread and marge. She couldn't shake free of that moment when she'd seen the man addressing the crowd. How could he have been so confident? He'd stood there, looking earnestly into their faces and it had been as though he were addressing every one of them personally. He was extraordinarily tall, a real streak of lightning. The spellbinding effect he exerted on everybody lay partly in the sweetness of his expression and in his complete lack of anything you might have called reserve. He hadn't spoken with a local accent. Would he have come from London? She wondered what would have happened to him and she shuddered in the heat. What did it all mean? Until that day, Sundays had all been the same with Mother's ample teas, church and Sunday School, and later hymn-singing at the piano. These were permanence, a settled state. But what if it came to fighting? She glanced at the faces around her: Bob, next to her, then Matty, whose friends called him Crippen after the murderer, because his pale eyes behind their wire-framed spectacles had a concentrated gleam which some might find unnerving. Joe sat by Matty. She felt the skin on her forearms growing cold. Again she looked round the room, as though to reassure herself of its continuing existence. On the mantelpiece sat the white-faced clock set in black marble and flanked by twin marble pyramids, which were inset with all manner of gilt and mother of pearl hieroglyphics. Shaggy horned cattle lumbered down to a brackish pool to drink. The family photographs stared back from the chiffonier and on the over-mantel an array of bevelled mirrors winked cheerfully at her, reflecting her dark hair and here and there a hand.

"What did the man mean?" she asked her father at last.

Amy watched her father's gaze rise from contemplating a jam tart. "That there's going to be a war," he said.

In that instant everything became highly charged: they were no longer dealing with the family and the church and Sunday tea and days at J.G. Graves addressing envelopes, and two evenings a week night school. Now the world, the universe was beginning to obtrude itself upon this personal life.

Amy noticed Bob staring out of the open window. She could hear a blackbird singing and the voices of children playing along the terraces. She could tell Bob's thoughts were elsewhere. *I bet it's that lass in the choir,* she thought, *and she's not his sort at all. And Joe's setting his cap at her as well ... it won't come to any good. She's not got much between her ears. Both of them, eyes like gob-stoppers staring after her ...*

* * *

Bob woke early and peered through the bedroom nets – *just let it be a fine day.* Rain would spoil everything. Mist spread a webby veil over the road. Later it should burn through and be really hot. They were to meet at one o'clock and that meant he'd a whole morning to live through before he would see her. He supposed he ought to get down to some French and German night class homework, and he did take his books into the parlour and set about doing a piece of German prose translation, but he couldn't concentrate, wanted to be out walking, being physically active, anything to liberate the suspense in his belly. Excitement wouldn't let him rest. All of him vibrated inside with the longing to be walking down that steep grey hill towards her.

"Where are you off to?" Joe said, appearing from nowhere at his side.

"Out with a few people."

"What about me?"

"It's not your sort of thing – anyway we're going walking ... you're not a great one for stirring your stumps."

"Oh I don't mind. Be nice to be out of the shop for a change."

"You'd not like it."

He didn't want Joe joining in. He'd be doing his daft acts and fooling about. It would spoil everything.

With relief, he heard Frank and Billy in the road. "Look, can't stop. See you when we get back."

In a scuffle, he hurried the other two off down the road. *Don't let anything spoil this now*, Bob prayed. He'd imagined that moment so many times, how he'd see her waiting lower down the street. Only that didn't happen. He had to knock on the door and face her mother. *Where were they going, when would they be back, she needed Lizzy to help at home?* Bob could hear younger girls squabbling behind the mother's back and two came peeking round her legs.

Ages later, Elizabeth and the cousins emerged giggling, tweaking their hair, and settling their blouses into their skirts. They smelled of cloth and shampoo.

On the tram ride out to the terminus Bob sat next to Elizabeth. On occasion the juddering of the tram threw him against her and his arm touched hers. What could he speak to her about; all topics of conversation dried up in his head and he found himself locked in the clamour of his insides.

"You've got a lovely voice," he said after there'd been silence for some time, filled with the zooming and clanking of the tram.

"Do you think so?" She burst out in giggles and studied her hands.

"Yes, I can always pick your voice out." Her answer was another burst of giggles.

When they piled out at the terminus, Bob felt an acute sense of anti-climax; they hadn't really talked, nothing had happened. He had been beside her, out of immediate earshot of the others, yet had drawn no closer to her. *But what did he expect?* he asked himself.

The girls soon flagged and they had to keep stopping because their shoes hurt.

"When are we going to get there?" Ruby, one of the cousins complained. "It's miles. Never thought it'd be like this."

"Want me to carry you?" Frank said.

"Don't be so forward!" Ruby said, giving him an arch look.

"Are you all right?" Bob asked.

"It is miles," Elizabeth said.

He thought she looked adorable with her flushed cheeks and the tendrils of blonde hair blowing about her face.

Once they reached the river, things seemed to get better and the girls stopped groaning. They sat down on the lads' jackets. Elizabeth lay back in the grass. The sun was a margarine ball in the blueness. Bob tickled her face with a blade of grass. She had closed her eyes and her eyelids were mauve shadowed. A few times she tried to brush the stalk away and then her eyes opened, and he saw their intricate mazy patterns. "Oh, it's you," she said. "You are a tease, Bob."

"I couldn't resist," he said, propping himself on his elbow so that he could lean over her. He wanted to cover her face with kisses, caress the white stalk of her throat and plant a kiss in the hollow at its base. "Your eyes aren't just one colour; I can see purple bits in them."

"You do say the strangest things."

"Do I?" He tickled her face again with the grass blade and she grabbed hold of his wrist. The urge to kiss her almost overpowered him. She gazed at him through half-closed eyes and he saw that her eyelashes were straw coloured, a tone darker than her hair. He looked at her rosebud mouth, lips parted in laughter. Her teeth, though white, were slightly irregular and that little imperfection pleased him.

The afternoon was languorous with heat and Bob sank into the lushness of it. The Rivelin gushing over boulders and tree roots was all part of the dream. He didn't want the moment to move on. He'd lain down beside her and the sun caught his face and his arms where he had rolled up his sleeves. The others were lying nearby and he became vaguely aware that Frank and Billy were discussing going in the army. It was Frank who drew their attention to the grey clouds bulging like smoke billows across the sky.

"We'd better be getting back – looks like a storm."

The afternoon ended in a scurry down the valley and onto the road, with the girls giggling and saying they didn't want to get soaked and whatever would they do if they got trapped in the open.

Bob reached home, still ensnared by the magic of that afternoon. The first person he saw was Amy. "You've caught the sun," she said. "Did you enjoy it?" He dismissed the deep look she sent him; it was only Amy being Amy. She always seemed to know everything about everybody.

Joe frowned at him. "You never said Lizzy Stanley was going, did you?" he said. Bob didn't reply.

Chapter Three

On the Tuesday evening when the family had just sat down to bread, margarine and cocoa and William was returning for the umpteenth time over Sunday evening's scene with the Reverend Price, Matthew came rushing in. His severe, aquiline face had flushed and his spectacle lenses glittered with agitation.

"Look," he said, flapping the late-night paper, "the Germans have gone into Belgium and Asquith's given them an ultimatum."

William sat for a few seconds watching as Lydia lit the gas. Her movements flowed into one another. She ran her hands over the antimacassars, straightening them, all part of her constant war on disorder. Chaos dwelt down the street and for her was some dreaded contagion threatening to engulf them without warning. He knew how she reasoned; but her defences, puny though they might be, comforted him. He took up the paper.

"And people are out in the streets. They're going wild with excitement."

"Are they?" William frowned. Everything was coming to a head. This added itself to Reverend Price's ultimatum.

I'm afraid, William, under the circumstances, it would be most inappropriate for you to use the, er, church premises for your, er, class.

Only three of the forty lads had been prepared to attend the Reverend's service.

So that was that – finished, severance.

William lost track of the Reverend in the flood of Matthew's news, and spurred by unease, rose. "I'll have to think about this for a bit," he said, and went into the hallway, put on his hat, took his stick from the stand and called back to them, "Bye bye folks!"

* * *

Bob sneaked a look at Mr Seebrooke's copy of The Times, and his skin went cold with shock.

"We are going into a war that is forced upon us as the defenders of the weak and the champions of the liberties of Europe," he read, and quickly refolded the paper and retired to his desk as he had spotted the black lump of Mr S. behind the frosted glass. The door surged open.

"So, we're at war," Mr Seebrooke announced and began to sing a new music hall number. "We don't want to fight, but by Jingo if we do, we've got the ships, we've got the men, we've got the money too." He bent over his desk, leafing through the correspondence stacked by the big blotting-pad. "Orders are really flowing in, Henderson," he breezed. "We shall have all on to meet them. I suppose lots of young chaps like you will be joining up now. They say you'll have it beaten by Christmas."

Bob made no comment but kept his eyes on the half-written letter in the type-writer. Further conversation was avoided by the arrival of more mail, which demanded instant action.

The war was on everybody's lips. People chortled with intoxication, charged with a new energy; the war had become some personal challenge. Langdale and Fletcher, who shared the same office, strode in. "We're joining up," Langdale announced, "well, I mean, it's the only decent thing to do – poor little Belgium, she's being over-run. They say the Boche are behaving like beasts."

"They've posted a mobilization order on the door of the Town Hall; have you seen it, Henderson?" Fletcher said.

"No," Bob said, now looking at the other two. They were four or five years older than he and had a worldly gloss of sophistication. Bob was known in the office as a book-worm, whereas they weren't interested in books. They far preferred a drink and a flutter on the horses.

"Everybody'll go, you watch. We'll show the dogs!" Langdale had drawn himself up to stand with his thumbs in his waistcoat pockets like a much older man. A Seebrooke pose, Bob noted.

With his profile turned to the window, he gazed out, blond, arrogant and yet attractive, so that Bob had to admire the figure he cut, whilst being totally out of sympathy with it.

In an instant everything had begun to skelter by. The war had speeded up the passage of time and made life more immediate, more alive. Bob saw it in the faces of the men in the works and out on the street. But he still wanted to linger in that Bank Holiday afternoon with the six of them down by the river and Elizabeth in the grass.

"We're joining the City Battalion," Frank and Billy announced on the Friday evening when they met for choir practice at the Victoria Hall. Their faces shone with pride, and Bob looked and wondered.

All this seemed to be happening to part of him, whilst the rest of him moved on a different plane: he was forever dreaming of Elizabeth. When he walked her and her cousin, Ruby, home after choir practice, he'd never managed to say what he wanted to her. They'd usually discussed the choir and how the evening's practice had gone and what the public performance would be like. Only occasionally had he managed to introduce what he'd considered a more intimate note, and it failed. Reviewing the situation later, he knew it had been a disaster.

Do you like Shaw? Have you read H.G. Wells?

No.

And then she'd given that charming, slightly disdainful smile. He had wanted to tell her about Shaw, share his enthusiasm, but Ruby had set up a low tittering, and the two had bent their heads together in girlishness, like two white geese nebbing in sand, and had flummoxed him. Amy was not their sort and never had been. She refused to hide behind coquetry of any sort. You'd get it straight from her. Oh yes, she'd laugh, but that was different, it was a laughter shared with him not apart from him.

Now though, since the afternoon at Rivelin Valley, things had changed in some subtle way. She'd sent messages through those half-closed lids and her laughing mouth. He wished he'd kissed her, felt sure she'd have welcomed it ... though like that out in the open with the others present it would have been considered wrong. There was just something so adorable about her big blue eyes and the way she smiled and the dimpling of her mouth and the stray curls of blonde hair nestling against her collar. You could forget the awkward bits when you fixed on those. He had been in love before, but this ... she had small slender hands and oval pink nails. Her hands fluttered to and fro settling a pearl brooch at her neck, adjusting her hair, stroking her skirt. When she sang, the pureness of her soprano made him ache, it was truly angelic. He had a dream of them singing together, just the two of them, his tenor, interweaving with her soprano. And then behind that, lay the lushness, the swell of her bosom beneath the white cotton.

It was after an evening's choir practice that he first saw the recruiting poster. Kitchener stared out from a bill-board, his finger pointing at the group of them.

Your Country Needs YOU.

Hundreds and thousands of young men his age were going.

* * *

William called the family together on Saturday evening after he had closed the shop. He was unusually serious. Normally even in his most earnest moods there was a bubbling exuberance in his tone.

They only used the parlour on important occasions like Sunday teas and the evenings when they would gather round the piano, hymn-singing. Now they sat on the straight-backed Sunday chairs, waiting. William took up a position before the black marble clock. The pyramids rose up behind his white shirt and stiff wing-collar. The back of his hair frothed in the over-mantel mirrors.

"You can see how it's going." He looked from one to the other of his family and his black eyes glowed. "They're war crazy. We're being asked to kill our fellow men. Mark my words, we shall hear it all tomorrow and from now on. The churches are becoming recruiting grounds. Now what we must do is visit as many as we can, listen to the sermon, see what line they're taking and then try to engage the minister in discussion on the evils of war. It's no use sitting here and accepting everything. We must offer resistance to this general hysteria. Do you see what I mean?"

"Oh do take care," Lydia said.

"This is not the time for doing nothing. Anyway, just the boys and I will go."

"But, Father, do let me as well!" Amy pleaded.

"No, I don't think it would be suitable."

"Please, please." Amy reached across and tugged his arm. "Do let me go as well. I don't want to miss anything."

In the end he agreed but with reluctance. The war feeling was running very high and people didn't want to hear anything to the contrary.

At midnight they were still discussing what they would say the next day.

* * *

Amy left her bedroom curtains wide open and watched the lights flickering out in the shops up the hill. It was a breathless night. She remembered lots of other nights in childhood when Bob had crept in to her. They being the youngest had to go to bed early. The others would be downstairs and the strains of 'Abide With Me' would drift up as Matthew played the piano. They'd watch people shopping on Spital Hill late into the night, until once Bob had fallen asleep on the floor, beside her bed and had been discovered by their mother in the early hours.

In the bottom of her wardrobe Amy still had the 'Snakes and Ladders' and a packet of milky marbles they'd played with up there in the evenings. Bob was very deliberate about things; he'd line up his marbles with precision and take steady aim. She was quick-quick. Sometimes it paid off, at others it didn't. Impetuosity landed her in no end of scuffles and skirmishes. When she said her prayers, she often asked forgiveness for her outbursts of sudden anger. Father's favourite text was: 'Let not the sun go down upon your wrath.' She did make an attempt when she remembered but she was usually caught up in a new project.

What could be happening to all those poor young men? She had passed the station that afternoon and had seen crowds of soldiers in uniform marching under the pillared frontage towards the barrier. The picture had remained with her: mothers, wives, girlfriends, parasols dangling from their wrists, their white blouses and light skirts brilliant in the sunlight, all smiling and glowing and waving as though they were seeing their loved ones off on some holiday-trip. She had wanted to cry. On the station hoarding she had glimpsed a recruiting poster. Two women and a child stood at a window. 'Women of Britain say "Go!"' It had amazed her. Why were they saying go? If you thought about it at all, you must realize immediately that the poster was asking women to do something terrible, demanding that they force their men-folk to kill. It had confused and frightened her. You were brought up to believe in King and Country and in obedience to your superiors, and you presumed that they knew better than you did but what if they didn't?

She lay on her back and watched the white patterns weaving on the ceiling. The last trams, great tumbling galleons, had long since rumbled down the hill. Her parents still moved about downstairs. The threads of office arguments at J.G. Graves churned through her head.

But Miss Henderson, how would you feel if a Hun attacked you, and

I and Mr Michelson merely turned our heads and did nothing?

Tiresome, idiotic arguments that made you spit, but you had to reply something to old Copeland with his warty nose and his lisp. They now expected her to come up with a retort, and had done ever since the suffragette business.

Did you know Miss Henderson's getting ready to lash herself to the railings outside the Town Hall ... and if you've got a horse then so much the better.

I don't expect anybody to save me.

Come, come Miss Henderson, you don't mean that.

Nobody would attack me anyway. People don't go round attacking one another.

* * *

On the verges of sleep, she still found herself wondering about the job of dispenser at Boots the Chemist for which she had applied. It would be an escape route from the world of J.G. Graves and old snoopy Copeland. Oh to be away from addressing envelopes!

Chapter Four

Amy watched her dad brushing his hair so hard it seemed to spark. The little grey spirals spumed and became waves dashing up spray. She could tell he was preparing himself for the struggle. Nobody talked much at breakfast but Amy had to swallow an urge to giggle. It would come on her when things were at their most serious.

Holy Trinity had never been so full. Dusty sunlight streamed through the scarlet and blue glass above the altar. Reverend Price, in his vestments, stood before them, his face bearing the composure of sanctity.

The opening hymn was 'Fight the Good Fight'. "Fight the fight with all thy might." The voices took the words and made them reverberate amongst the pillars. Many uniforms were in evidence. Amy looked at the backs of the soldiers' necks, and their scrubbed vulnerability brought the tears to her eyes. Emotion see-sawed in her chest and she was on edge. You could let yourself go in the hymn-singing and be borne aloft on an unthinking wave of emotion, but that wasn't the way. Everything battered at you – there'd been the women poster at the station, everywhere you looked messages screamed; people talked of nothing else but the war, the war. How could they ever resist the mounting pressure to move with mass opinion? Looking around her in the church, she could see nobody apart from her own family, who would not be prepared to support the war. At the end of the pew were her father and mother and she found herself admiring their single-mindedness. Often she felt at odds with her mother because she thought daughters should above all be obedient and domesticated; their main aim was of course marriage and the raising of a family. Respectability was her watchword. But Amy knew that her mother had another side, which yearned after the exotic and sometimes emerged in a pair of long glass earrings, a feather boa, a black velvet dress with georgette sleeves covered with blobs like gold sixpences. She loved jewellery and silks and velvets. Amy didn't. She wanted to know about things ... the world, about plants, how things worked ... perhaps in a chemist's shop she'd be able to learn about cures. Mother must find her disappointing; she didn't want to have cosy chats at the dressmakers and discuss which pair of earrings – the jet or the glass – looked better. There her mother was in her pew, splendid in a pale grey and blue silk dress and matching wide-brimmed hat. Long blue-glass beads threaded on gold wire gleamed against her pale throat. Nobody would imagine she'd oppose the war; rather they'd expect her to wave off battalions to the front.

Reverend Price, Amy realized, had based his sermon on the words of the hymn, 'Fight the Good Fight'. She only tuned into it at the end when he was rounding off with, "We have a great and noble cause to espouse and we must do so with our lives if necessary ... nothing can be more noble than to sacrifice one's life for one's country."

The organ boomed into 'Onward Christian Soldiers' and everybody creaked up to sing. Amy glanced along the row and saw that all her family were silent. They continued to stand gazing towards the altar and the gleaming cross. She wanted to cry. *All these words,* she thought *and what do they mean?*

Amy, just behind her father as they were leaving at the end of the service, saw him take hold of the clergyman's proffered hand.

"Surely," her father said, "Christianity is about loving one's neighbour, not killing him?"

"William, we cannot stand by and see our country pillaged and our wives and daughters ... er, threatened."

"I don't think wives and daughters are being threatened, are they, Reverend Price?"

"Belgium has been overrun, you must realize that. She is a small and defenceless country, we have to save democracy."

"Whatever you like to say, one cannot justify the taking of a life."

Amy's chest blazed. She wanted to storm at Reverend Price but she bit her lip and stared at the sunlight outside. Other members of the congregation had gathered there and lay in wait for them. Amy's pulse throbbed; now she focussed on the humping grey grave-stones and the small urns filled with bunches of asters and stocks. People shook their heads and muttered.

"So you're prepared to leave your wife and daughter to the Hun, Mr Henderson, are you?"

"No sense of proper pride, a traitor. I wouldn't have thought it of you, Barber Henderson."

"He just wants to save his sons."

Amy's cheeks felt hot. How dared they say these things? She wanted to shriek at them, let out the rage that lay on her chest like indigestion. Her father faced it all and didn't attempt to defend himself, and her mother continued to stare away to the spiky metal railings surrounding the church yard.

"Only shirkers and cowards refuse to fight," a furnace man, one of her father's customers, shouted.

"Thou shalt not kill, Frank," her father said.

"But what about an eye for an eye," someone else bellowed.

"Well, good morning to you, my friends," Reverend Price interrupted, moving down the flagged path towards the road.

As they walked back home, Amy comforted herself by remembering the tall man addressing the crowd that Sunday. Now she thought she had an inkling of how he must have felt. The excitability amongst people fed upon itself, and you could imagine how in a very short time they would have been prepared to strike out physically. What did you do if someone began pelting you with stones?

* * *

After tea and bread and marge Amy listened as her father drew up a plan of action. They would spread out and attend evening service at as many churches as they could reach. She would visit St. Cuthbert's with him, Matthew would take St. John's and Bob and Joe St. Mungo's.

"What a lot of chortle," Joe guffawed after the morning's episode.

"I felt embarrassed," Bob said as he and Amy leaned on the wall in the yard.

"Why," Amy said, "because they were attacking Father?"

"He's so well known, that's the trouble – I mean he does all that stuff for The Guild of Help – as well as his business. Anyway, I suppose this isn't anything yet, we've really only just started."

* * *

"But, Father," Amy asked as they made their way through the warm evening, "how can we ever convince people if they've made their minds up?"

"They may change their minds – people do. At the moment they're mesmerized ... but we have to help them out of it. A lot are going to war because they haven't thought about it properly. We must have faith."

Listening to him and looking up at the side of his face, Amy thought, *yes, he's right, it's the truth. It will be possible to give them a different vision.* Her shoulders tensed with excitement and she drew the four feet nine of herself up pencil-straight as they entered the unfamiliar church.

The sermon carried a similar message to the morning's one. The clergyman looked like Moses descending with the tablets of stone. He leaned over the pulpit and surveyed his parishioners. "The call of our great country is the call of God. Do not fail Him!"

Amy studied the straight backs in the pews and the firm

profiles. A few women dabbed their eyes and many seemed moved by the exhortations and the preceding rhetoric. Her father, beside her in his dark suit, had his hat on his knees. She watched the slight tremor in the fingers of his left hand. She loved his pale, firm hands that spent their days wielding scissors and razors and gestured when he spoke, flying up like doves to emphasize a word. He knew people by their hair, could tell their lives through it, so he said.

"Let us say the prayer that Our Lord taught us." Skirts rustled as the congregation sank onto the hassocks, and the movement sounded like fire settling in a grate. Soon the moment would come. Kneeling, her head bowed, the sneezy smell of old hymnals in her nostrils, Amy could scarcely join in the words of the Lord's Prayer, such was the gnawing anxiety in her belly.

The congregation rose and streamed out to the triumphant rumbling and churning of the organ. They continued to sit in the pew, waiting. At last her father got up and made his way down the aisle and when he reached the church door where the parson took leave of his flock, he stopped. Amy hovered by his side. The clergyman looked at William as though he expected a congratulatory remark.

Oh let them get it over with, Amy prayed. *Please God let it be over fast.*

"Good evening, Reverend Marshall, I have listened to your sermon with great interest, but I am afraid I cannot agree with the sentiment expressed in it."

"No?" Reverend Marshall's white brows rose. They had a life of their own. Amy watched, feeling a giggle welling up inside her. They were furry caterpillars, the hairy type destined to flap off as big hairy moths. "And why would that be?"

"Didn't Jesus say, 'Resist not evil but if any man smite thee on one cheek, turn to him the other also'? And what about, 'My Kingdom is not of this world, else would my servants fight'? It is quite clear if we are Christians that we should not be at war, or ..."

"Now my dear chap – what, by the way, is your name – though I think I probably know?"

"Henderson."

"Ah yes, you have been causing my friend, Reverend Price, problems over the Immaculate Conception, I believe." He smiled at them. Amy saw her father return the smile. Her heart plunged to and fro in her chest.

"Have I?"

"My dear fellow, you must be able to see that we cannot leave Belgium in the lurch – it is our beholden duty to render assistance. We are fighting for a sacred principle, for our liberty." Reverend Marshall's manner swung between the gutsy and the benevolent. Amy could see how he would easily convince his listeners. He had a way of smiling and easing his points forward. If you raised any objections to what he was propounding, you would appear most ill-mannered. But her father stuck to his central argument, his voice always remaining low and pleasant, though he gave no ground.

"Are you saying that only you have the right interpretation of the Bible?"

"No, I wouldn't presume – but there can be no justification for the taking of a life."

They ended up drinking tea with Reverend Marshall in his manse. His wife had made currant buns and offered them round on an elegant cake-stand, but Amy who would normally have polished off a couple, felt quite sick and refrained altogether.

"Oh my dear chap," the Reverend Marshall was saying, opening his eyes very wide, so that the two white creatures shot up an inch quite magically, "the very essence of Christianity is to fight – think of the hymns, 'Fight the Good Fight', 'Onward Christian Soldiers', we are always fighting against the devil, are we not?"

Resisting on the Reverend's home territory with the currant

buns and tea before them, seemed to Amy to be even more bad-mannered, but her father didn't let it silence him.

"All this is purely figurative, just to make things more vivid – fighting is the activity of savages."

"Indeed."

As they were leaving Reverend Marshall turned to her father at the door and laid a hand on his shoulder.

"Well, my dear fellow, you've got spirit, I must hand it to you. But you are seriously misguided and I shall pray for you."

"That's very kind of you and thank you for the tea and buns."

Once more out in the street Amy wanted to caper about and screech, anything to be rid of the awful tension, but instead she began to giggle.

"What's the matter, Little Bits?" her father said.

"His eyebrows," Amy spluttered, "I thought they might go crawling off."

"Well, we've started. I think I could probably pay a visit to Firth Browns and catch the men when they knock off and talk to them about the evils of the armaments industry."

"Goodness!" Amy said. "That's not going to be popular; won't it be like going into the lion's den?" She heard a wheezy buzzing in his chest and realized he had begun to hum 'The Rock of Ages' and that meant a new venture had seized him. Her mother moaned privately, *I do wish your father weren't so enthusiastic.* This latest proposal brought the goose-pimples up on Amy's arms and her hands felt clammy.

When they arrived home, they found the boys stuffing down Mother's currant loaf and drinking cocoa.

"Couldn't get shut of us fast enough," Joe said. "They were all on about 'poor little Belgium' and what would we do if you and Mother got attacked."

"It would have helped if you hadn't grinned so inanely," Matthew said.

"Matty, it's not easy, we had Reverend Marshall's eyebrows,"

Amy said. Matthew always had to play big brother and disapprove.

Amy listened to her father enlarging on his idea of visiting the armament firms and heard how her mother sighed. "William," she said, "they'll attack you."

"I don't see how we can continue working at Browns," Bob said.

Matthew didn't say anything but scooped up the dregs of cocoa and the sprinkling of sugar granules in the bottom of his cup with a teaspoon. "Waste not, want not," he muttered.

Amy, watching him, thought, *typical Matty, always has to have everything tied up and no rebellious bits. But what was he thinking? All right, he was a lot more important at work than Bob. Being Dr Ziegelmann's private secretary and supposed to be moving up in the firm's export department was much better than Bob in the general office.*

As they said family prayers together before going to bed, Amy could scarcely concentrate. She found herself back in the church that morning, hearing the furious voices of the congregation and feeling the hot desperate plunging inside her. What was going to happen to the boys?

Chapter Five

Matthew had slept very little that night. To resign or not to resign, and therein lay the problem. Three night classes a week, head crammed with French, German and Spanish verbs, years learning about the steel process, the acquisition of business knowledge and impeccable English skills – he'd been honed by the process, felt he had become like a bar of Sheffield stainless steel. And now to give it all up? Career finished. How could he? But this was about more than a career, this was a moral issue. Was he such a poor worm that he'd want to hang on?

Dr Ziegelmann summoned him not long after his arrival in the office. Matthew expected to take dictation and brought his shorthand pad. He waited to be told to sit down but the other man had a distracted air, and paced back and forth, seeming almost unaware of him.

"Were you wanting to dictate a letter, Dr Ziegelmann?" Matthew asked.

"No, Matthew, not at the moment. I have something to tell you."

Matthew felt his skin prickling with coldness.

"I am having to go."

"But why?"

"I am a German, nicht wahr? What else is there to say? Now I have to put everything in order. I have to finish today."

Matthew stood staring at the other man. What did it all mean? Fragments tumbled in his head; a whole structure was about to come crashing down.

"Sit down, Matthew, sit down."

Matthew subsided into the chair facing the desk but Ziegelmann continued to pace. He was a huge man, about six foot four with a leonine head and his thick grey hair rose helmet-like about his skull. No matter the season he always wore either a pink carnation or a rose in his button hole, and even today a pink carnation was there.

"I shall need you to work at my house this evening. Can you do that?"

"Yes, of course." Matthew had sometimes been out to Dr Ziegelmann's house at the weekends to take dictation of pressing letters. He lived in a fine blond stone villa surrounded by lawns and shrubberies. In summer the rhododendron bushes formed purple billows around the tennis courts and the lilacs made your head reel with their sweetness. Only Ziegelmann, a widower, and his housekeeper occupied the mansion. On the grand-piano Matthew had noticed a framed photograph of a young woman with an exquisite ivory face and large dark eyes. Her hair was swept up in a chignon. Such a face was unforgettable.

* * *

The morning passed in a strange whirl and Matthew felt relieved to be escaping home for lunch but as soon as he walked into the kitchen, he knew his mother was upset.

"They've smashed up Lindenberg's, the pork butcher's on Spital Hill," she said.

"Why for heaven's sake?"

"He's a German, isn't he? Smashed everything, a regular mob, and the police did nothing. Stood by and let it happen. And that family down Shoreham Street, the Rauschwergs, they're having to go. Mr Rauschwerg's been sacked from the bakery. Can you imagine what'll happen to them – they've six young children."

"But they're doing exactly what they're accusing the Germans of."

Joe waltzed in from the shop. "My belly thinks its throat's cut, Mother dear ... what's for grub?"

"Your belly always does," Lydia said, smiling. "It's lentil soup."

"Shall we have an ear-wiggling competition, or would you prefer a handstand or a cart-wheel?" In an instant Joe cart-wheeled across the kitchen floor whilst pennies cascaded from his pocket.

"Do you have to behave like that?" Matthew said.

"Yes, it's no good everybody going round like a wet Monday."

Matthew scowled at his brother. Joe always had to trivialize everything.

"Are you all right, Matty?" his mother said.

"They've sacked Dr Ziegelmann."

"Goodness!" Lydia clicked her tongue.

"I shall be late home tonight, Mother. I'm helping him to get his papers in order." Matthew tried to eat his soup, failed to and took a long swallow of water. There weren't going to be any more sessions with his boss, in the middle of giving dictation, bursting into poetry. 'Am grauen Strand, am grauen Meer ...' or discussions about Goethe and Schiller. Even Ziegelmann's insistence on absolute perfection in all matters appertaining to the foreign department appealed to him. He didn't think he'd ever met anyone he admired more.

Amy, who had been eating in silence all the while, shot her head up. "What'll happen to him then?"

"I don't know," he said, glancing across at her. Amy had a tendency to be forward, he thought, was far too curious for her own good. Irritated, he wanted to upbraid her but didn't.

Joe, going to relieve their father in the shop, blew a sardonic kiss at Matthew. He scowled back and then set off with Bob for the tram. Looking out of the window, he was arrested by yet another poster, 'Britain wants you. Join your country's army! God save the King'. Another couple of stops and they passed Kitchener's staring eyes and pointing finger. How could Dr Ziegelmann become a fugitive? He felt bruised inside, as though someone dear to him had died, and he was shocked when Bob said, "When shall we hand in our notices?"

"Today," Matthew said, though he hadn't realized such was his intention.

"Today!"

"Yes, I shall at any rate. I can't just sit there and let them sack my boss. It would seem like condoning it."

* * *

At the works Matthew found Dr Ziegelmann going through sheaves of documents in his room. No breeze came through the open window to disturb the turgid air.

Ziegelmann muttered to himself now and then, "Ich verstehe es nicht ... zwecklos. Ah da ist es!" He appeared to be following along some hidden thread of thought. "You know the German band has gone, some say to the Isle of Man. All the waiters too, all gone. I am in good company."

Matthew felt himself blushing with embarrassment ... was it shame?

"I'm very sorry," was all he could find to say.

* * *

After six, Ziegelmann's chauffeur arrived with the Bentley. Matthew had ridden in the motor car a couple of times before and always with a mixture of trepidation and amazement. He sat up very straight as it roared along.

Arriving at the house, Matthew experienced his usual feelings of awe at the size and beauty of it. Blackbirds warbled in the larch grove and on the croquet lawn two thrushes hopped. Matthew admired their speckled plumage and enquiring black eyes. The air was heavy with the dark sweet scent of roses. It had been a very hot day and the heat still rose from the grey crazy-paved path. The housekeeper greeted them in the hallway and took Dr Ziegelmann's silver-topped cane.

"We shall have a drink first." Ziegelmann led the way to a room facing the garden. The French windows opened onto a patio where chairs had been arranged. Matthew glimpsed oil paintings in heavy gilt frames and handsome mahogany furniture, bookshelves filled with row upon row of leather-bound volumes.

Dr Ziegelmann poured himself a whisky and handed Matthew, a non-drinker, a glass of cordial.

"It is strange that it should end in this way. I hear you have resigned."

"Yes." Matthew flushed.

"Ah well – I hope not because of me?"

"I cannot agree with war and Browns is making armaments."

They sipped their drinks. Matthew couldn't believe that he and Dr Ziegelmann would never again concern themselves with work for Browns. They had crossed the foundry yard for the last time. All finished, the end of something ... and furthermore, he would miss Ziegelmann, miss the conversations about music and literature.

"I think after this war our world will change very much," the older man mused, and then began to quote: "'Herr: es ist Zeit. Der Sommer war sehr groß. Leg deinen Schatten auf die Sonnenuhren ...und auf den Fluren laß die Winde los.'"

As he spoke, he looked away to the purple rhododendrons. Matthew listened to the sonorous roll of the words.

"It is a poem by a modern poet, one whom I like very much, Rainer Maria Rilke. I shall give you a volume of his poetry. 'Wer jetzt kein Haus hat, baut sich keines mehr. Wer jetzt allein ist, wird es lange bleiben' ...Oh," he sighed, "the disaster of it all."

It had such a sorrowful ring that Matthew had to blow his nose and surreptitiously wipe his eyes.

"Come, let us to work!" the other man announced, seeming to make an effort to overcome his melancholy.

They spent the next three hours in the study where Matthew

wrote letters on the Olivetti and answered correspondence. Ziegelmann dictated and at the same time tore up letters and tossed them into the waster-paper basket.

At ten o'clock he stood up. "So, es ist gut. You have been a very good secretary, Matthew, and I shall miss you." At this he handed Matthew a small packet and the book of Rilke's poems. "Ein kleines Andenken. Grayson will drive you home."

Again Matthew felt the tears constricting his throat as he held out his hand and grasped the other man's. "Goodbye, I hope we shall meet again." The older man only nodded.

The last Matthew saw of him, he was standing smiling on the top step before the front-door, just the same faultlessly dressed, commanding figure as always, but now somehow detached, the angle of his head slightly sunken.

* * *

When Matthew arrived home, he found his mother ironing in the cellar kitchen. She slapped away at his father's shirts and pressed her lips together with concentration as she flattened the cuffs and eased away at the creases on the front.

"That's it," he announced, sitting down on a cane chair by the table.

"What, my love?"

"Ziegelmann's finished. I've handed my notice in. He's given me this." Matthew began unwrapping the square object. "Heavens ... but it's his gold Hunter!"

"What!" Lydia dropped the iron.

"His own watch."

"But ..."

"I don't understand." Matthew sat gazing at the pattern of twining flowers engraved on the gold case. The watch weighed heavily in his hand, as did the thick gold Albert. He felt incapable of saying any more about it.

'Herr: es ist Zeit. Der Sommer war sehr groß …' The words sounded in his head and he heard Ziegelmann's voice reading them. Without another word he went upstairs into the parlour and sat on the horse-hair sofa, staring unseeing at the black marble clock. He had no idea what he would do.

* * *

It was perhaps an hour later that there was a staccato knocking on the front-door. William answered the summons. On the doorstep stood two police officers.

"Good evening. Does Matthew Henderson live here?"

"Indeed."

"Can we come in?"

"Of course."

William showed them into the parlour and Lydia went to fetch Matthew.

"Is something the matter?"

"Yes, there is." They were being very mysterious and officious. Their eyes leapt to and fro like fleas.

"Might I ask …?"

At that moment Matthew appeared. "Good evening," he said. "May I ask what's the matter?"

"Matthew Henderson, where were you at nine thirty this evening?"

"I was working at the house of Dr Ziegelmann."

"And when did you leave?"

"I've probably been home about an hour."

"Yes," Lydia said, "that's true."

"You are sure?"

"Perfectly. But why do you ask?"

"Ziegelmann has been found shot dead."

"What!" Matthew felt as though all the blood had drained from his heart and he gripped the back of dining chair. It made sense, that was it. 'Als Andenken, ein kleines Andenken,' he had said. "He must have intended to shoot himself. Look, he gave me his watch."

"You'll have to come with us to the station to be examined."

They think I've murdered him, he registered with amazement. He wondered if they'd put handcuffs on him. *Let them*, he thought. What did that matter when it was set against Ziegelmann's death? He saw the tall grey figure standing on the doorstep in the dusk; moths fluttering over evening primroses. He heard the late breeze rustling the larches and smelt roses. The pity of it got him in the gut and he wanted to weep. As they led him away, he bit his lower lip and forced the nails of his right hand into his clenched palm.

* * *

Bob had just typed in the addresses and written, *Dear Sirs*, when he noticed the grey blob of Seebrooke looming behind the glass.

"Ah ... er ... Henderson, I have some very sad news. Our friend Langdale has fallen."

There followed an awful silence. Bob didn't know what to say. He saw Langdale standing by the window a few weeks before, his fine profile turned to the yard.

It's the only decent thing to do.

Bob felt obscurely that in some peculiar way Seebrooke held him responsible for Langdale's death and however genuine his own sorrow might be, nothing he could say would cause Seebrooke to review his opinion. He sat stunned, staring at the iron-rib cage of the type-writer.

Seebrooke made no further comment, he simply went to stand for a few seconds by Langdale's desk and then sighed. "He was a fine young man, very fine."

Back home for lunch and spooning down Mother's ham bone and lentil soup and dunking in chunks of bread Bob found his thoughts leapfrogging about: *Langdale was dead.* He'd never walk through that office door again, or stand by the window discussing racing results and what he'd chanced on the 4.30. Over that slid dreams of the Victoria Hall performance swiftly approaching. Elizabeth of the heavy honey-coloured hair and porcelain skin would send him seductive glances and smile. How would he react if a German threatened her honour? But that was a personal question. What he might do on the spur of the moment could hardly be placed beside his principles operating on a national level. He worried at it – heard Langdale: *It's the only decent thing to do.*

Back in the office that afternoon, he knew this must be the day of his resignation. What on earth he would do afterwards, he had no idea, but that wasn't going to deter him.

Bob glanced across at Langdale's bare desk and swallowed. This was it, he'd better go to Seebrooke's office and get it over with.

"Mr Seebrooke," Bob said, as he stood by the door, glancing across at Seebrooke who was busy poking out his nails with a paper clip and looked quite absorbed.

"Yes, Henderson, what is it?"

"I've come to say I want to resign."

"Ah." Seebrooke did raise his eyes at this point. "You'll be joining up I suppose ... after young Langdale. Of course you may be back at your desk by Christmas."

"No," Bob said.

"No? I don't quite understand."

Bob looked at him squarely and tried to keep his voice calm. "But Mr Seebrooke, we're manufacturing armaments. I'm supporting that by working here."

"But have you no feelings for your country, man?"

"Yes, but I think it's wrong to fight."

"Well I think you're a fool. I shall tell Mr Forrester that you wish to leave. I must say Henderson, I expected more of you. It is really quite disgraceful."

Bob listened to his superior's reprimand. His heart banged hard with anger but he kept quiet and began looking through the papers on his desk. *Pacifists don't start snarling and warlike in the face of attack,* he told himself. Pacifism forced you to examine your behaviour all the time. Just acknowledging its demands stopped him from wanting to level a volley of abuse at Seebrooke, the creepy, sanctimonious office manager.

Chapter Six

Bob hummed to himself, enjoying the special occasion feel of his best clothes. They were all spruced up in their starched white shirts and dark suits for the performance in the Victoria Hall. He felt alert, tense with excitement and yet at the same time caught up in an extra awareness of everything around him. The evening had a pellucid splendour and the light was clear and rosy. All the people they passed in the street appeared to be drawn into this spell. It was both languorous and focused. He had to stop himself from grinning. It wouldn't be right, not with Matthew being so depressed. Joe jogged on as usual, dropping out garrulous remarks. Matthew, striding between them, didn't speak. Ever since Ziegelmann's death and the business in the police station he had barely spoken. The police had evidently decided that he hadn't been lying, but Bob knew all the neighbours thought Matthew must be a criminal. They'd been nebbing at their nets when the police arrived.

As they mounted the steep stone steps to the choir seats and took their accustomed places beside the other men, Bob listened to the secret notes of Bach spiralling and flowing. In a few minutes he would see Elizabeth of the fine honey-coloured hair and blue eyes with their amazing violet centres. She would glance across and meet his gaze, send him a special message ... He could scarcely wait.

"Look at Henshaw," Joe whispered. "He's like a mad wasp."

Bob forced himself to watch the choir master, who was darting along the rows of older men asking them something, and they appeared to be nodding in agreement. Looking at them, Bob realized that almost all his age-group must already have joined up. Some of the older men turned now to stare at Bob and his brothers. Bob detected a coldness in their glances. He began to feel uncomfortable. Minutes ticked by and nothing happened but

Bob could sense an atmosphere gathering. He stared down at the bank of scarlet salvias and geraniums and the opulence of the sage green palms surrounding the stage. The auditorium had filled up and everywhere rippled with movement, programmes rattled, ladies adjusted their hats, men removed theirs, children fidgeted. Waves of restiveness stirred the audience. The female members of the choir had still not come onto the platform. Henshaw bustled off. Bob noticed how the men glanced at one another. It seemed very hot. He stared at the mighty silver organ pipes and up at the domed roof and the treacle coloured seats and balcony rails. What could be happening? Ben looked across at him and pulled a face. Matthew didn't turn his head or look about.

Finally when public sentiment had started to express itself as a hoarse muttering behind hands and programmes, Henshaw bounced up the steps onto the stage. Bob realized he was making directly for them. His heart pounded when he noticed how Henshaw had Matthew in his sights. He heard him say, "Er, Mr Henderson, I'm afraid I must tell you that the ladies are all refusing to come on the platform if you remain here." Matthew didn't appear to reply. Bob felt the heat surging up his neck, this was too embarrassing.

"What shall I …" Henshaw, face red as a rooster's comb, stared at Matthew. The male members of the choir were all silent, trying to hear the exchange. The audience had realized too that something untoward was happening.

"Why would that be?" Matthew said. Bob saw the sweat shining on the choir master's forehead.

"You're not … er, joining up. They say you're cowards and shirkers."

"In which case."

With that Matthew rose and Bob got up too. Joe stumbled out behind them. They found the rest of the family waiting by one of the exits.

"So that's it," Matthew said.

"The poor ladies wouldn't come on the stage because of us!" Joe gave a snort of laughter.

"Ah well ..." William sighed.

"The poor, poor things," Amy said. "I'm sorry for them. It'll not be half as nice without you." Bob felt his hand being seized and given a squeeze.

All the way back home on the tram Bob didn't speak. *What must Elizabeth be thinking? Did it mean that she too thought him a coward and a shirker? Was he a coward? But how could you join up if you thought it was wrong?* She would be singing at that very moment, letting her voice soar up into the hall. And he wasn't there ... couldn't look along the row and meet her gaze; was debarred from doing so ever again. *But if you join up*, a voice whispered, *if you join up, she'll admire you, you'll no longer feel an outcast. It's no good, you can't go against what you believe in your heart. This is a mere pin-prick, it'll get a lot worse yet ...* only it wasn't, and it hurt like hell.

Chapter Seven

William had been preparing himself for the big onslaught on the steel works, but what finally galvanized him to action was an article in that September's Labour Leader by a Dr Alfred Salter.

He had finished work at 1pm that Thursday and sat down in the parlour after dinner to look at the paper. As he read, devouring the words, his excitement flared.

"There are two main religions in the world – though each of them has many forms. 1. The religion which trusts in the power and ultimate triumph of material forces – the faith of materialism. 2. The religion which trusts in the power and ultimate triumph of spiritual forces and faith in God …

"The materialist religion believes in the big battalions, the millions of armed men, the might of battleships, the superiority of artillery, the efficiency of organizations, the adequacy of food supplies, the stability of financial resources … The scene which you now have is one in which God does not count. Force alone matters. That is the gospel of materialism …"

William paused. He thought of the Sheffield slums, the married couples living separated in the workhouse, and on the other side of the city the steel manufacturers residing in their handsome villas. They were making a fortune out of the war. The injustice smashed into his chest like an iron fist. But what to do? He continued reading.

"The other religion is the simple faith that the only thing that matters is the doing of God's will … For the man who believes in God there is only one sure means of defence … obedience to God's command."

By the time William reached the last paragraphs he found tears plopping onto the paper.

"In the matter of this war I must try and picture to myself Christ as an Englishman at war with Germany. The Germans have overrun France and Belgium and very possibly may invade England by airship and drop bombs on London. What am I to do? Am I to answer the Prime Minister's call, make myself proficient in arms and hurry to the continent to beat the Germans off?

"Look! Christ in khaki, out in France thrusting his bayonet into the body of a German workman. See! The son of God with a machine-gun, ambushing a column of German infantry, catching them unawares in a lane, mowing them down in their helplessness. Hark! The man of sorrows in a cavalry charge, cutting, hacking, thrusting, crushing, cheering. No. No!

"There is a great place in history waiting for the first nation that will dare to save its life by losing it."

William sat deep in thought and then he took out his handkerchief, wiped his forehead, called down to Lydia that he was going out for a while, put on his hat and set off. He walked right across the city looking for news-stands selling The Labour Leader and he bought up any copies he could find before returning home.

At home he saw the three boys sitting talking in the back yard. "Come and see this!" he called. "I'm going to Browns this evening. I shall stand outside and speak and I'll give out these papers to anybody who seems interested."

William didn't ask any of them to join him, in fact, he thought, it might be better if they didn't, but they all insisted they wanted to be there.

"In for a penny in for a pound," Joe grinned. "There's bound to be fur and feathers flying."

"I could have phrased that differently," Matthew said, casting a disapproving glance in Joe's direction.

* * *

An hour later they were positioned at the gates as a trickle of men began to leave. William took a deep breath. "I wonder, friends, whether you have thought about what you're making here. Do you realize that the steel you're producing is being used to make bayonets, battleships and all manner of objects intended for the destruction of your fellow men? The Bible tells us that God is love – we're called to live in love as Christian brethren … is this what we're doing? We're sending our young men, the flower of our youth, your sons and brothers, to certain death. And for what?" As William overcame his initial nervousness and the banging of his heart quietened the words came tumbling out. "Think of those German mothers, they too are sending their sons to die. We've been manipulated by the government, by those with wealth and position, they're using us against our fellows. It's not the industrialist who's out in the trenches, is it? No, he's sitting comfortably in his office, making fat profits with the lives of your sons."

Bob saw how his father's black eyes flashed and his grey hair spumed in the slight breeze. His voice welled up full of passion. A crowd had gathered, their begrimed faces turned towards his father. Bob knew many of them by sight. Bob felt the knot of tension in his middle screwing tighter. He was forgetting to breathe. His father had moved onto 'The Prince of Peace'. Abuse began to rumble but his father took no notice except to raise his voice.

"Each one of you must search his conscience … the way of Christ is the way of peace. Look, he was crucified, he didn't lift a hand against his persecutors."

"Hun lover!" someone bellowed. "Hun lover! Get him down! Foreigner! Spy!"

Bob saw a surge in the crowd. Pushing and shoving started. His father continued to stand facing the onrush, still trying to be heard. Bob at his side stared into yelling faces. Fists jabbed, a hand shot out and shoved him so that he lurched against Matthew. Pushing, dragging, a hand wrenched his arm. Now stones whizzed about. Something hard got him on the cheek and he winced with pain. A flying object hit Matthew in the face and smashed his spectacles.

"Na then ... look, it's Mester Henderson, t'barber and his lads ... stop it!" a voice roared. Bob watched the old foundry-man elbowing his way into the centre of the mob. His massive head poked above them. Anger, laughter and poverty had ploughed deep lines on his forehead and cheeks. He raised a gristly arm in the air. "I say, let the man speak!"

"Thank you, Alec," his father shouted.

They continued a while longer and dispersed after giving out their copies of the newspaper.

* * *

"Thank God you're back," Lydia said when they walked in.

"Oh I do wish I could have gone," Amy said, her eyes shining.

"Heavens, it's not for girls ... whatever do you think. Matty, where are your spectacles?"

"Broken." Matthew produced the smashed lenses from his pocket.

"We were saved by Alec Ford," William said.

"I wonder if it did any good?" Bob mused, fingering his bruised cheek.

"You never can tell," his father said, "remember, some seed fell on stony ground, but some fell on fertile soil and flourished."

They'd got onto cocoa and bread and dripping when a heavy knock sounded on the street door. William went down to answer. Bob heard the dull, smudged sound of men's voices as his father conducted someone into the parlour.

"I bet it's the police," Bob said.

A few minutes later William reappeared; behind him were two policemen. "These gentlemen want to search the house," he announced.

"Whatever for?" Lydia said.

Bob felt a rush of pride for his mother, who stood so erect and unafraid, surveying the policemen. Even in her print work-day overall she looked imposing.

"Papers, Ma'am," the leading policeman said.

"What sort of papers?"

"Subversive literature."

"Goodness! I'm sure we won't have anything like that here. Still, carry on."

Bob remembered that they'd only returned with a single copy which they'd left on the hall table.

Whilst the policemen wandered about the kitchen and mounted the stairs to the parlour, Bob sneaked out into the hall, seized the offending newspaper and folded it up so small that it fitted into his inside jacket pocket.

Two hours later the men left empty handed.

"I told you we wouldn't have such things here," Lydia said as she accompanied them to the door.

"Goodnight, Ma'am."

They all gathered in the cellar kitchen.

"Where is it?" William asked.

"Where is what?" Lydia said.

"In my pocket," Bob said.

"I thought I'd have heart failure." His father guffawed.

"Subversive literature!" Joe mimicked. "Bed-time stories ..." He caught Bob a light cuff on the ear and they fell about in a mild bout of wrestling. Amy giggled until the tears ran down her cheeks.

Chapter Eight

Amy had left J.G. Graves to start work as an assistant at Boots, the Chemist. She loved the special smell of the shop and the Winchesters massed on the dispensary shelves, containing pink, mauve, white and cream liquid. Ruby-coloured cough mixture sparkled like some elixir of life in bulbous bottles. Lines of sky-blue jars with strange Latin names inscribed in gold on white scrolls stood on another shelf above the dispensary bench. There were little brown varnished drawers with glass knobs and they all bore labels inscribed with gold letters. The brass scales were polished every day by a cleaning woman. The chemist weighed up powders and crystals on them, gently sliding increasing quantities onto the glistening heap until the thin counter swung up to the centre of the arch and remained there, quivering.

Everywhere she turned, Amy spotted some new and intriguing objects. Lines of glass jars held cough pastilles and barley sugar lozenges. There were barley sugar sticks as smooth and yellow as amber. Sometimes mothers brought their babies to be weighed on the scales, and the children would lie in the baby-basket, gurgling, like the pictures of Moses in the bulrushes in her children's Bible.

There was another dispenser in the shop, a girl called Daisy. The Manager, Mr Dows, was a very precise, middle-aged man. Amy liked him because he tended to be distant, and treated her views with respect, unlike Snoopy Copeland at J.G. Graves.

* * *

Amy, as she weighed up quarters of Friars' Balsam lozenges on the handsome brass scales, wondered about the suffragette movement. She had been following its activities passionately and enshrined Emily Davison in her thoughts as a martyr, and her flesh could still creep at the idea of Emily being kicked to death as the horse's hooves pounded over her. Now she had just come across a report about Christabel Pankhurst addressing a meeting in London. She had cut out the article in order to digest it. According to Christabel's speech, women were to accept their duty, which was to make their men-folk flock to the colours. The men were to go into battle like 'knights of old' and 'uphold the honour of the nation'. *All cackle*, Amy decided, *cackle and tosh*. She tweaked the corners of the white paper bag and placed it on one side and began letting a fresh pile of lozenges trickle into the scale pan. They made a tinny patter as they hit the metal.

"Miss Henderson, would you serve please." Amy left the dispensary and entered the shop to stand smiling behind the counter.

"Can I help you, please?" she said.

"Court plasters, please, Miss."

In a twinkling she'd located the plasters in one of the shiny chestnut drawers, and made the sale, interspersing it with bits about the splendid weather, lovely to be out, all bracing stuff. She enjoyed the challenge of finding articles and listening to customers' stories as she gave them their change, but most of all she wanted to learn how to make the magic potions. The big Winchesters of medicine had to be restocked. She would see Mr Dows pouring dark liquid into a measure as he prepared to make *Mist Expect Nig*. Then there was the white powder to be weighed out for *Mist Kaolin Sed* and *Mist Kaolin et Morph*. When you had a stomach upset you'd be prescribed *Mist Kaolin Sed* and the chlorodyne in it gave your tummy a warm glow. There were also chlorodyne lozenges in the big glass jars. They were thin, smooth brown oblongs and they gave you a pleasant burning sensation in your chest and you'd heard people could become addicted to chlorodyne. That was an addiction you could understand but others were different. A shabby bloke in a raincoat would shamble in for a bottle of methylated spirits. Mr Dows ahemmed and stared over his spectacles at the man when Amy was serving him. Later he asked her to come into the dispensary.

"He's er ... he drinks it, Miss Henderson ... but there's nothing we can do." Amy felt sympathetic to the man, though she couldn't imagine drinking methylated spirits, but chlorodyne, that might be different ...

The making of pills was another fascinating occupation and as soon as Mr Dows brought out the handsome machine with its brass finish, she knew what was afoot.

Everything in the shop, but particularly in the dispensary, had its own intoxicating odour. Kaolin had a dull, blunt, powdery smell, whereas when Mr Dows made up *Mist Tussi Nig* and *Mist Expect Nig* the smell had an edge to it, a bit vinegary and not altogether pleasant. When people said they had a cough, you had to ask if it was a dry or a productive one. If they wanted to expectorate, you'd reach for the *Mist Expect Nig*. The word 'spit' was not used. You had to acquire the correct terminology, but Amy had almost choked trying to suppress the desire to giggle when she listened to Mr Dows asking a foundry-man whether or not he could expectorate and the foundry-man had looked very puzzled and said, *I don't rightly know.* There had followed an elaborate skirting round of the word whilst Mr Dows' cheeks grew from pink to tomato and Amy had finally intervened with, *You know, get stuff up, spit.* The man had looked relieved and grinned at her.

* * *

The decision came to her gradually, as she watched Mr Dows' thin dry hands holding the medicine phials up to the gas light to check the level of the liquid: she intended to be a pharmaceutical chemist. She wanted to be able to make up those mixtures and read the Latin on the prescriptions by herself – she would penetrate that foreign country and know its secrets. But how? Mr Dows had obviously come from the sort of family who could afford to send him to study pharmacy. You knew it from his gently honking accents, so different from the local ones. He was looked on by many as a wise man.

Have you got anything for warts, earache, biliousness, headache, rheumatism?

They believed in what he could provide and liked the bitterness of *Mist Expect* because they were sure it would cure them. And Mr Dows stood there like a pillar of white soap, fingers trembling as though with an excess of sensibility. Amy, positioned at his elbow, would feel how stalwart she was by comparison. She realized that she must make herself indispensable to Mr Dows and in that way she might find some possibility of achieving her ambition. *How ...* she wrestled constantly with the how of it. You were imprisoned in the family, mainly because you were female. As you grew older it became ever clearer.

It was: *Miss Henderson, wash the measures will you please! Miss Henderson, get the sterilizer on. Miss Henderson, shop! Miss Henderson, get the order up for Lofthouses and Saltmer ...*

Daisy didn't mind. She was one of thirteen children and knew all about babies and household chores and running a tribe of men and boys. Her big doughy face was perpetually creased in a good humoured smile.

"Oh well, he *is* the boss ... and I mean, Amy, we're just the girls."

"'Just the girls!'" Amy snorted.

"He's in charge ... Amy, you *are* dreadful!"

"I want to be a chemist."

"*You* ... but you never could, girls don't."

* * *

Amy thought a lot when she sat on the lower deck of the tram travelling to and from work. She wouldn't support Christabel

Pankhurst any longer, nor did she think the Reverend Price had anything to offer, so what next? Daisy talked about the price of calico and her young man who'd gone to the front.

He's fighting for his country – I'm that proud of him.

What could you say to that? You had to keep quiet. It would be wrong to make her question what he was doing.

I've heard about your father, Amy, and your brothers …

When she walked up the hill home, people gave her an extra hard look. *Your brothers, Amy … and your father … outside Browns, all that business … well.*

Yes, well? She wanted to pull a funny face and wiggle her ears to them like Joe did, but she kept her sphinx-like smile and pressed forward.

Daisy had a smug look. All the girls from Firshill School, her old school, seemed to be blooming. There was a spate of sudden marriages, white dresses and veils were set off splendidly by khaki, but Amy read in The Sheffield Guardian 'For Black Millinery at popular prices go to Daniel Evans & Co., The Millinery Emporium.' You might not have known that men were dying all the time except for little hints like that.

* * *

After Amy had been working at Boots for several months, one day Mr Dows didn't appear. In the course of the morning they learnt that he was suffering from 'nervous indisposition' and would be unable to resume his duties for some time.

Throughout the morning Amy took charge and was able to sell cough lozenges, Beechams pills and powders and anything which didn't require dispensing. Although she knew by now how to make up bottles of cough linctus and stomach medicine, she was not allowed to do so without supervision. The poison cupboard remained locked and Mr Dows kept the key on his chain.

Amy enjoyed those hours. She felt herself growing into the role. She imagined advising countless customers on sprains, runny noses, sore eyes and stomach aches. The cure of illness had always fascinated her. Bessie, her doll, with the pot head and speedwell-blue eyes, had received hot poultices made from breadcrumbs and boiling water on numerous occasions, much to her mother's disgust. *Why do you have to be messing about like that? Must be getting the doll's clothes off every five minutes – never a second before you're undressing it and slapping something on it. So messy!* Mother had never been able to understand the satisfaction of preparing poultices.

After the lunch break when Amy had just opened the shop, she was always first there anyway, a person in a brown suit and stiff white collar arrived. With his rimless spectacles and his air of idle cleverness, he irritated Amy from the moment she saw him.

"Hah, good afternoon, I'm Godfrey Campbell. I'm coming to manage the shop until Mr Dows recovers from his indisposition."

"I see." *What a jumped up snob ... so there he was, just like that, the one in charge.*

"You must be Miss Henderson?"

"Yes and this is Miss Wilson."

There was a burst of how do you doing with Daisy beaming as though the Angel Gabriel had descended. Amy listened to his cultured tones and surveyed his finely chiselled features with disgust. He was another like Dows, she supposed, used to commanding. He could walk into the shop and take over and soon it would be, *Wash the measures, Miss Henderson, get the sterilizer out. Have you made up this week's order? Have you checked the stock?*

They tottered through the afternoon with Mr Godfrey Campbell dispensing medicines and demanding to know the layout of this and that. Daisy Wilson obviously loved it. She thrust her well-cushioned bosom at him and it seemed to palpitate and thrill under the careful pin-tucking of her white blouse. To and fro she swanned, "Yes, Mr Campbell, no Mr Campbell." And Amy set herself to wash up the measures, and stood at the sink in the dispensary with the phials piled in a bowl of suddy water, and attacked them with a bottle brush that reminded her of Mr Dows' moustache. *Idiot,* she thought, *idiot – just because he's young and a man! Dows' dithering was infinitely preferable, at least it allowed you to get on.*

When she arrived home, her mother's blue and grey Sunday dress and dangling earrings told her they'd got visitors.

"Your cousin Freddie Brown's come to see us."

"Oh yes." Amy didn't feel like visitors, she'd sunk into a glowering mood because of Mr G. Campbell, the new lord and master. An advance into the world of magic potions was growing increasingly remote.

"He's in the parlour with Matty and Bob. Can you take the tray up for me? I must look in the oven. I've made a batch of buns, just as a treat."

The treats and Sunday teas grew more infrequent these days what with the shortage of sugar and it being so expensive.

"He's been wounded and he's on leave from the front."

"Hm." Amy glared at the bone-china, rose-sprigged tea-set. Best things – there were always best things. People seemed to embalm part of their lives. She'd never cared for the stuffed owls and tropical birds some families had perched on the mantel-piece under glass domes in their parlours. In the same way she detested fur capes and those bits of fur with little snarling fox heads upon them, which her maternal aunt, Freddie's mother, wore on important occasions. The creature's spiny fangs and bright, frantic eyes turned her stomach with pity. Creatures should be free and roaming in the open, or allowed to die and disintegrate naturally. In that spirit she had once let out Aunt Bessie's canary, much to everyone's consternation. *What a child, what a child! She'll come to a bad end, mark my words.*

Upstairs she clomped with the tray. They'd certainly hear something from Freddie and she didn't know whether she wanted to. "Tea!" she announced, entering the gloomy parlour which felt cold and smelt of lavender furniture polish. Freddie, dressed in his uniform, sat on the horse-hair sofa.

"Well if it isn't Amy." Freddie grinned palely. "Quite the young Miss."

"None of that." Amy set the tray down on the table and began to arrange cups and saucers. "What's been happening then, Freddie?"

"Not what you'd like to hear."

"You've been telling Bob and Matty, I'm sure."

Bob, leaning back in an armchair, looked rather ill.

* * *

Amy's arrival came as a relief to Bob. With Amy present Freddie wouldn't give them any more details. He'd arrived joking, trying to make everything seem fine and dandy, but then as the afternoon wore on, fragments had poked through. Mounds and mounds of rotting corpses, he'd said, with big black flies laying eggs in their eyes and maggots hatching and crawling, and the stench, a sweet rotten reek. *Oh, if I hadn't seen it*, he'd kept repeating, *if only I hadn't. You had your rum tot and you went over the top and then you saw your battalion struggling in front of you and going down as the bullets hit 'em, seeming to fall real slow. It was like a dream and you thought you'd wake up. And the moaning and screaming, like souls in purgatory. No reason in it, nothing. All that death. Things you'd never seen in your life. We'd marched down that road singing.*

With Amy pouring out the tea, things edged back from a precipice. Freddie started recounting pleasanter stories.

"Last Christmas we played football with 'em, the Hun, they

were no different from us. Very nice in fact. This chap from Hanover showed me these photographs of his wife and family and we swapped cigarettes. We got a rocket from headquarters about it though. Next day we were killing one another again. As though it hadn't happened."

"Have a bun, Freddie," Lydia said, presenting him with the glass cake-stand.

"Thank you, Aunt Lydia, we could have done with a few of these out there."

"I thought they said it would all be over by Christmas," Amy said. Bob wished she wouldn't poke about now that Freddie had stopped telling the dire stuff.

"Once the Hun got dug into the trenches, that was it. It'll be a long time, a long time."

Freddie had a wedge-shaped head and carroty hair. His mouth was a narrow line beneath a ginger moustache. He'd been a cheerful, cocky sort, now he was old somehow. Bob noticed the way Amy was taking little peeks at him; she'd be weighing him up.

Whilst the conversation wound in and out of the tea cups, Bob struggled with the gruesome details. In those heaps of bodies were Langdale and Ian Crawford. To think of them rotting made a wave of hot dizziness sweep over him. His palms sweated. He remembered the words in The Labour Leader: 'Christ in khaki out in France thrusting his bayonet into the body of a German workman.' Why had they insisted on walking straight into this suicide? Was the human race set on its own destruction?

It was going dark already and his mother lit the gas. Freddie's hands shook as he drank his tea or replaced the cup on the saucer. Lydia pressed buns on him.

"You're so thin, Freddie, you need all the food you can get."

"That's what Mother says. It's funny to be back."

"Why's that?"

"Kind of. You forget that things can go on like this." He gesticulated round the table at the tea things. "You wouldn't understand. Whatever you do," he twisted to look at Bob and Matty, "don't join up. It's quite different when you get there."

He didn't really mean that. Instead he was telling them that they were lucky blighters who'd worked it, so they could escape whilst others died. Bob felt the hot blood in his cheeks. He couldn't say anything. It was like sinking into a swamp. He felt the sucking sticky mass clinging to his ankles – you had to grasp hold of what you believed, keep firm, or you'd be clawed under. He watched the flickering of the gas in the milky globe. This was bound to get worse.

"Well, I'd best be off back up home."

"Won't you go down into the shop and see your Uncle?"

"No, best get off. I'll be round again." He hauled himself up with some difficulty and Bob went downstairs to see him off. They stood for a few seconds on the doorstep looking up the steep grey hill. It was a cool spring evening.

"I didn't expect to come back."

"No," Bob said. He was aware of Matthew standing beside him, looking very pale in that light.

"Cheerio, pal!" Freddie gave Bob's shoulder a friendly slap, nodded at Matthew and lurched slowly up the incline.

Chapter Nine

Amy still couldn't suppress her overpowering feeling of dislike for the new lord and master. Daisy had fallen in love with him from the first. "Yes, Mr Campbell, really, Mr Campbell, you don't say." And then, "Well, if it wasn't for my young man, Herbert, I can't think …"

Amy was scornful. "What's so special about him – not got a thought in his head. He's just one of those accountant types, always scurrying after farthings and working things out like a cash register."

One afternoon Amy and Godfrey Campbell were alone stock-taking, between serving customers, and Daisy had gone to post some orders. Amy, at the top of a ladder, called down, "Thirteen boxes of Bile Beans, twelve of Doan's Back and Kidney Pills, five bottles Sloan's liniments." Pause. Godfrey Campbell looked up.

"You enjoy your work, don't you, Miss Henderson?"

Amy stared down at him, surprised. She had a smear of dust down the front of her white overall and knew she'd got some on her face. What did it matter! "Yes, why do you ask?"

"Oh, I just thought, you're very quick; don't you think you might be more than just …?"

"Yes." In her eagerness, she almost slipped off the ladder, and it swayed perilously.

"Steady."

"What were you saying?"

"Hah, there's a customer, we shall have to break off for a while."

Amy climbed down the ladder.

"I should, er, clean your face, Miss Henderson."

Amy squinted at herself in the mirror advertising some back and kidney pills. *Cheeky pig, telling me I'm …* she giggled at the sight she presented and scrubbed at the grey patches.

Mr Campbell strode back into the dispensary whistling 'If you were the only girl in the world'.

"We were having a serious conversation," Amy insisted.

"Were we? It was the Sloan's we'd got to, hadn't we?"

"About me."

"Oh heavens, yes, about you. I gather you don't like me, that you're a little creature of some fury when you choose to be ... and that ..." He held up his hand, regarding her sardonically with his head on one side. "I'm telling you Miss Henderson, only you won't wait for the coup de grace, will you?"

"I don't know what that means because I wasn't privileged to stay at school and study French, but I just thought, just for a second that ..." She glared at him, wanting to wither him with fury.

He smiled at her. He evidently thought she was funny, some weird little creature – perhaps he'd never encountered someone like her before. No doubt his usual ladies flattered his ego and danced round after him like Daisy did.

Further conversation was interrupted by a peculiar noise out in the street.

"Heavens," he muttered, "I wonder if it's a Zeppelin. Stay here ..."

They'd been hearing about Zeppelin raids since April. People said you could be incinerated without warning. All you'd glimpse would be a great conical object hurtling towards you to cause a mighty apocalypse. There'd been a lot of stories about apocalypses ending in Armageddon. Amy forgot what she'd been saying as she listened. Perhaps they would be blown to pieces. She recalled what Freddie Brown had said about exchanging the snaps and cigarettes with the German soldiers. They'd just be ordinary people who incinerated you. Did that make it any less awful? Fragments whizzed through her head as she stood there staring. Godfrey Campbell returned and she noticed that his face was rather pink.

"Actually er ... it's just a dray that's shed its load."

They both doubled up with laughter. Amy held onto the dispensary bench and giggled until the tears streamed down her cheeks. "So it's not the apocalypse this time! Oh there's everything happening now," she said. "Russians travelling about Britain in trains and Zeppelins over the horizon ..."

"I'm sorry, Miss Henderson, I seem to have got Zeppelins on the brain."

"It's not surprising."

"Tell me why you don't like me."

"Who said I didn't?" She could feel herself blushing.

"It's quite obvious."

"Go on."

"Anyway, what I was going to say, why don't you try for a Boots' scholarship to study pharmacy?"

Amy stood quite still. She could feel the racing of her heart – why not? Why ever not? "Where do I find out about it?"

"I'll see what I can dig up."

"Thanks."

They were about to resume the stock-taking when he turned to her. "Miss Henderson, dare I suggest that after the Zeppelin, we should have some tea?"

"All right, I'll get the kettle on." Amy went through to the old stove in the back of the shop, filled the kettle and set it on the burner. Whilst she waited for it to boil, she speculated on the possibility of the Boots' scholarship. This was what she'd been waiting for; here, here was a chance, a microscopic one perhaps, but nevertheless something. 'If I was the only girl in the world' she hummed, hardly daring to probe what it might mean. Really, perhaps old Campbell wasn't too bad after all, but one had better wait and see. Amy was by nature sceptical, people rarely conned her. She had a way of seeing through pretence and flattery, and enjoyed speculating on people's motives. *I'm not a nice biddable girl*, she thought as she spooned the tea into the brown pot, *I'm spiky and I can't bear cackle.*

"Do you want your tea in the dispensary?"

"Yes please – you are actually smiling at me."

"Am I? I wasn't aware of it."

"They'll be having to train women for this job, the way things are going. You realize now they've passed the National Registration Bill we'll all be required to register in August – men of military age, I mean?"

"Yes." Amy frowned. "My brothers think it's a trick. Asquith seems to be hinting there'll be conscription and this is just the first stage ... he denied it for ages."

"You seem very well informed, what do you know about politics, Miss Henderson? I didn't know young ladies were interested in such topics."

"Why would that be?"

"You're a proper card, Miss Henderson ..."

"Are you a pacifist, Mr. Campbell?"

"No. Are you going to present me with a white feather?"

"That's the last thing I would do."

"But I thought the suffragettes were handing out white feathers?"

"I have an independent mind." Amy was standing in the dispensary doorway, and she could feel how her face burned.

Just then Daisy bounced in. "Oh what a mess in the street. Amy, you aren't on about politics again are you?" She rushed breathlessly on in her usual way. "Tea, oh good!"

When they closed Godfrey Campbell waited until Daisy was out of earshot and then he turned to Amy. "I shall not forget about the scholarship, Miss Henderson."

"Thank you." She grinned at him. "I appreciate it." *Yes, after all he was quite reasonable and human.*

She hummed 'If I was the only girl in the world' all the way home on the tram, breaking off now and then to stare at people in the street, the lines of houses, the rows of bill-boards with their urgent notices: *Women of Britain Say "Go!" Your Country Needs YOU!* Kitchener's finger pointed at her and his eyes glared. Was conscription coming closer? What would happen? Poor Freddie Brown and Daisy's Herbert and Mildred Shields' young man, Michael ... all those young men, and Freddie like a ghost. It wasn't as though things were any easier at home: nobody would employ Matthew. He'd come in drooping with exhaustion after tramping round. If he wasn't out looking for work, he went to the library and worked on perfecting his French, German and Spanish. Bob disappeared there as well when he wasn't helping in the shop. Mother didn't cook any more Thursday joints because they couldn't afford them but performed miracles with a few lentils and a ham bone. Father said they'd lost some trade because of their speaking out for pacifism – but at least he reckoned it wasn't as bad as he'd expected.

When she arrived home, she found Aunt Bessie and her mother sitting in the parlour crying.

"Freddie's gone," her mother said.

"Oh dear. But I don't understand – he was injured, I thought he'd not go back for a long while?" She found the tears sloshing on her hands.

"They sent him back – he should never have gone. He couldn't run, not now."

"Your Auntie got the telegram this morning."

"Oh dear, oh dear!" Auntie Bessie rocked to and fro, her handkerchief thrust before her eyes. She'd given birth to eight children but only Freddie had reached manhood and now he too was gone ...

Amy felt glad that Matty and Bob weren't around. Joe was in the shop with Father. She was sure they'd have taken it very badly. Each death seemed like a reproach that they were still alive when their contemporaries were dead.

Chapter Ten

It was the waiting that wore you down, Bob thought, *and the uncertainty and the constant accounts from the front.* News vendors screamed, 'British break through ... heavy enemy losses.' And that brought back Freddie and his accounts of men lying black and bloated in the shell holes with gigantic rats gnawing at their entrails and the screams of the dying in No-Man's-Land; Freddie himself now part of the dead out there somewhere. What had this got to do with honour and glory and freedom?

Most mornings he cleaned in the barber's shop, brushing up the multi-coloured piles of hair, gazing at its texture as he swept it into the shovel, whilst his father shaved customers or cut their hair and Joe worked nearby, interspersing Father's homilies with garrulousness and grinning. Even then, and later on his way to the library, Bob couldn't let the three words go: honour, glory, freedom. Whom could they possibly be freeing with all this slaughter – neither those taking part in it nor those like himself who had refused could be free of guilt? He knew that everyone who saw him must be thinking, *what is that shirker doing, how dare he, what a coward.* Their glances stuck in his skin like darts.

Engrossed in such thoughts, he strode hatless towards the big white stone block of the central library. Somebody had called his name and he swung round. Since the night in the Victoria Hall he had not seen Elizabeth Stanley. Now there she was, splendid in a dove-grey costume and a high-necked white blouse. His smile at the sight of her died when she approached him. "Coward," she hissed, and thrust a white feather at him. "I thought you'd got more about you, Bob."

"Thank you," he said, "kind of you, Elizabeth." He stuck the feather in his button hole and climbed the library steps, feeling neither angry nor sad, that was just how it would be.

In the library he looked straight at a new poster pinned up on the cork board. 'Volunteer or be fetched!'

It's coming, he thought, *sooner or later, they're bound to try coercion.*

Inside the oak panelled reading room where elderly men nodded over thick books Bob's eyes met yet another notice board: 'What did you do in the Great War, Daddy?'

It would be far easier to don khaki and go over the top with the rest sooner than suffer this constant attempt to force you to act against your conscience.

The room was quiet enough except for the sticky asthmatic breathing of old men and the turning of pages. Now and then somebody scraped his throat. One or two offered him a malevolent stare. Everything was scratchy – where could he escape the stares? Could he never be someone the gaze would leap over, just how it used to be? No, he was guilty, they had all decided he was sitting pretty whilst all the others, his old school mates, went to their death. Sooner be dead than this …

He made for the newspaper and periodical table, where he found The Labour Leader.

"Whatever the purpose to be achieved by war, however high the ideals for which belligerent nations may struggle, for us 'Thou shalt not kill' means what it says. The destruction of our fellow men, young men like ourselves – appals us, we cannot assist in the cutting off of one generation from life's opportunities. Insistence upon individual obligations in the interest of national well-being has no terrors for us, we gladly admit – we could even extend – the right of community to impose duties upon its members for the common good, but we deny the right of any Government to make the slaughter of our fellows a bounden duty."

This was evidently the first manifesto from a group calling itself 'The No Conscription Fellowship'. So there were other people sharing their views, perhaps thousands of them, not just the Hendersons. He could scarcely believe it. Here in this library that almost vibrated with poisonous glances, rescue at last. Now it didn't matter, let them pour scorn on him ... none of it mattered, unknown people were out there no doubt sharing the same fate but not giving in. Fancy there being a newspaper bearing such news! Most papers on the table had been banging Horatio Bottomley's drum for recruiting meetings where society ladies presided to encourage the dear boys. In The Daily Mail he'd seen conscientious objectors called 'pasty faces'. In The Times personal column the previous month he'd noticed:

'Jack FG – if you are not in khaki by the 20th, I shall cut you dead – Ethel M.' Such things stuck in your memory even though they belonged to someone else's lives. Would Jack FG now perhaps be in uniform, or would he already be dead? And Ethel M, how would she feel when she heard the news of his passing? What would all these women do, when the supply of young men had dried up?

* * *

That was a peculiar summer. Lydia complained about food prices, eggs were getting scarce and sugar increasingly costly and difficult to come by. Meat had become so expensive that they were forced to eat much less of it. She'd stopped cooking William's favourite dish, roast mutton, because they couldn't afford it.

When she was out shopping Lydia began seeing posters on the hoardings exhorting people to economize. 'We risk our lives to bring you food. It's up to you not to waste it.– A message from the seamen.'

She consoled herself with the thought that it was a household where very little was thrown away. Years of near poverty had encouraged thrift.

In the shops Lydia listened to the other women's gossip. A lot were now in mourning and those who weren't talked of the letters they had received from their sons and husbands at the front.

They don't say very much, can't I suppose, you never know where they are – mind you, he's allus cheerful.

Did you hear about young Albert West? Only been out five minutes, such a fine lad.

When they saw Lydia nearby, they drew into a tighter group, huddling in their black so that she would feel excluded. She tried to ignore it, look the other way, but if she knew someone had lost a son or a husband, she would make herself approach them to offer condolences and they would stare at her with angry eyes. She knew what they thought ... *hah she's got her boys, why should they still be alive?*

She'd find herself washing towels in the cellar kitchen, not seeing the suddy water but with Matthew in her head, his pale face and his flashing spectacle lenses. He said little most of the time and read his foreign language books, or he'd play the piano, often hymn tunes. But when Ziegelmann had killed himself, a change came over him. She could only sense what that might be but she saw a deadness in his eyes. And Bob, dear Bob, wrong to have favourites, but she'd got a soft spot for him, he had such winning ways, would bring her a bunch of violets he'd spent his last coppers on, recite a line of poetry to her. It pained her to see how over the weeks his face had set in lines of despair; he looked older. Joe was different, he was in there day in day out beside his father – he could be caustic and he'd laugh, though she sometimes heard an edge to that laughter. No, he wouldn't let them fetch him down. He'd boomerang into the kitchen, seize her round the waist and dance her round whilst she protested.

William, though, was her deepest worry. He didn't know how to spare himself. If he wasn't working then he was out with the Guild of Help or preaching pacifism. At night he'd started waking with pains in his chest. *Nobut wind*, he said. *No*; she'd insisted bringing him a glass of water, *you're working yourself into the ground.* Of course he wouldn't have it, but it came again. And now the doctor said angina and he must rest, but how could he? He would never rest. All those years ago she'd been swept away by his preachifying, his passion, his great dark eyes, Bob's eyes. He was going to make the Kingdom, he believed it. Only she'd known even then that he never would, but she hadn't realized the power of his longing and his determination. At times she thought it possessed him, and there was nothing could gainsay it.

* * *

Amy kept the possibility of training to be a pharmaceutical chemist secret and she waited. Had it just been hot air? Would Godfrey Campbell really find out about it? She tried to pretend that she wasn't waiting, hoping ... It was a strain to be her normal self; she didn't want to let herself beam or fawn. No, she would be resolute, glower if necessary. And then one morning when Daisy had been despatched to the post office, she heard him calling her into the dispensary and went, trying to suppress any hope.

"Miss Henderson, I've got some news for you – not particularly marvellous but it may help."

Oh come on, come on, the jumping jack inside her chafed.

"That sounds interesting," she said.

"I discovered if you continue with your night classes and matriculate there's a possibility of Boots awarding you a scholarship to a School of Pharmacy. It would mean, and here's the snag, you would have to cover in three months what other students might in two years."

"Thank you for finding out," she said. "Whatever happens I shall try for it." She found she was grinning and couldn't stop. This was where it started. She had been in the dream of her own shop, an independent chemist, for a long time. If ever Godfrey

Campbell happened to be off the premises briefly, she would let herself sink into the dream of being in her own shop. She was dressing windows, arranging different displays depending on the time of year: green and purple for Easter, crape paper forming a series of effective panels, mauve, lilac, purple against which the show cards and packets would be a perfect foil. Build yourself up for the winter: gold and cheerful orange, cod liver oil, cold remedies, chest rubs. There would be a horticultural section as well and the pavement before the shop would flower with seed packets, canes, watering cans, plant-pots, fertilizers. All aids to growing things, creating a thriving plant life. Perhaps one day she might have a garden, a plot of earth where you could plant green things.

When people wanted advice, she tried to give it. Above all they interested her, each person contained a new story; the days were like the turning pages of a story book.

Daisy left to marry Herbert on one of his home-leaves from the front. I'd like to have invited you, Amy, but I can't really ... what with, you know ... I mean Herbert and all that ...

Yes, yes, of course.

All that drifted by, and then one October morning when Amy was on her way to work, she heard bands blaring and saw soldiers marching in the city centre and there was Horatio Bottomley waving his fists.

"I take it you'll follow the herd?" Amy said as soon as she saw Godfrey Campbell. She knew this might have been considered rude, but she didn't care. She couldn't stop herself.

"Boots have asked me to stay on until Mr D. is well enough to come back. After that, I don't know. These are strange times."

Amy, who had been sticking labels on pill-boxes, happened to look up and met his eyes. Their expression was curiously veiled and concentrated.

"Yes," she said, "I often think the war will go on for ever. I'm sick of seeing the newspapers and looking at posters."

"Shall you miss me?" he said.

The question ricocheted round the dispensary and took Amy by surprise. She coloured and let the pill-box roll off the dispensary bench. They were royal-blue ones with a gold rim round their lids and Amy found them very pretty. "Yes … if I'm to be truthful, I shall, but then again …"

"Then again what?"

Amy gave him a wicked smile. "Never mind."

Further conversation was prevented by a customer, who rapped a coin on the counter and screeched, "Shop!"

* * *

Most days he walked with her to the tram stop.

"Someday, we shall get the vote."

"But you're not a suffragette."

"They aren't all supporting the war. There's Sylvia Pankhurst anyway."

"But what about Mrs P. and Christabel?"

"They're misguided. I want to be able to vote, there are lots of things I'd change."

"What then?"

"Oh masses of things – for one thing everybody ought to be able to go to secondary school … oh, and have free medical treatment … and no more workhouses."

After these conversations Amy would ride home on the tram in an inner fury. She felt hemmed in, with years and years of struggle ahead – why was it that whenever she spoke out, showed she had an opinion, people stared at her, made her feel she shouldn't be saying anything because she was *only* a woman?

Chapter Eleven

Life, Bob felt, since he had resigned from Browns, seemed on one level scarcely to move. Once he'd realized that nobody would employ him, he embarked on a new routine: if Father didn't need any extra labour, he walked to the central library and took his place in the asthmatic stillness amongst the dozing old men. Some hid behind the pages of The Times but would let them sink from time to time in order to send him a poisoned glance. It was the same procedure day after day. He waited, just as he knew Matty did, for a reckoning, because it would come. Joe, labouring away beside Father, hadn't experienced this existence, where the days appeared somnolent but inside them a spring wound tighter and tighter. In the end it would snap. Anyway Joe took things easier ... He turned them off with a jocular remark and a guffaw.

Even whilst this life limped along in Sheffield, Bob knew that over there in France those same moments were crammed with raw noise that could split your eardrums, and everywhere hung the stench of putrefaction from suppurating wounds and rotting bodies. Freddie had told how the reek became a taste that turned your stomach. And all this was only part of the constant tumbling and scrambling through shell holes full of stinking water and body parts mired in mud to advance on the enemy lines. When he pictured such scenes, Bob felt sick to his guts. Sitting there, studying, waiting, could send you mad. The worst was always when he'd see a familiar figure, now in khaki, swinging himself along on crutches, who would wave at him, and haul himself over. That was how it happened one Friday morning in December on his way to the library.

"Bob! Thought it was you."

"Len, good to see you." He couldn't say, *You look well*. Couldn't ask him how he was – he'd lost a leg. There was the empty khaki trouser folded up and pinned. Len, who'd been such a nippy football player. His tackles were legendary. Bob glimpsed the shadow of that bow-legged boy who couldn't wait to be out in the school yard, playing in the street until darkness fell. What did you say?

"Did you know Frank and Billy never made it?"

"No," Bob said, tears filling his eyes, so that he had to look away. "I'd no idea."

"A lot of them from our class have gone. I've been lucky."

"Though you can hardly call that 'lucky', Len," Bob said, indicating Len's leg.

"Oh you can, pal, believe me. I heard your Freddie never came back."

"That's right."

Once installed in the library with the books spread out in front of him, Bob still saw Len before him, leaning awkwardly on his crutches. He was a foundry man's son and had gone into the works like his father but had joined up soon after the outbreak of war. Frank and Billy dead. They lay in the grass in Rivelin Valley, joshing the cousins, eager-faced, springy, their faces dappled by the sun. But they wouldn't traverse that hill any longer, would never suggest a walk ... 'gone' he said ... gone.

He wanted to lay his head on his arms and weep out the pity that lay on his heart like a great chunk of lead, causing him to sink ever lower.

* * *

In the evening of that day Bob, together with Matty and Joe, walked to the Temperance Hall where the No Conscription Fellowship was holding a meeting. William had been keen to accompany them but was having to rest in bed.

After that morning's meeting with his old school mate, Bob felt as though a quick-sand was sucking him under. He'd been monosyllabic on the way there – not that Matty spoke, so it had been left to Joe to keep them afloat with his barber's tales.

Once in the hall Bob was amazed to see how many were gathered there – several he knew from the Independent Labour Party meetings. They'd been there a few minutes when the main speaker, Clifford Allen, mounted the platform. He was a tall, very arresting looking man with a gentle face.

"We yield to no one in our admiration, of the self-sacrifice, the courage and the unflagging devotion of those of our fellow countrymen who have felt it their duty to take up arms ...

"All of us, however we may have come to this conviction, believe in the value and sacredness of human personality and are prepared to sacrifice as much in the cause of the world's peace as our fellows are sacrificing in the cause of the nation's war."

Clapping broke out in a great surge, and Bob clapped until his palms stung. Now he had been hurtled high in exhilaration. He'd heard that evening what he had felt inside him over months working at Browns, and later helping his father or in the library reading room. How he admired Freddie and Langdale and Ian and Billy and Frank for carrying out remorselessly what their consciences dictated, but he couldn't agree with them. His pulse didn't quicken at the call of 'defend' his country, or 'fight for freedom'.

Matthew, Bob noticed, clapped but without enthusiasm, and remained sunk in moroseness.

"Got the shutters up, have you?" Joe said, grinning at his older brother. "Look, I hear 'em all the time – snip, swipe, swipe ... 'The Lord said, thou shalt not kill'. The other lot say, 'An eye for an eye, a tooth for a tooth'. It's like ping-pong. There's Dad giving them the big eye look and smiling all the time, 'and I say unto you if any man smite thee on one cheek, turn to him the other also'; 'it is through meekness that a man may attain to eternal life', and they rumble on about freedom and defending your women folk. I just want freedom to think my own ruddy thoughts."

That was a big speech for Joe, and Bob looked at him in surprise. Even Matthew had turned to smile at him.

"It's been a good evening," Bob said, buttoning his jacket as they filed out into the freezing street. But seconds later, a chunk of wood struck him on the shoulder. A mob blocked the exit, surrounded them, and had begun hurling rubbish.

"There they come, pasty faces, shirkers, dogs! Fetch the fuckers down! Need teaching a lesson. Think they can swan around while our lads die."

Matthew took no notice and walked on through the crowd, and because he remained so indifferent to them, they left him alone. Bob saw Joe kicked to the ground and tried to reach him but got stuck in a mêlée of punching, thrusting bodies, which only drew apart because a group of police had come on the scene. By this time he had lost his collar, his best shirt was torn open and he bled from a gash to the temples.

Father wanted to hear the full story and his eyes glowed when he heard about Clifford Allen. Mother shook her head. "I don't like you going to these gatherings, you're going to get badly injured. All the time you've been out I couldn't rest."

Bob drank his cocoa and ate his bread and marge and gazed round at them all. He met Amy's eyes. She had two spots of pink in her usually sallow cheeks and her eyes sparkled. "Wish I'd been there," she said. Mother looked at her with disapproval.

Chapter Twelve

They'd been very busy that morning with people streaming in for cold remedies and advice on what to do with chilblains. A mother came with a child whose thumb was septic. It kept them occupied until lunch time and then Amy heard Godfrey Campbell addressing her.

"Do you see French has been recalled and now Haig is Commander-in-Chief of the army in France?"

"How very interesting!"

"There's no need to be sarcastic."

"But quite honestly, what does it matter?"

"It might matter a great deal."

Amy noticed that he seemed rather snappy, which was unusual for him. He generally like to argue, debate and feel himself opposed. Today he was different, she sensed, and she waited, wondering.

They were standing behind the counter side by side, staring down the empty shop, deciding to lock up, when he announced, without looking at her. "Oh, by the way, my parents received a telegram this morning to say my brother, John, fell in action."

"How simply awful!" Amy felt the tears stinging her eyes. "I'm so ... so sorry ... why ever didn't you say?" She put out her hand and touched his white overall.

They were silent for a while. "It's all right ... just the shock you see ... the shock. I can't believe it, not yet. I feel he's really around somewhere."

Amy thought of Freddie and the things he wouldn't tell in front of her and which Bob and Matty refused to recount. Not knowing the exact demarcations of horror made it worse, so that it lingered in the memory like some veiled threat, which menaced but never actually revealed itself.

"Amy," he said, "I think I should tell you, I feel I must

volunteer at once, now that John ... If I don't, if I wait until conscription comes, which it will, I'm sure ... I'll feel unworthy. Do you understand?" He'd turned to look at her then.

Amy wanted to say, *'unworthy', what do you mean? How can fighting increase a person's worthiness? All these big words, 'freedom', 'justice', big abstract words, they issued so easily from men's mouths ... but what were they in the end?* Yes, his news shocked her, but she supposed she could see its logic. Again as when Daisy used to speak of Herbert and Herbert's heroism in joining up, she saw that it was better to remain silent, and so she stood there with her head whirling with words she might have said.

"You do understand, don't you?" He was no longer someone languid and amused, Mr Godfrey Campbell, Pharmaceutical Chemist, cleverly playing at life. Amy was astounded at the change. An odd tension arose between them, different from the sessions of argument and banter, which even though they'd dealt with ticklish subjects at times, had nevertheless remained comradely and without threat or ambiguity ... at least she had thought so.

So you believe in free love, Miss Henderson?

Absolutely.

You will do away with marriage?

Definitely.

Yes, she believed in all of it – well, theoretically. Why not?

But the children? Bastards?

They had both known that these were theories; you could explain, explore, probe, enjoy the intellectual exercise.

Click into the present, and he was still looking at her, waiting for a response. "Well, you've always believed in big words."

"Don't put it like that!"

"I don't mean to ... I don't at all. It's just that we consider different things important. I want *this* to be dominant!" Amy tapped her temples.

"You fool yourself."

"Do I?"

"Your response is more emotional than mine ... more irrational perhaps."

"Go on!"

"Anyway, Amy, I've no way out. I must join up." He went to lock the shop door and turn the closed for lunch notice to face the street.

For some time now Amy had stopped returning home for the midday meal. Instead she ate her sandwiches in the back-premises, along with Godfrey, and it was mostly whilst they chewed their sandwiches that the arguments broke out. They lit the gas light in the kitchen for it was always so gloomy and cold.

"Almost Christmas," Amy said.

"Yes, somehow that makes it worse. They'll get Dows to come back, I suppose."

Amy, sitting opposite him, opening her bread and dripping sandwiches, had an awful hollow feeling in the pit of her stomach, as though what she was experiencing in that moment had already passed and she must look back with regret.

"Were you close to your brother?"

"Close, not close, what can you call it? When you've grown up together, there's a tie, there must be, if only through shared experience. John was always far more impetuous though. He went as soon as war broke out, seemed charmed somehow, every time he survived. He was at Mons, Ypres, got gassed but they sent him back again. When he came home on leave, he couldn't wait to return to the front, but somehow you know, he seemed happier than before. He was a Maths teacher. War made him live."

"How dreadful!" was all Amy could say. "Don't you see how terrible that is?"

"But to defend one's country isn't terrible."

"I'm not meaning that. I mean that someone needs a war before he can be happy." Amy the campaigner was speaking. Her eyes flashed, she took big bites into her bread and dripping and mourned. He gave up any pretence of trying to eat his own potted meat sandwiches.

"Will you write to me?" he asked, during the ensuing silence.

"Yes, of course I will."

"I shall need you to keep talking."

The following week Mr Dows was back, looking very doddery and subject to sudden flushes of colour and spasms of trembling whenever customers behaved with any show of firmness. He constantly called, "Shop, shop, Miss Henderson!" so that she would serve and he wouldn't have to face the customers.

* * *

On Christmas Eve, Godfrey was to leave for an army camp down south from whence he would by degrees go to the front. He had sent Amy a letter asking whether she would see him off at the railway station in her lunch hour.

So it was then that she found herself passing under the same grey stone arches, where months before she had seen summer crowds of smiling women waving off their young men. She shivered, wondering where they would all be now; how many lying buried in some unmarked grave out there in France or Belgium. The very station had a spectral air about it. A freezing wind blew and the ground shone with patches of frost like mica. Gone were the martial bands and streamers. Such people as bustled about there looked distracted. She saw Godfrey by the barrier. He was some stranger in uniform, and not the companion of stock-taking sessions and picnics in the damp, dark kitchen in the back premises.

"I'm glad you've come," he said. "I've thought of you a lot."

She wanted to tell him that it was madness, that he was a fool, but she didn't. Instead she seethed with irritation and despair.

He took her hand, something he had never done before. She was allowed to go through the barrier with him and approach the train. It was already packed with troops, some stupefied with drink, or was it grief, or both? ... difficult to tell. Amy felt awkward and unsure what to do. Already she thought he had left and that like Freddie, he would return no more. His hand felt hot and alive.

"Well, Miss Henderson," he joked, smiling down at her, "I hope the next time I see you, you will have settled the problems of the world!"

"Don't be so pompous," she said, aware that he was still holding her hand.

"I shall get on that train. Don't make life too difficult for old Dows mind, Amy. When I come back, I'll invite you to dinner ... and we can talk more about free love."

Amy, glad of his jokes, blushed and grinned. She had never been to dinner with anyone. In her family the midday meal was dinner and what you ate in the evening was known as 'tea'. Dinner, his sort of dinner, would be quite superior. But she knew they never would sit down together. Already he was a ghost and had joined all those others ... and she felt her skin prickling with coldness. Christmas, another year almost over and what if conscription came?

She stomped all the way back to the shop with the wind driving snow flurries in her face and tugging at her coat. The wafers settled on her cheeks, and caught on her eyelashes. She tried to fix on the weaving and winding of the white veils and not think about that train hissing and snorting down the country, taking those young men closer by the hour to their doom. Better to concentrate on the last Organic Chemistry lesson.

Chapter Thirteen

Matthew had been sitting in the library reading when he happened to look up and saw the headline in his neighbour's Times. He rose and made his way out into the snow. Slithering and lurching he hurried to the nearest newspaper stand, bought a paper and set off for home.

He called to the house in general as he came in. "They've passed a bill to bring in conscription." The warm air from the Yorkshire range caused his spectacle lenses to mist over and he stumbled into the newel post.

His mother came out of the basement kitchen, her hands caked in fawn-coloured dough from bread-making. "Lord help us," she said. "Who are they asking for?"

"All unmarried men between eighteen and forty-one and widowers without children."

"When will it be from?"

"March second."

"Go through, Matty, and tell your dad and Joe."

* * *

That evening whilst he ate his lentil and ham stew and forked up a white mound of mashed potato, Matty felt himself catapulted into alertness. Months of blank time had tottered by, each day a replica of the one before. And now on this evening everything came at him clear in outline, making his pulse race. He heard Bob say, "I'm just glad it's come to it at last – I'd sooner face it, let it happen."

"I hate it," Amy said. "I knew it would be like this, and I've been dreading it."

He saw how his little sister's thick dark brows crozzled in a frown. Her sallow cheeks had turned pink. She was irritating and loveable. Then there was Joe. His reaction was a guffaw. "Oh be buggered," was all he said as he slid up a forkful of potato. Matty saw how his father bridled, he didn't tolerate swearing in his presence, but Joe at times had a demon in him.

"Joe, don't you ever use language like that – not in this house," his father said.

But somehow, Matty thought, his father seemed softer that evening, the swearing didn't shock him as much as it might have done, and it slipped away without much ado, but he caught Amy hiding a smile.

* * *

The act hadn't been passed long before the brown envelopes arrived. They were to present themselves at the Town Hall on a Thursday morning to appear before a Tribunal. In their best suits and white shirts they stood in the hall and Amy, eyes glassy with tears, reached up to kiss them all before she set out for work. Their mother gave them a hug and smudged tears from her cheeks, then she came out with them and stood on the doorstep, watching them leave. Their father was already in the shop cutting hair but he'd prayed with them the night before.

"I wonder what Sir Reginald Northwich looks like?" Bob mused. "He's got his finger in plenty of pies – chairman of this Tribunal, Education Committee, Tramways Committee and he's a big noise in the Football League Association. He'll have a lot of power. I just dry up when I have to speak out in front of people like that – it was bad enough with the priests."

"He's only another chap like you and me, farts, belches – but he's got a few more pennies and a louder voice," Joe said.

Instead of getting a tram, they walked to the Town Hall. It was a day to make you shiver, with a raw east wind belting into your face and driving the breath away.

"Wonder if Dad's busy?" Joe said. "Seems funny to be out at

this time."

They were told to wait in a corridor on bench seating to be called. Matthew was summoned first. He took in the high wooden benches, the platform above, where he supposed the magistrates would have sat during a court hearing. Now it was occupied by the chairman and someone in khaki, who must be the military representative from the War Office. Both men's faces were carved in stone – he could have expected nothing else, he told himself. They stared down at him. Sir Reginald had blood-pressured cheeks, the army man had a brisk black moustache and bulldog jaws.

"You are Matthew Henderson?"

"Yes, Sir."

"What is your reason for refusing to answer your call to the colours?"

"As a Christian I cannot take a life."

No muscle flickered in the chairman's face. Matthew waited. He could hear the pounding of his heart and thought they must be able to hear it too. Then, like a shot, the military man turned to him.

"It says in the Bible, 'I come not to bring peace but a sword.'"

Matthew answered, "'Ye have heard it said, *An eye for an eye a tooth for a tooth*, but I say unto you, love your enemies, bless them that curse you ... pray for them that despitefully use you.'"

The military man held Matthew in a buzzard's gaze. "That was personal, not national."

"My position is a personal one."

"Mere rhetoric. Objection over-ruled."

Before Matthew had understood it, he was out in the corridor and the court usher was saying to him, "They'll be coming for you soon, mate."

The whole procedure had taken less than two and a half minutes.

* * *

Bob went in next. Just the sight of the court shocked him and he had to remind himself that this was only the beginning, there would be far worse to come.

"Are you not prepared to protect your mother and sister from the enemy?" Sir Reginald asked, gimleting Bob, who gazed back as though mesmerized.

"I don't think war does protect women and children. The manhood of two nations is opposing each other simply because the governments have declared war – what will happen – thousands and thousands of widows and orphans are created. I don't call that protecting women and children and I will not be party to it."

"You are an insolent young shirker and deserve to be shot. Objection over-ruled."

Bob felt the anger bubbling in his chest and wanted to shout back at Northwich, *Shoot me then, I'd sooner that than have a gun in my hand.* But then he was being ushered out into the corridor in a haze of emotion.

* * *

Joe, having seen his brothers' faces, braced himself for what would come. It was all a big charade, more ping pong, just like the churches' visits had been.

"And what would you do, if a criminal assaulted your mother?"

Joe decided that the chairman was a vile looking fellow. "Nothing," he said, and waited for the explosion.

"You are a liar and a humbug – and your claims to exemption from military service are false."

Joe hadn't expected any other outcome. "Just like a Christmas charade," he said as they left the Town Hall.

"I thought I'd bust a gut," Bob said.

"Why bother," Joe said. Matthew didn't speak.

"But that's it," Bob said, "that's the end of it ... they didn't even listen."

"What did you expect?" Matthew said. "This is just the beginning. It will be like this onto the finish."

"Perhaps we shall be shot."

"Let 'em get on with it," Bob said. "Fancy trying like that to decide whether we're serious or not! I mean, how can you prove your sincerity to someone who doesn't believe in the idea anyway?"

* * *

That evening when they were drinking cocoa and eating Mother's new bread and marge, William called them together. "Whatever happens to you, boys, you know we shall be with you in spirit. I expect you'll go to prison. They'll try to break your spirits with it."

"I wonder what colour the arrows are?" Joe said, grinning. "I can just see myself in one of those suits like pyjamas with the arrows on."

Part II

Chapter Fourteen

Rendel Watson looked at the man in khaki who sat at a desk facing him. Across his chest ran an imposing array of ribbons.

"Hah, now you've been through the police court, I have to make a soldier of you."

"I am afraid that I shall have to refuse."

"Indeed, we'll see about that. I've had thousands through here. They take it in the end. It's best to go quietly. Now give me your full name and address."

"I decline to reply."

The Sergeant Major's pen remained suspended. "Come along now, don't let's have any unpleasantness. You're in the army and if you continue to cause a nuisance there could be some exceedingly nasty consequences."

"I'm sorry, but I can take no part in any sort of military service."

"You've brought it all on yourself. Take him to be attested!"

A soldier gave Rendel a shove and they left the room and crossed the yard where a number of men sat at trestle tables filling in forms.

"Your full name?"

"I'm sorry, I've already stated, I can give no information."

"Take him for examination!"

Rendel found himself in a cubicle where he sat down on a bench and took off his hat, wondering what would happen next. It wasn't bad whilst things were moving but the quiet spells were the ones that might wear you down. He tried to keep himself steady inside, but all manner of incidentals came to him. There was Henry out in France somewhere, and his letters from the trenches; his sister, Lucy, knitting bed socks and sleeping helmets for the soldiers; and his mother conducting sewing parties and inviting the local women up to Heyford Manor to take part. She dabbled in Red Cross work too, much to his amazement, though perhaps that wasn't kind of him. They all seemed incredibly distant from him, and they were. Heyford was like some dream place: the attic, with its gable window, which had been the day nursery; the lovely ancient trees, the Wellingtonia, the elm and chestnut over two hundred years old, his father used to say. In spring the waxen magnolia blossoms curved against dark branches, wisteria, blue as the heavens, formed swathes upon the walls of the eighteenth century stables. The clear chimes of the clock set under the eaves had reached him even in his bedroom. Heyford had belonged to his family for a hundred and seventy years and the Watson commemorative burial plaques lined the church walls. Watsons had been squires longer than anyone could remember.

Looking round the cubicle he almost laughed – Heyford and this! Some might consider Heyford paradise, and indeed it was: picnics, with food hampers brought up in the donkey cart; shooting parties in September and October when they traversed the corn-stubble chasing coveys of partridges, hares and rabbits. At midday they'd sat in the shade and eaten cold turkey sandwiches and pork pie and drunk cider.

Childhood had been very pleasant – parties at the houses of other landowners, tobogganing and skating on icy ponds until the sun sank scarlet behind the black winter trees and stained the ponds and the snow pink and purple; great black birds flying into the crimson sunset.

The door of the cubicle burst open. Rendel jerked alert.

"Get undressed!"

"I'm sorry, I cannot."

"I advise you to."

Rendel smiled at the officer. "Look, please, don't think I've anything against you personally, but my conscience makes it impossible for me to undress."

"Take him to the recruiting officer!"

Once more they marched him off. A man in a brass hat with red on it and with red lapels, whom Rendel discovered later to be a Brigadier-General, sat before another enormous desk.

"You're under military law and you'd better obey or it will be the worse for you."

"I contest, Sir, that I am under military law."

Again they returned to the doctor. He was once more commanded to strip and refused. Violence rippled beneath the surface and Rendel felt it in the heavy, thrusting hands which propelled him forward. He concentrated on memories to strengthen him: Keir Hardie addressing a meeting in St. George's Hall on a Saturday afternoon and explaining to children that they should love flowers and animals and their mates. They should abhor cruelty and injustice and never do underhand or spiteful things, but be generous in their relations with others. And then his final words, 'Live for that better day'.

Rendel didn't like to think of that too often because memories could lose their power by being revived too frequently. No, he kept it inside him and it was a treasure only to be enjoyed at rare times. Keir Hardie had shown him an example, a way of life and it would remain with him always; it made nonsense of balls and hunting parties and that soft, spoiled thoughtless existence.

There were certain events whose impact upon him had been so great as to place their seal on him for life. During the No Conscription Fellowship convention at Devonshire House the previous month, he'd recognised it. He, along with two thousand others, had been gathered inside the hall to listen to Clifford Allen, and at the end of his speech, when they'd stood in silence waving their handkerchiefs so as not to provoke the mob outside the building by applauding, he had felt the power of people united by a conviction: together they could live that better day.

"Take him away and prepare the charge!"

For the second time he faced the recruiting officer. They progressed through a scene similar to the previous one and

Rendel again maintained that he was not subject to military law.

"You are under arrest!" the Brigadier finally pronounced, and Rendel was marched into a dungeon. It was about fifteen foot high by twelve wide, with walls of glazed white brick and concrete floor. He had plenty of time to survey everything. His gaze went first to the windows, but they were set over six foot from the ground, covered with corrugated iron within eighteen inches of the top, and even the glass not obscured by the metal mesh was so dirty that very little light could enter. Everything was filthy, but worst was the stench from the urine bucket, and the rusty animal reek left behind by unwashed bodies. Prisoners had spat gobs of greyish yellow slime on the floor. Did that betoken TB, pneumonia ...? Better not to think of the disease rampant in all this, pretend it wasn't there. Not see it, ignore it – after all this was just the start. You couldn't quail at this point just because of a bit of squalor ... You were just being the spoiled squire's son, and should be ashamed. They thought they would break you by making you feel degraded – if they couldn't do it with interviews, they intended to succeed with physical deprivation and conditions which would eat away at your morale.

How would the others be faring? It was unbalancing suddenly to lose the momentum of everyday life. Where a few hours before there had been London under rain, a taxi speeding down Marlborough Street to the recruiting station and everywhere colour, movement, life – now, nothing but uncertainty and waiting and an all-pervading dullness and drabness. He'd be in trains listening to their rhythmic throbbing and the pipping of their whistles as they thundered under bridges, off to another city for another ILP meeting, where the most important thing on earth was to convince people that war caused a suppression of democracy and liberty, and when it would be over the same spirit of violence would still be reflected in the peace treaties and that would cause a still greater suppression of democracy and liberty and in the end give rise to further bloodshed.

When it went well, he'd feel he could float in air currents – it was like his flying dream. He'd have such a certainty inside him that they would see 'that better day', that he was for brushing all objections aside. *Rendel, you are far too impulsive, too much so for your own good,* he remembered his father telling him. His brother Henry had taken over the reprimand. When they must duck to avoid being pelted with stones and rubbish from hecklers at public meetings, or narrowly avoid being dragged from platforms, he would wonder if he had misjudged the tone of the gathering – but anyway, opposition became pretty widespread once war had been declared.

On the days when he wasn't travelling the country to address meetings, he'd been composing editorials for The Labour Leader.

Being cut off now from this world chivvied him so that he couldn't be still, and he paced up and down, trying to swallow his impatience.

Where would Henry be now? In France for sure ... Sad that Henry and he could no longer be close. It had been different when they were children; being the younger brother he'd often followed Henry, tried to copy him. But that hadn't always worked out, it couldn't. For one thing Henry was a stickler for exactitude and planning, demanded perfection in all things. That kind of personality clashed with the spontaneous, impulsive person, who took snap decisions and didn't count the cost. Henry knew the weight and cost of everything. A gulf had been caused between them by the Sunday morning church services, which Rendel had refused to attend.

I'd sooner think about God on my own at home. God can equally well be here as there – he must be if he's omnipresent and omniscient.

Henry had gone with the rest, leaving Rendel to roam the Heyford woods. Already he had been rebelling against the high pious tone adopted by the clergymen. Religion had seemed such a dreadfully serious business with so many things you could do wrong.

By the time they'd been at Balliol for three years, they'd drawn completely apart. Henry had become a barrister. Rendel tried to picture him, a tall young man, a couple of inches shorter than himself with straight black hair and a square jaw; a very precise and eloquent speaker, but he didn't examine what he regarded as his birthright. It would never have occurred to him to question his place in society.

Being alone with only the walls to stare at made you grub around in your past life. The visit to Heyford in that fatal August, after such a long absence, had been a mistake. He'd only agreed to go because Henry was leaving for the front. Of course Henry had been one of the first to volunteer. How could it have been otherwise? With Henry it was all about serving one's country, defending honour, freedom. They'd sat at tea on the white wicker-work chairs set under the trees. The air had shimmered with a blond beautiful heat. Lucy and his mother had been smiling tremulously.

I do hope you'll be all right, dear. I've packed the chest-warmer and I've put in a little surprise from Fortnum's. You've got Kipling, Hardy and Tennyson at the bottom.

And Rendel sitting there sipping scented tea from paper-thin china and eating wafer-like cucumber and salmon sandwiches, had watched the dappled shadows swaying and had felt guilty about his own thoughts.

There was his brother bound perhaps for a terrible death and yet he couldn't stop feeling impatient with him. As he lingered with them in that idyllic setting until the evening had crept up the rim of the parkland and the first owls hooted, he had been torn by an immense sadness: here they were, the squire's family, the two upright sons, the pretty daughter in her white muslin dress, the charming mother. They were church-goers, good kind people, and yet when at seventeen he had seen London's East End for the first time on a visit to a 'School Mission' founded by some old Etonians, and had been deeply shocked, his mother had dismissed the horror.

My dear, it's necessary to the economy. Anyway, such people are used to their way of life.

He hadn't argued with her because it would have been disrespectful, and besides he hadn't known how to put his feelings into words, but he had felt instinctively that she was wrong. There could be no justification for poverty like that.

If it had been as simple as that, wholesale condemnation of his family, it would have been easy. But no, he loved them, he loved Heyford, he had grown up there, and it was uncongenial to live in a small room somewhere – but that very war was about poverty. Rendel continued pacing. He kept before himself the facts and never wanted to forget them: the average farm labourer worked a twelve hour day, starting at five or six am and earned for it between ten and fourteen shillings a week. His cottage rent would be 1/6 per week. He knew that the large families in the village were reared on potatoes, bread, jam and cheap tea. Now with the war they wouldn't even have jam.

The poor devils working the land of his father's nine tenant farmers were being told they would be fighting for *their* freedom. 'Freedom:' they'd never known it, they were donkeys, pack-horses …

His long-running train of thought was interrupted by the slamming open of the cell door. A soldier pushed a mug of tea and three slices of bread and margarine at him and then the door clanged shut.

The overpowering stench made him think the very idea of food nauseating, but he ate nevertheless.

In the course of the evening some soldiers were thrust into the cell. They all told their stories to one another and Rendel thought of the Canterbury Tales.

First came a massive Irishman, reeling with drunkenness. He kept up a frantic hammering on the iron-reinforced door. "Water, water," he bellowed, his neck straining into knots of rage, and

Rendel thought he would drag the door off its hinges, but three huge soldiers muscled up, one handed him a mug of water and glared at him. "Now then shut your bleeding mouth!" At that the drunk subsided against the wall, whimpering to himself.

A freckle-faced man from the Argyll and Sutherland Highlanders had been caught at the coast trying to stow away on a troop ship bound for France. He'd absconded because he wasn't allowed to go with the rest of his regiment off to the front.

A scrawny youth who looked about sixteen had been caught in Hyde Park with a prostitute. Rendel couldn't believe he was old enough to be in the army.

The next time the door jerked open a sergeant shouted, "Fetch your bloody biscuits!"

With that they had to go out and haul in three mattresses each that were spotted with holes like giant dog biscuits.

"Them who isn't tried get three biscuits and two blankets."

Late on the cell door rattled again and a small man in civilian clothes was pushed in. He was an attractive little chap with big dark eyes and thick black hair which lay flat against his skull from a central parting. In the half light from the flickering corridor gas-lamp he appeared gypsyish.

The soldiers, who'd hastily hidden their cards at the sound of approaching footsteps, cursed and resumed their game after re-lighting their candle.

Rendel took a good look at the newcomer. "Hello, I'm Rendel Watson." He held out his hand. The dark young man took it. Rendel became aware that the dealing of cards behind him had stopped.

"Bob Henderson," the newcomer said. "I say, I know I've seen you before. You were addressing a meeting in Sheffield once. I thought they were going to set on you."

Rendel smiled. "They probably did as well. I'm used to it by now. So what are you doing here?"

"I'm er ... actually a CO."

"Pleased to meet you, Comrade."

"Bloody conchies!" the freckled faced Scot grunted.

"That's right." Rendel grinned across at them.

"The save their skin brigade."

"The very ones."

The new chap took a postcard from his pocket. "I'm just going to drop Little Bits a line."

"Little Bits?"

"Oh just my sister, Amy. That's what we call her."

"Why?"

"Because she's tiny, but she's a ball of dynamite."

Rendel liked the little chap's smile but struggled somewhat with his flat Northern accent. Assailed by an overpowering weariness, Rendel turned on his side, muttered, "Good night, Comrades," and lulled by the mumble of the soldiers' voices and the slap of cards, he drifted off to sleep.

Chapter Fifteen

Bob glanced over at the sleeping Rendel. *You had to admire his imperturbable good humour.* In a situation like this, corralled with a bunch of unlikely looking soldiers and with the possibility of violence festering under the surface, he seemed at ease. It amazed him that he should find himself together with this man whom he had only ever seen once before and yet whose face he could not forget.

Rendel had told him that until he was court-martialled and sentenced, he could have visitors. The thought of seeing someone from home, preferably Amy, had made him decide to tell her where he was and about the meeting with Rendel Watson. Perhaps there was some remote possibility that she would manage to visit him. After finishing the card to Amy, he decided he'd better try to sleep, though his head whirled and his stomach ached. At least he'd remembered the advice of the No Conscription Fellowship to take a stamped and addressed postcard when they were first arrested. Now Dad and Mother and Amy would know where he was.

The soldiers finished playing cards and snuffed out their candle. Bob was about to take off his trousers and get under the blankets but a soldier called to him.

"Keep your togs on, mate, they took a chap from here with VD yesterday. Place is full of it. Nearly everybody you fuckin' meet's got it."

"Thanks, pal," Bob muttered, hastily dragging up his trousers. VD, he'd barely heard the word. Just the name made him blush and he was thankful for the darkness.

He lay sleepless listening to the snores of a big Irishman. They started low and rose to grinding honks. Someone else belched and broke wind in any peaceful stretches. Outside in the courtyard the sentry's boots clattered as he marched back and forth.

Where would Matty and Joe be? After the police court they had been separated as though on purpose, and now here he was, down south, miles from home and from anywhere he had ever been. Brief stays in guard rooms. Barked commands. Always being shunted further and further – and never knowing the end destination. Disjointed fragments slid through his head as he lay on his back, watching the weird patterns on the ceiling and on the concrete floor thrown by the gas-light outside the cell door. There had been the brawny soldier, who had threatened to give him a hiding, *Come on you little bugger, you won't-fight-funk, let's see what you're made of!*

And then, just as had happened when Alec Ford had saved his father from the mob outside Browns, another soldier got up. *You'll do it over my dead body, pal. I don't agree with him, but by God he's got the right to his own opinion.*

Get your kit. Take your kit, sign, sign!

I am a CO.

The hell you are. Sign! Sign!

Get the fucker to sign!

The boots clonked across the courtyard. His stomach rumbled with hunger. He felt filthy. This was the first night he had thought of removing his clothes. He'd been advised to keep them on, otherwise they might force him into khaki.

* * *

Next morning a guard collected the blankets and they were unlocked to wash in the yard and go to the lavatory, and afterwards they breakfasted in the cell on three chunks of bread and margarine and a mug of tea apiece.

"Have you got a lively group in Sheffield then, Comrade?" Rendel said.

"Not really – until we joined the No Conscription Fellowship we were just on our own … when my father tried to distribute copies of The Labour Leader with that Dr Salter article in them at the steel works, we had the police round."

"What did they do?" Rendel was grinning.

"Searched the house, but they didn't find anything. I'd got the last copy in my pocket."

"You had a lucky escape. In Australia men have been sentenced to ten years' hard labour for distributing it!"

Bob gasped. "We were so innocent. Even my sister Amy's set the cat among the pigeons arguing about COs. If we'd lived down south, she'd have been a suffragette, I reckon, but not like Christabel Pankhurst."

"This is such a hellish shame, this war – there we are, killing our fellow working men … and for what?"

"How are your family taking it?" Bob asked. "I mean, being in prison?"

"They've probably given me up for lost. My brother Henry's at the front. Still never mind, perhaps one day, they'll think again."

Just then the post arrived. Rendel had withdrawn to a corner to read a letter from his mother, when the door crashed open and Bob saw a whole array of military. He distinguished a sergeant, private and an officer. All the soldiers in the cell jumped to attention as though someone had touched them with a magic wand. Being uncertain what to do, Bob likewise stood up, but he observed that Rendel hadn't moved and didn't even glance round.

"Hey, you there in the corner – do you hear? Fall in! Come on, you're in the army now."

At that Rendel turned round, folded up his letter, pocketed it and approached the officer. Bob found he was holding his breath, sure that there would be an explosion.

"Hello, I'm sorry, Sir. I don't want to be rude in any way but I'm afraid I can't obey military orders."

"You're for solitary until you learn how to behave!"

* * *

When the officer and his retinue had withdrawn, the cell mates gathered round Rendel, grinning in amazement. The big Scot said, "Fancy that – never knew I'd see it, the old colonel told to bugger off. Well, you're not scared, I'll say that for you. Why won't you fight, mate?"

Bob, listening to Rendel, was back in the barber's shop hearing his father moving onto building the New Jerusalem – or he was down in Attercliffe outside the steel works sweating, whilst his dad moved into the evils of militarism, and waiting for the first punches to be thrown, and wondering how he could protect him. If only Dad and Ma and Amy and the other two didn't seem so far away! They belonged to a different country, somewhere known and yet not treasured enough until now. You could move through life without seeing its texture, studying it, being it, having it – only you didn't realize it until it was irretrievable. But that world could never return. To dwell on the loss was dangerous. *You mustn't think of it. Face forward!*

Rendel was saying, "A strong nation would simply get rid of all arms. It doesn't need arms to defend itself ... and see, in this war people talk as though only German militarism is responsible – it's never so simple. There's always some element of aggression on the other side. Look mate, I belong to the world." He was addressing his remarks mostly to the big Scot. "My brothers aren't just Englishmen. How can I possibly kill my fellow men?" Rendel's eyes blazed, his spectacles flashed. He might have been speaking before a hall full of people. The soldiers listened, obviously unused to hearing these kinds of sentiments.

"Think of all the young chaps dying ... and for what, eh? Just imagine, we could eventually wipe out the entire world population. Killing brutalizes people. We've got to try to unite in friendship." He was looking at them all now and smiling, and Bob glimpsed the sweetness he'd seen that day in Sheffield when he'd watched Rendel charming the crowd. And the remarkable thing was, even when the crowd turned on him, he didn't seem to care, he just went on …

"Aye, sounds good, man," the big Scot remarked, rubbing his face as though coming out of a dream, "yer ken plenty words …"

Next they got involved in speculating on what would happen at their court martial.

"It'll be two years' hard, whatever …" the Scot said.

The door crashed open again and another soldier was shoved in. He tripped and fell flat on his face. "They won't send me back, will they? They won't … they can't."

The others crowded round. "Look, look, it's me hand." He was a pitiful frightened lad, Bob thought, terrified out of his wits.

"You did it yoursel, mate, we know."

"'Course I didn't."

"Ye need nae lie," the Scot said. "We ken. Come on, own up, laddie, we'll not tell on ye. Oh lots of 'em do." He had turned to Bob who'd expressed surprise. "Cut their bleedin' hands off at times so they won't have to fight."

Bob had begun reproaching himself for not having remained seated along with Rendel when the officer had appeared. He felt he'd let Rendel down without realizing it, simply because it hadn't occurred to him not to rise. Here, codes you'd obeyed all your life were cancelled; being a CO demanded a different set of precepts. If you daydreamed at all, you were lost. He'd just reached this conclusion when the door crashed open again, and a sergeant and two soldiers seized Rendel and without more ado marched him off, leaving Bob appalled.

Once Rendel had been snatched, gloom descended again, like a Sheffield pea-souper fog. The sour stench of sweat and the ammoniac gassiness of stagnant urine stuck in his nostrils. Outside boots cracked on paving stones, a cracking voice barked commands. There was an endless yelling and banging and whistle blasts from a regimental sergeant major. "Shun!" bang, bang, bang, grate – and then it would all begin again. The soldiers grumbled amongst themselves, yawned and scratched and talked about courts martial. Bob found himself scratching too. His back itched, his groin itched, his armpits itched. He knew he must stink because he'd been sleeping fully dressed for days – how many, he didn't know. Perhaps he'd got lice, bugs of some sort, an infestation such as the homeless suffered, those who slept rough under bridges, the ones his dad tried to help. He raked his nails through his hair. His head itched. This must surely be lice. He shuddered. What would they be doing to Rendel Watson? If only he'd been with him!

Sometime in the late afternoon a sergeant unlocked the cell door and shouted. "Henderson, as you aren't prepared to be medically examined, you're deemed fit for service. You'll go to the Rifle Brigade at Harwich."

What bliss to be out in the open, even for a brief time! He stood blinking and drawing in deep lungfuls of air. The sun shone and it was a balmy May day with a pale blue sky and clouds like bolsters. He could scarcely believe that the stench and the gloom had vanished at a stroke. But part of him pulled back from surrendering to the morning's bedazzlement. He would go with it at his peril – that way lay weakness. They would surely imprison him again and when incarceration came, it would crush him. This was a mere temporary intermission.

The military policeman was quite a decent sort of chap. "You've a right to your own opinion I expect ... mind you, they'll make it hard for you. Easiest to give in and get on with it, you know. This war's making a lot of palaver. Hardly get to see my wife and the children. It's always the ordinary man that pays. Never been no different ..."

Bob nodded and said *yes, he was right,* and kept on agreeing until the train chugged in. The train was packed with troops and

Bob stood jammed in a corridor between bodies and kitbags. "Want a ciggy mate?" they'd ask him. Some wondered why he wasn't in uniform. "CO," he said. "Fuckin hell, mate, they'll crucify you!" Not encouraging tidings. "Want some, pal?" Bob was luckier this time and received four squares of chocolate, which he adored. What could be happening to Matty and Joe? Of course Amy would now have no idea where he was. He just hoped she wouldn't have decided to make the journey to see him. And what about Rendel? For sure they'd see he suffered and Bob understood now that Rendel would never back down. His determination was inspirational. Whenever Bob sensed a weakening in himself, he thought of Rendel.

Being in the train lulled by the rhythmic beat of the wheels, and the sibilant rush of steam from time to time, Bob found himself in a reflective state where he wandered in the past. He saw himself in the cellar kitchen with his mother when the police came for him.

I want to give you this, Ma, he'd said, handing her his last gold sovereign. He had kept it since the introduction of paper money in 1914. *You might need it sometime.* Her only answer had been a nod, and she had pressed him more tightly to her.

Be strong, lad, she'd said, the tears in her eyes.

All that had happened a million years ago, and to someone else. He felt ingrained with dirt and sour sweat and itchy with vermin. His thoughts refused to settle and he dozed on his feet, sedated by the background babble of soldiers' chatter, but was woken now and then when the train lurched and he stumbled into the military policeman.

It took the policeman some time to locate the barracks once they had left the train, and Bob plodded along beside him enjoying the evening air and hoping they would never find it.

Alas a brick building with sentries on duty at the gate came into sight! They had arrived and Bob was handed over and the policeman left with a receipt. Bob was locked in a cell and had a plate of cold beef, two slices of bread and marge and a mug of cold tea thrust at him.

The next morning he was awakened by a bugle call. He stared round. The other occupants were mostly soldiers but there were also a couple of COs. "I'm fucking fed up with this war," one chap railed. "I just got me leave and they cancelled it."

"They're running out of manpower," somebody else said. They presented such a gloomy picture that Bob couldn't find the right words to sympathize.

Before he could speculate on his next trial, a sergeant fetched him and took him before an officer. Again they went through the business of telling him he must attest, and with him refusing.

"Do you know that you are under military law?"

"No," Bob said. This had all begun to appear like an absurd charade. Except that behind it lay a menace, and every time, the threat of a violent end was implied. Eventually it would happen. They made him sense that he would provoke the ultimate. But what might that be?

They marched him to the Quartermaster's store.

"Are you aware of the consequences of disobeying an order?" the officer probed him with an unwavering stare. Bob felt how his heart pounded and he broke out in sweat that crawled from under his hair line and down his forehead. "Well?"

"Take your clothes off and put on this military uniform!"

"I'm sorry, I can't."

"We'll see about that!"

You wanted to fight back, struggle with them ... but if you did, you'd be finished. They thought they'd drive you to it. When the officers, the toffs, with their clever, posh voices didn't subdue you, then it was going to be a physical onslaught. Three soldiers had surrounded him and now they jabbed at him and had his jacket, shirt and trousers off in a trice. Next they forced his limbs into khaki. The cloth smelt musty and rubbed his skin like emery paper. He let it all happen, and tried to offer no resistance.

"Left right, left right!" one chanted as they frogmarched him into a bare cell. The only window, of frosted glass, was set six foot from the ground. A ventilator in the ceiling allowed some passage of air to circulate. Every now and then the spy hole in the door clattered as an eye like a giant blob of frog spawn peered at him. He sat down on the floor, back against the wall, and waited for what would happen. They'd regard this of course as a weapon for breaking him down. In such a situation, you had to work out a thought strategy; decide in what sequence you would examine everything you knew or had ever experienced. Just thinking about the chaps in the last cell should occupy him for quite a while ... The big Scot had already been out twice. He'd described frying bacon and eating it in a trench, whilst talking to the chap from Glasgow next to him, and then the shell whizzing over, and wee Malcolm becoming only a soggy mess of bright red, brains and bits of body splattered in the mud ... and he'd vomited his breakfast back up. The bacon was still frying but now flavoured with bits of brain. You could understand why the big Scot had been so drunk he'd missed returning with his unit to the front.

When the young kid, who'd harmed himself, heard the story, he asked again, *They'll not send me, will they?* And the other soldiers had looked at him and said nothing.

Apart from the one hour exercise, Bob remained in the cell twenty-three hours a day, and it was only at such times that he saw the other COs but they couldn't speak, because eyes gimleted; guards stood ready to pounce.

When he finally appeared before the court martial, he was charged with Number 2 crime, refusing to put on the uniform whilst on active service. Bob maintained that he was not in the army, so could not be called upon to wear uniform. They didn't listen to what he said. The whole event ran on mechanical channels just like the Sheffield Tribunal had; you were condemned from the start, so there was really no point in holding a tribunal, or a court martial. You did not have the right to protest, and anything you said was regarded as totally irrelevant.

Two more days passed. Bob had grown used to being in his own head all the time and was shocked when keys clonked on the wall, and the door crashed open to reveal the sergeant, flanked by two other soldiers.

"Henderson ..." and he gabbled a number, "you are to be read out."

They marched him to the parade ground, which was a square of tarmac where lines of soldiers were drawn up on all sides. Their chins stuck out, their legs were braced. How serious they were! An officer read out his crimes and announced that he was sentenced to two years' hard labour.

Back once more to the cell where it was gloomy and stiflingly hot. The floor burned the backs of his legs. His stomach churned with hunger and his head ached. He was too hot even to think and had let himself subside into a torpor, when he heard the bang and crack of approaching boots, a key grated in the lock and the door crashed open again. The sergeant and the two privates were back. One soldier held some handcuffs, the other a sword-bayonet and a kit bag.

"Take your kit and this!"

"I'm sorry, I can't."

"All right, then you'll wear these!" The sergeant strode up to him and snapped handcuffs on his wrists. "Tie that round his neck!" he commanded a private, and with that they lashed the kit bag about his body. "Forward march!"

Bob took his time. A group of fellow COs waited outside. The sunlight blinded him for a few seconds. Breeze on his face and sunshine made him smile; they defeated the metal biting into his wrists and the kit fastened round his neck. Perhaps these were the last days of his life, but the thought didn't disturb him. As he shuffled forward, he grinned at his neighbour and felt like singing.

Through signs and whispers from the CO nearest to him, Bob learned that they were bound for a redoubt built by French prisoners during the Napoleonic wars.

* * *

On arrival at the redoubt a sergeant instructed them to drill. Bob and the rest refused and had their hands clamped in irons and Bob was thrust into a cell and told to face the wall.

"You're in the army now and we don't tolerate insubordination," an officer's voice told him.

The cell was bare of everything like the other one had been, except for a small sheet of iron, which let into the wall and had to be used as a table. At night he was allowed to have his overcoat and some blankets but during the day these were removed.

For the next three days he was confined to this cell on a diet of bread and water. Eight hard biscuits and the jug of water doled out in the morning were the day's rations. You dared not think about food. Once you started imagining Mother's steak and kidney pie, or ham bone soup, or sago and stewed apple, or Sunday teas in the old days, you were lost. The longing turned into a craving that nothing would assuage. It consumed you, devoured your very thoughts ... No, the way to survive was by imagining that the biscuits were a great delicacy, which you could only allow yourself to eat by degrees. Hunger made you weak, so that you wanted to lie down on the cell floor and sleep, but it was cold, damp and flea infested. You took to watching the black beetles and woodlice that shared your cell. The black beetles had bodies shiny as coal and looked aggressive, whilst the woodlice were grey, had lots of little legs, and squatted passively in crevices, only moving when disturbed. They had a primeval appearance as though they'd been in the universe a long time. You fell to wondering how they organized their existence, whether the woodlice feared the black-clocks.

He kept thinking he'd be let out for exercise, but nobody ever opened the cell door. Darkness fell and he heard boots grating on the path outside. They stopped, a key rattled in the lock. "Excuse me, will there be exercise today?"

"You don't get no exercise on punishment. You'll be let out first thing for a wash, but that's it." The soldier slung a coat and blanket at him and made off.

He'd spent all those solitary hours, at times reading the Bible, picking out old favourites, the Gospel of St. John, Revelations and the Psalms, at others in a daze, hardly conscious.

When Sunday came round, he was let out to attend a Friends' Meeting for Worship. He'd never been to a Quaker Meeting before and found it strange at first to be sitting in silence. They'd formed a circle, sitting on kit bags and overcoats, but from time to time someone would stand up and minister. Nobody seemed to be in charge and there were no hymns. At the end a fellow CO shook his hand and smiled at him. "I'm James Crawshaw," he said, "from Leeds." Bob exchanged names with him and had to choke down an urge to cry. The complete naturalness of them all disarmed him. He'd spent so many hours alone or struggling against efforts intended to break him that now he didn't know how to respond to kindness. They must all be suffering similar things, though you would never have known it, because they were so cheerful.

It wasn't yet light on the following day when an officer and some soldiers unlocked him. "You're going to Southampton," he was told. "And you'll go from there to France to be shot."

It was May 7th he registered, and for some reason that seemed important.

Chapter Sixteen

Lydia experienced an uneasy feeling when Sunday morning came round. No church. Not to be going there anymore gave her an unpleasant anxious sensation in her middle that wouldn't let her rest and she found herself fiddling with a handkerchief, pleating and re-pleating it. Church was where you went every Sunday. She looked across at William and his face was nipped tight and gave nothing away. The church was his life. William led the way upstairs and they went to sit in the parlour. Lydia had put on her best blue dress and dangly earrings as though she were prepared for the morning service. Amy joined them.

William opened the Bible and read from Corinthians. "'I may speak in tongues of men or of angels, but if I have no love, I am a sounding gong or a clanging cymbal...'" And Lydia, listening to his deep voice that throbbed with passion, wanted to cry. Where were the boys? What could be happening to them at that very moment? The piano had been silent since Matty went. No more hymns, no more music. No voices raised in laughter or argument. No Joe being silly. No Bob, with his arm round her waist, or a kiss on the cheek.

Everybody round about knew that they'd come for the Hendersons' boys, and that was their just deserts. She'd seen them crowding their doorsteps to watch the boys leaving with the police escort, and she heard someone say, *They should have shot 'em, that's what they deserve, cowards!*

It was as though those black-clad women held her responsible for the loss of their own sons. Lydia never said anything, she simply turned away and went indoors, but she grew to dread leaving the house to go shopping.

All sort of things happened which made her brood, as she washed the towels in the basement kitchen. One day she'd been out shopping when a German Zeppelin had been hit by an anti-aircraft gun. It had fallen on a slope above the city, disintegrating in flames, whilst the men on board were incinerated alive. Some reckoned there'd been thirty men. Vomit had risen up her throat. In a daze she had stood there, whilst around her people went wild and roared with delight at the sight of the burning plane. She had been almost overcome by faintness and had forgotten why she was there and what she had intended doing and had returned home, white-faced and sweating.

William, coming in from the shop at lunch time, had found her collapsed in a chair. She had become aware of his face bending over her, creased with concern. Only then did she realise that no food was steaming in the fire oven, nothing was ready. He asked her what the matter was and she tried to describe what she had seen, and he put his arms round her and rocked her.

* * *

Amy found it almost unbearable being the only one left. The boys had vanished as though into thin air. Their clothes remained disconcertingly behind: Joe's overalls in the barber's shop, a pair of his boots waiting to be cobbled, a pile of Matty's German books, Bob's dictionaries. Mealtimes were the worst. She would sit down with her parents and try to avert her gaze from the empty seats.

Letters kept on arriving from Godfrey, and then he wrote to say he would be coming on leave prior to his departure for the front and he hoped they would manage to have their long-postponed dinner.

"But what exactly are your intentions regarding this young man, Bits?" William asked when she had said he wanted to invite her out for the evening.

Amy blushed. "I haven't got any intentions."

"Well, why do you encourage him?"

"I'm not encouraging him. It is possible for men and women

to have a friendship you know …?"

"I just hope he's thinking in the same way."

* * *

Amy awaited Godfrey's appearance on Tuesday evening in a state of suspense. He had never been to her house before, and she would have to introduce him to her father and mother. It was bound to be awkward … he would not fit in. It would be like the time when Freddie had appeared in his khaki and she had thought, *you and us … we are both fighting different wars.*

When she saw him standing outside in the street, she was caught up in a muddle of emotions. Godfrey belonged to the chemist's shop and to that time. He was essentially a conventional man. But then friendship flooded her and gladness that he had survived thus far.

"Amy," he said, smiling.

"Hello … do come in, you'll have to be introduced to my parents."

Mother had put on her best dress and sparkly earrings and Father was wearing his Sunday suit. They sat in the parlour beneath the clock with its white face. The hieroglyphics on the pyramids gleamed as the gas light caught them. They all shook hands.

"I'm very grateful to you for helping Amy," William said. Amy could see he was weighing Godfrey up, not certain what to make of him. It was obvious her mother approved of him straight away.

There were difficult areas: what did you say about the boys? What could you ask him about his own life? Amy wriggled inside with the discomfort of all the hidden currents she could feel criss-crossing the room. Silences elongated and teased into weird shapes like amoeba, and Amy sweated. At last she was able to get him out into the street, where she took a deep breath.

"Sorry about that! Tell me what's been happening to you."

"A great deal of boring, useless drilling. I'd sooner be out there. I can't wait to be in France. I shall know then."

"Know what?" Amy asked, and her voice sounded dry. They dawdled down the hill in the warm evening.

"I shall have accepted the challenge."

"What challenge?" Amy couldn't conceal an element of scorn. "I don't see why killing people is a challenge."

"You are so simple-minded in some respects, Amy."

"You've changed, you know."

"Have I? How would that be?"

She realized she'd liked his cool, clever way, she hadn't wanted him to show her anything else – certainly not this shift into patriotism.

"Oh, I can't say." She tried to brush the question aside.

"I've imagined you so often."

"The shop's more or less the same. Old Dows doesn't improve. My night-classes are plodding along." She talked about organic chemistry for a while, hoping to divert him.

He took her to a restaurant, an absolutely new experience for her, but she bluffed her way through it. People glanced at Godfrey with respect because he was in khaki, and that made her think of Bob, Matty and Joe. Had she been in their company, the reaction would have been cold hostility and unpleasantness. She ate her roast beef and choked down her anger.

Quite abruptly he stopped eating, wiped his mouth with his napkin and turned to her. "Amy, the idea of asking you here was so that I could ... er, speak to you privately about ... I want you to marry me now, marry me before I go to France."

Amy was so shocked that for a few seconds she didn't respond. This was what happened, it was the usual way – Daisy and her Herbert, so many more. What on earth would she reply?

"You've actually given me a shock ... I mean ... I ..."

"Will you, then?"

"It's very nice of you ... I mean, you've paid me a terrific compliment, only I have to say I can't."

"Why not?" His nostrils dilated, his eyes looked hurt. She hated the feeling of having distressed him. She realized then that a person might do lots of things merely for pity's sake, even agreeing to marry someone. It was a struggle to reply.

"I'm going to be a chemist, you know that. I'm only just starting out. I've exams to take, I'll perhaps get that scholarship to Manchester."

"You'd put that before ...?"

She knew he was thinking; *and what if I get killed.* She blushed.

"Oh, Amy, I look at your face ... you're not pretty, but you're riveting – you're so alive ... you've so much energy, I can't ever imagine you being old. I think of you all the time ..."

"Look, Godfrey." She leaned her elbows on the table and supported her chin in her hand and focussed on his face. "You're qualified, you've done all these things. They came first. I want the chance. If I married you, I'd never have it."

"But what about love?"

"Friendship."

"I know that I should marry you."

That awful hollow feeling returned to her. She had experienced that moment before and it had already passed. Perhaps he had a premonition of his own death. She had to hold on tight so as not to weaken ... far easier to have said yes. "Godfrey, forgive me, I can't." She could have wept for him, for Bob and Joe and Matty, for all those young men of her generation. The war took charge of your life and wiped out your individuality. You became a microscopic, scurrying insect on a vast wall.

It was late when she arrived back and her parents still sat on in the parlour, waiting.

"I shall write to you," she'd told Godfrey as they parted outside the door, and he had nodded and turned away and Amy had felt very old, old and aloof from what had taken place.

"Now, Bits, how did it go?" William asked.

"He asked me to marry him, and I refused."

"Goodness!" her mother said. "And why was that?"

"I'm going to be a chemist." Amy stood in the doorway, feeling the hot blood in her cheeks.

"Oh," her mother said, "you're just like your father!"

What she meant by that, Amy didn't know but could guess. "I think I'll go up to bed, if you don't mind," she said.

She sat on her bed, fully dressed and gazed at Spital Hill. It was a haunted place now with no lights and the black-outs.

Poor, poor Godfrey! She didn't want to be married to him ... nor to anybody for that matter, but it had been so painful having to tell him so. She wanted a different sort of life from the one her mother led ... but she was sure she'd only achieve it if she dared to work out her own destiny.

When she'd taken off her costume and undressed, she said her prayers for the boys and her mother and father, and then she wondered if she in fact really believed any longer ... perhaps she didn't. What would people say when they came to write the history of those times? Would they see the hysteria, that mesmerized state of being, for what it was?

Chapter Seventeen

The day following Amy's evening with Godfrey Campbell, Bob's card arrived. Amy had to open it before leaving for work. This was an event! It caught her up, made her pulse quicken and her head whirl, but at the same time, she seemed to see everything with astonishing clarity.

She rushed into the barber's shop and caught William just as he was sliding his arms into his white overall. "Father," she said, now quite certain what she ought to do, "I want to travel down to see Bob at the barracks – after that, I mean, once they sentence him, we might not see him again for …"

"Yes," William interrupted the flow. "I suppose you're really the only one who can go, Bits – I can't leave the shop. Got to earn our living … but I don't like the idea of you going alone. Anyway, what about your work?"

"I shall ask for a day's compassionate leave."

* * *

Dows dithered and doddered a little about letting her go but finally agreed to her taking the next day off. Once she knew she could travel down, she planned how she would walk to the station in her lunch break, find out train times and book a seat. She moved in a flurry of activity. It bubbled inside her all the day as she served customers. "Can I help you, please?" over and over she said the refrain, smiling into their faces. She searched on shelves and in drawers for potions and pills; headache tablets, ointments for sore ears, cuts and grazes … But she wasn't really there, she was on that train zooming down the country, listening to the throbbing of the wheels and the pipping of the whistle. Oh what an adventure it would be! And at the end of it, she would see Bob, and he might know what had happened to Matty and

Joe. All kinds of rumours were rife, and they kept worming their way into her head. But she tried not to think about them ... she guessed Father had let her go, because they were in his mind too. It could be the last chance ever of seeing them ...

* * *

The train began to gather speed. You could hear the chug-chug of the pistons, the hiss of steam. The grey stone walls of the station slid by, seeming to be in motion. The engine sank into its inner rhythm. First time ever alone on a train ... trains meant occasional holidays before the war when they'd visited Morecambe and Bridlington. They'd paid 4/- a night and taken their own food with them in big hampers. Almost sick with excitement they'd craned at the first glimpses of the sea. The air rushing through the open windows had brought in black smuts, making Mother complain because they settled on her white collar, but it had smelt of sea and salt and strangeness that had given her belly ache. The train had been packed with excited holiday-makers, peeping into bulging holdalls and opening packets of sandwiches. But today the train was jammed with soldiers who drowsed in the compartments, or sat on kitbags in the corridors and stood smoking by the windows. Amy tried to gaze over their heads at the prints of sea-side towns set in oval frames above their seats. Kit-bags threatened to burst the luggage nets and protruded from every available corner and made it difficult to leave the compartment. The soldiers played endless games of cards and sometimes quarrelled. The compartment smelled of men, of cigarettes and the flat beery odour that you'd notice if you happened to be passing the Ball Inn when the men came staggering out at turning-out time. Some wrote letters and didn't take any part in the talk. Now and then Amy found soldiers staring at her. She pretended to be unaware of them, and concentrated on her physics book.

Although it was still early May, it seemed very warm that day and Amy felt stifled, wedged in amid the many bodies. Sometimes a wave of fear would cause her heart to race, but then she reprimanded herself for her weakness. There were her brothers, locked up somewhere in prison, perhaps in solitary confinement, and she couldn't even face a train journey alone. Spurred on by the thought of the three boys entombed in a dungeon somewhere, she made herself study the physics book with renewed vigour. No good wasting time dreaming ... this was good studying time. Only it wasn't, because the men's voices impinged on her efforts to understand and remember ... chemistry had been easy, but this ... Billows of cigarette smoke drifted over her and made her cough. They hawked up and she heard the phlegm rumbling in their chests and thought, *Mist Expect Nig ... or should it be Mist Tussi Nig? What if these were their last hours? How would it be to spend your final moments just playing cards and smoking? Oh Lord* ... their faces looked young, her age, perhaps a bit older. *Would they be struck down now before they'd ever lived?* Mortality was in their faces. *No, it couldn't be.* This was madness and brought on a burst of sweating.

A soldier had fixed her with his eyes and she didn't like the way he smiled ... but perhaps she'd been staring at him. Eyes down! This was a whole study-day and she must use it. At this time she'd be at the counter ... *Can I help you please? Something for wind? Piles? Back ache? Let me wave a magic wand!*

How good it would have been to have sat there reading a new H.G. Wells' or one of her favourite Jane Austen's rather than physics. What a traitorous thought!

* * *

At last she'd arrived and was swallowed up in the mêlée of bodies and kitbags as the train disgorged the soldiers in a cloud of steam. *Be sure to take a taxi to the barracks,* Father had said. *Oh*

I don't like you going all that way. Mother had wrung her hands. *Anything could happen.*

After the taxi drove off, she surveyed the high brick walls and the imposing metal gate of the barracks, and she heard her mother's voice, *Anything could happen* ... She swallowed, breathed in and chomped on a peppermint the size of a large hail-stone. Mama had given her a bagful to suck on the journey; she often relied on mints to calm her dyspepsia. The bell was an imposing black splodge set in an array of brass scrolling. In other circumstances she would have enjoyed pressing such a bell, but on this occasion she did so with trembling fingers. She waited. Minutes dragged by, and then a small side door shot open and a soldier stared at her.

"Yes?"

"I've come to see my brother, Robert Henderson. He's a CO."

"Right, you'd better come in."

He led her into a paved yard. Two sentries manned a gate. Beyond that people in uniform strode by, all with a determined, purposeful walk, their boots banging on the flags. From somewhere behind a screen of buildings, she could hear a voice bellowing, "Shun ...shun!" Feet stamped, a whistle blasted, boots pounded, more whistles blasted.

She was conducted into an office, where another soldier sat behind a desk.

"Yes?"

She explained her mission and the man consulted a thick ledger like those they used in the shop.

"Been moved on ... gone. He'll have been court-martialled by now."

"Gone!" Amy exclaimed, aghast. Tears came into her eyes ... all this way, and just to be told she was too late. She struggled to keep her tears in check and rubbed her hand across her face. The soldier's attitude thawed.

"Sorry, Miss."

"Where has he gone?"

"I'm not allowed to say."

And then a sudden idea came to her. "Excuse me, I'd like to see Mr Rendel Watson."

He seemed to be making his mind up.

"What's he to you?"

"A friend."

"I'll see."

She was left waiting in a fever of excitement, barely able to sit still. Suppose the soldier decided she could see Rendel Watson, what on earth would she say to him? It might be highly embarrassing.

When the soldier returned, she was led down a maze of official-looking corridors where soldiers saluted one another for no apparent reason.

"You can see him in here." The soldiers unlocked a door and showed her into a bleak room. As she entered, the tall, bespectacled man, whom she remembered from that day in 1914, rose to greet her. She was aware of the guard behind her and she prayed that Rendel Watson wouldn't betray the fact of their being strangers to each other.

"Hello, Miss Henderson," he said, shaking her hand.

"I'll wait outside if you like?" the guard said, and surprisingly left them.

Amy was weak with relief. "I thought that ..."

"It's all right ..." He smiled at her. "You must be Little Bits."

Amy blushed and giggled. "Please, what's happened to my brother?"

"They moved him along with the rest when I was in solitary. I'm not sure where to."

"How was he?"

"In fine fettle. Don't worry about him. I'm sure I'll catch up with him later on. You see, once they've finished with us here, we'll be court-martialled and given a prison sentence. You'll see, we'll come through all right ... but what about you?"

He was sitting at a rough table in the middle of the room and she had taken a seat opposite him. She liked his smiling eyes, his cheerfulness; the way he seemed to centre his entire attention on her. He was unlike anyone she had ever known.

"Oh it makes me so mad – I mean, there's not much we can do. You see, I'm a dispenser in a chemist's shop ... but ..." Amy looked down at her hands, reluctant to share her dreams with a stranger, because after all that was what he was.

"And?"

"If you want to know the truth ... I intend to be a pharmaceutical chemist."

"What about college then?"

"Night classes ... and perhaps college one day."

"You're a bit different from my sister, Lucy. She'll just stay at home until she marries some local squire, and that will be that."

"That must be quite boring," Amy said, feeling her cheeks going hot. "I don't mean to be rude."

"You aren't being – my sentiments entirely."

"I want to work for myself. Anyway, don't let me ramble on. Tell me about you; tell me why you were addressing that meeting in Sheffield when I saw you."

"Trying to convert people to socialism ... it's my religion, you see."

"But how did it start?"

"I had to interview Keir Hardie for a newspaper article ... that was one thing ... oh, and then living in big cities ... and there was the day this young girl fainted in the street. When we got her to the hospital, the doctors discovered she was dying of starvation. You see, I grew up with plenty of everything: it made me ashamed."

"You have to have a lot of energy," Amy mused. "The trouble is that when you're struggling to educate yourself, your energy's sort of limited ... do you see?"

"Yes, my dear, I do." And he put his hands out and held hers, just for a second, so that her cheeks flamed.

They heard the guard at the door.

"May I write to you?" Amy asked.

"I'd be honoured, Little Bits."

Amy rose, her face redder than ever.

"Write to the No Conscription Fellowship, they'll trace your brothers."

As the soldier led her out, Amy turned once and smiled at Rendel. It had been the strangest meeting. He had stood up and was staring after her. Their eyes met. She wanted to clutch onto the moment, hold it there, stop it sliding from her. She had a pain in her chest. *Dear God, don't let anything bad happen to him.* She wanted to say goodbye but couldn't. "Go well!" she said.

The long wait on the station didn't flummox her. The physics book lay on her lap but she didn't look at it. *The brotherhood of man,* she thought ... the words re-echoed over and over in her head. Whenever she started sweating and panicking and got the collywobbles, she'd think of all those men who were resisting and whatever happened, they'd give her courage.

Chapter Eighteen

As soon as they arrived in the barracks in Catterick, Joe realized they were in for a trouncing. Sergeant Thomas, who'd been put in charge of him and Matty and a group of soldiers, centred all his attention on Matty from the start. He fixed a stare on Matty like a flame thrower. He reminded Joe of one of the foundry men who'd come in for a shave and a hair cut. He had massive shoulders and strutted like a bantam cock.

"Is your objection religious?" he said.

"Very much so," Matty came back.

"Answer me then. You can't call that an answer!"

"I went through all that at the Tribunal."

Joe got stomach ache listening to the exchange. He noticed how the soldiers strained to hear too but they kept their faces blank. Sergeant Thomas would be playing up to them no doubt.

"Right turn! Quick march!" the sergeant barked. Matty didn't move. Joe, who'd set off with the rest, heard Sergeant Thomas say, "I'll settle him!" He didn't know what to do. *I'll go for 'em*, he thought, *drag the buggers off him if they try anything* ... His heart pounded with fury when he saw three soldiers hurling a kitbag at Matty, then a mattress and blankets. Matty staggered and went down as the kitbag hit him. Someone dragged him up. Joe clenched his fists. *I mustn't hit out, if I do they'll say I'm not a CO and they'll force me to join up. I won't, I won't* ... Sweat drenched his armpits, all of him ran in sweat. He hated it, couldn't bear having to watch them put Matty through it. All right, Matty could be priggish and liked to take him down a peg or two but he loved him ... hadn't known how much until now.

"Private Henderson, we've broken a lot of COs in here, and we shall do the same with you. I advise you to give in. You are a disgrace to your country, man."

Joe held his breath, waiting. Matty made no response. "On

parade!" the sergeant commanded.

When the two soldiers set to work on Matty, one kicking his legs and the other twisting his head in whatever direction they were supposed to be marching, Joe felt sick. It was like the most refined torture – better to have suffered it all himself than to have to stand by and watch his brother being hurt and humiliated.

Joe reckoned that Matty must have endured this for a good half hour, when another sergeant appeared and said they were to be marched off for vaccination. At this point Joe heard Matty say, "I'm afraid I must decline vaccination, as I am not in the army." "I don't want vaccinating either, thank you," he said.

"Right Privates Henderson, a bit of gym will sort you both out!" was Sergeant Thomas's parting shot.

The gym instructor was a nippy sort of fellow who ordered them to be pushed before a vaulting horse. At the sight of him Joe had guessed he'd be a provider of rare tortures. Matty was slammed up against the horse five times but refused to jump and Joe followed suit.

"Give it to 'em, chaps!" the instructor shouted, and they were both pitched over a seven foot hoarding to be kicked and punched down the six foot slope on the other side by two soldiers. After half a dozen repetitions of that, they were pushed into separate cells.

Next day Joe was let out on exercise, but there was no sign of Matty. Perhaps they'd moved him on like they'd done Bob. But they'd been after Matty right from the start. Anything could be happening to him ... You had to stop yourself dwelling on it. Just thinking about the way they'd battered Matty made him boil with fury ... he wanted to hit out, make them pay. Why should they get away with it? As a CO he was meant to live a life that was an example to others ... big laugh, his never would be.

"I don't know what's happened to my brother," he managed to ask a fellow CO when they were out on exercise.

"He'll have been stopped exercise because of refusing to

parade," the CO whispered.

Joe started wondering whether he too should refuse ... but then if he did, he would have no means of knowing what was happening. No, better to play the fox, prowl and watch out for an advantage. All around him he could hear a constant noise of bullying and commands. It went on until the last bugle call, a long-drawn out throaty note, at 10pm. Then the guards came round inspecting and rattling the bolts. He'd had a day spent padding back and forth in the cell, sweating with impatience. The best plan would be to try to thaw Sergeant Thomas out by a show of geniality; that would be a way of discovering Matty's where-abouts, and if Thomas opened up a bit, he might also spill the beans about the COs' fate.

* * *

The days settled into a stultifying routine: unlock in the morning to go through to wash in the guard room; breakfast of bread and tea; wash plate and mug in cookhouse. Whilst trundling about the camp, he took everything in. The cookhouse staggered him. Half sides of oxen, sheep, huge crates of chops and steaks filled up one side of the building. Sacks of potatoes, beans, flour, cabbages in enormous nets were all being unloaded from lorries. Men rushed here and there pushing trolleys, washing, peeling vegetables, slicing them up. Water hissed and gushed at full pressure from hundreds of taps into a series of big sinks. Steam twined up from great cauldrons. Fires blazed, heating the mighty ovens. The men were scarlet faced as they worked, and so sucked into their routine that they didn't notice Joe staring at them.

On this pilgrimage to the cookhouse to wash his plate, he sometimes observed the dining-hall routine. Meal over, a bugle sounded and all the men lined up in platoons and companies. After another bugle call, they were marched into the parade ground. The regimental sergeant major blew his whistle three times and the company sergeants ran to him. Joe watched them receiving their orders from the big man, and sprinting back to their places. A further bugle call meant the commencement of drilling.

What must they all be thinking about when they scurried hither and yon? But perhaps they'd stopped thinking? If you became so used to taking orders, in the end you'd surely lose any will to act by yourself ... *they're getting trained into absolute obedience so they'll be able to kill a group of fellows who'll be doing equally stupid drilling for the same purpose.*

Even stranger was the scene when the brass-band played twirly tunes, whilst the men produced feet the colour of dead fowl flesh to have their corns and toe-nails cut. The soldier conducting the foot-inspection glared at the extended feet and everybody stared straight ahead, faces set in funereal lines.

On another journey to and from the cookhouse, he turned his head at the sound of a voice bellowing, "One, head, two heart, three guts!" An instructor stood behind a line of men whom he was training to stab bayonets into sacks. On three, eighteen or nineteen men thrust eighteen inches of steel into the sack representing the enemies' entrails. "Twist the bayonet as you pull it out to make a jagged gash!" the instructor commanded.

As he walked back to his cell, Joe could still hear the dull impact of the bayonet blades slicing into the stuffed sacks, and he wanted to throw up.

* * *

There was still no sign of Matty. During the hour's exercise, he managed clandestine conversations with a fellow CO called Zacky, a Jehovah's Witness. "Two got sent on last week to Wakefield," he said. "Oh they've had it bad. It's broken them so they say ... one joined up in the end because he couldn't bear the punishment."

Joe thought of the bayonet blades plunging into the sacks and the sergeant's voice droning on, and he thought ... *never, that's beyond my limit*. He'd discovered that he had boundaries and he could not move outside them. But how would he cope in a civilian prison, because that was where he would eventually end up?

As he waited and wondered in his cell, he let his thoughts idle on his life in his father's shop: the scissors snipping, his comb stroking the hair against the skull before he cut, the ebony handled brush dusting away the nest of hairs. The customers talked, told you things they might not say otherwise. The garrulous old foundry men like Alec Ford were the best, *Na Mester Henderson, what is it this week as you're preachin' against?* And his father would give a deep guffaw. He could boom with hilarity and then turn those blazing eyes on them so that sometimes Joe almost expected the big sheet of mirror to shatter.

Things happened that you had to keep to yourself – like the business with Lizzy Stanley. Bob had her stuck up on a pedestal somewhere. She could do that with her big blue eyes and the swing of her hips ... but she wasn't just what she seemed. Her dad was a regular but he liked a jar at the Wayfarer and there were times when his missus would send Lizzy up to the shop to see if he was there where he'd said he'd be. Only of course he wasn't. The time she called in when Father was upstairs having a rest, he'd been alone with her for a while before the next customer turned up.

She'd been billing and cooing at him as he'd seen her do with Bob, fixing him with those big eyes and beaming, and he'd told her she was a little flirt and she'd said she wasn't and that he was staring at her and he said he'd like to have a closer look at her. She'd started giggling and then she'd asked him if he ever did ladies' hair. He'd told her he could do hers. At that her cheeks went all rosy. Somehow or other they'd ended up kissing ... After that there'd been some more times. Of course, when she gave Bob the white feather that was the end of it. But he'd never tell Bob any of this.

* * *

By the time Joe actually arrived at the prison, he was braced for the worst. The sergeant had tried to persuade him to give up. "They'll break you ... give it up ... it won't be so bad!" Over and over he tried. The trouble was that the sergeant seemed to like him, probably because they'd shared a joke or two and Joe had made an effort to be pleasant. He didn't like having to upset him, but there was nothing else for it.

Immediately he entered the prison precincts, a warder growled, "No more talking in here. Disobey and you'll be on bread and water."

A guard buttoned a yellow badge inscribed with a letter and numerals onto his jacket.

The great body of the prison with the tiers of cells rising up above it struck dread into him. The silence was eerie. A warder locked him into a cell and left. *Dear God*, he thought, looking round. The cell was about seven feet by thirteen and its sole furniture was a wooden table, a stool and a bed-board. On a shelf stood a pint pot, a blunt knife, a spoon, a pot of salt, some prayer cards and prison notices.

Joe studied the rules. *Rule 1: No talking. 2: No communication between prisoners. 3: prisoners should not have pens or pencils in their possession.*

So that was it. Everywhere steeped in a creaky silence. School days and Mr Greene thwacked boys with the cane on their hands and backsides for talking ... but this, this silence, this was full of despair. He stood in the centre of the cell and stared at the tiny barred window, and listened to the clamouring of his heart. What if he were to go mad? A breathy silence. Somewhere he heard a man shout, "Speak to me! Somebody speak to me!"

Chapter Nineteen

Bob shuffled up the gang plank in the middle of a throng of soldiers. "Your crimes have been overlooked," the sergeant had told him and the other COs. "You're free men now." What did that mean? There must be a catch in it somewhere.

Eureka, there was food! Bully-beef, biscuits and tea. Bob, stomach aching and groaning with hunger and wind after ten hours fasting, gobbled the food down so fast he hardly tasted it. "That's better," he remarked to the CO sitting near him, who'd likewise been jamming provisions into his mouth.

"Best take all you can," the other chap said through his bully-beef sandwich, "never know when the next chance will come. Well, we got that note thrown out of the window, didn't we ... don't know whether it'll do any good."

They'd tossed a note out to a porter. It was addressed to The No Conscription Fellowship, telling them they were bound for France.

"I wonder," Bob mused. He had begun to notice the happenings about him. The deck was packed with a huddle of men who all had a doomed look and Bob noticed how manic tomfoolery alternated with moroseness. Some evidently knew already what was waiting for them on the other side.

A soldier sitting close by struck up a conversation with him. "You're a conchie?"

"That's right."

"Don't go on with it, mate, they'll half murder you. They do out there. Crucifixion, you know. They have to make it look bad or they'd find three quarters of us joining you."

Bob listened and looked into the centreless eyes of the soldier. *Freddie's eyes*, he thought. *He had seen too much.* "Thanks for warning me anyway."

Breeze blew off the channel. It was the first crossing Bob had ever made. Oh what heaven to be out in the open air, to smell the salty tang of the sea and hear the gulls mewing like babies. The sun had always meant those longed-for and infrequent holidays of childhood. Land-locked Sheffield had seemed so far away from any water that the first sight of it had invariably been tinged with magic. He watched the surging of the waves and the way they churned about the vessel like fizzy lemonade in a pale green bottle.

So there lay the sea oiling and spuming and about him pressed suffering humanity. It was all happening like some strange dream, in which there was no sense or cohesion behind outward events: they simply took place. He had been told they were bound for France where they would be shot. In his light-headed condition that state of non-being did not seem hard to imagine. There would be the awful flash of pain as the bullet struck him, but after that nothing more – release. The difficult bit was obviously the period immediately before the execution; the imagination would make it twice as dreadful as the reality.

When they reached Le Havre, Bob saw how they must be gradually nearing the battle zone because everywhere were detachments of soldiers. Trucks without windows and with sliding doors at the side waited in a siding. On the railway trucks he read '40 hommes 8 chevaux', and grinned with pleasure that he could understand the words. He'd written hundreds of letters to firms in French, but never been able to visit France, and now here he was. There'd been all those German letters too – *Sehr geehrte Herren!* The words returned to him from another life: Browns, where typewriters clacked and Seebrooke posed, his thumbs caught in his little waistcoat pockets as he surveyed their industry. Blond Langdale dusted his lapels in the battle against non-existent dandruff ... but Langdale was a ghost, like Matty's old boss Ziegelmann. Did God differentiate between Langdale and Ziegelmann?

At Harfleur they were ordered out onto the parade ground

with the company. Bob looked at his fellow COs, and Graham, a very active NCF member from Leeds, winked at him and Bob winked back and then gazed past all of them to the barbed wire fence enclosing the camp. They were grinding towards the climax. It had become a struggle to the death between them and the army. The air smelled different over there. It would be bliss to have a walking holiday in France, to ramble through high grass spotted with golden enamelled water blobs, cranesbill and fragrant meadow-sweet; use his French, *Comment ça va?* Or German, *Wie geht es Ihnen?* Words, beautiful words, and the symmetry of such languages, these things created magic.

The company had formed up. "Right turn! Quick march!" the order came.

Bob winced and remained standing. The company marched off, leaving a handful of COs behind. *Now for it!*

Punishment came very fast; it always did in the army. He was sentenced to twenty-eight days' Field Punishment No. 1.

At the sight of the rows of strong willow stumps, he understood what was about to happen. The poles were six to eight inches in diameter and twelve foot high. He had to stand with his back to a pole and was tied by his ankles, knees and wrists to it. Very soon the rope stopped his circulation. The worst was that he couldn't get a grip with his feet on the ground round the pole as it had been worn away, so his toes were much lower than his heels. When the sergeant had left him, the burning grew fiercer and fiercer, like rope burns that chafed his legs and arms until they were raw, and he thought he could no longer bear it. But he wouldn't groan – that way the guards would think he was cracking, and they'd finally broken him. They spoke so often of 'breaking' him that he wondered what they expected to see ... him perhaps crying and pleading with them to cut him down and his agreeing then to fight. It reminded him of school times when bullies twisted your arm back until you begged for mercy. He'd no idea how long they would leave him there. How could he endure it? The burning ache ground into his bones, his wrists and ankles throbbed with pain. There had been trials before … perhaps the first time he was locked in a cell had been the worst. It had hit him then like a dart: he was on his own. Nobody else would help him. At the end only *he* could bear it, only *he* could die. Somehow even when the crowd had been pelting his father and his brothers and him with stones and rubbish, he hadn't thought it would come to this. His head ached, his skin felt clammy but inside his bones a fire blazed … how could he hold on …? It was then that the St. Francis of Assisi prayer came to him and he clung onto it like a talisman and began to repeat it silently to himself.

'Lord make me an instrument of Thy peace
Where there is hatred, let me sow love.
Where there is injury, pardon …'

He got down to, *'O Divine Master, grant that I may not so much seek to be consoled as to console.'*

The pain threatened to engulf him at times and he thought it would obsess him to the point of madness, but he kept on. *'For it is giving, that we receive …'*

How were the others faring? Matty and Joe … they seemed so far away … the pain, the aching and dragging … numbness. What would happen to Rendel Watson?

Way beyond the camp, he glimpsed a road where peasants plodded by with carts, some walking, others riding. They all averted their faces as they passed. With officers it was different; they slowed their cars so as to stare across at him. Really though, as a CO he had nothing to complain of, after all this was what they put the soldiers through if they'd been found guilty of some petty offence. If you thought of it like that, you felt ashamed of your own weakness.

Everything jumbled in his head and he thought at times that he was back at home in Sheffield. He began to tell Amy about the ferry trip and seeing the giant crucifixes as they neared land;

about the wayside shrines; about the spicy smell of France and then the choking reek of cordite ...

When at last they cut him down, he stumbled and crumpled up in a heap on the ground and couldn't stand for a while.

Dazed and confused he was led back to his cell and collapsed there for several hours, still battling with the pain in his wrists and ankles.

Next morning the cell door crashed open and a sergeant poked his head in. "You lot are for the quarry to work!"

Bob joined the other COs waiting outside to be marched to the quarry. At the sight of them he began to feel better. As they clomped along the chalky road, he told himself it wasn't so bad after all. Solitary confinement had eaten away at him, made him doubt himself, and at times despair. It felt like struggling up a rocky outcrop, hanging on by his nails and feeling his feet slipping back, and knowing that beneath him a precipice yawned.

Sunlight glittered on white boulders. Yellow ragwort poked up here and there. Bob luxuriated in the warmth. He accepted the stone-breaking hammer and the pick-axe which were thrust at him.

"Get working!" the sergeant bellowed.

They all stood about in the sunlight. Bob felt the familiar agitated clamour of his heart. Again the sergeant shouted, his neck muscles straining in cords. Nobody moved. A blue-bottle buzzed. Cabbage white butterflies flitted over the surface of the bleached stones. The voice echoed in the stillness. The sergeant raged, blood pumping up his neck and face. Bob was embarrassed by the scene, sorry to be causing the chap to lose his temper. He wished the whole painful situation could disappear – this constant battle of wills, the fury, the impotence, the sense of growing determination to overcome opposition, even if it had to be by death.

"No offence, sergeant," Graham said.

"Right, you bastards!"

They were dragged before the Commandant, who pronounced, "I have no special instructions regarding COs, and I shall deal with you as ordinary soldiers."

A short while later Bob, along with the rest of them, was fastened to a frame-work which had cross-beams and was about five feet from the ground. He found this more excruciating than the stringing up on the previous evening, because his ankles were bound together and his arms were roped to the cross-beam so tightly that he felt he had been skewered to it. They were left like this for two hours.

The next evening they were strung up again in another part of the camp. This time Bob faced an inner barbed wire fence. The ropes tying him were bound to the barbed wire and this allowed them to be fastened more tightly than before, so that he could turn his head only with difficulty without harpooning himself by the wire spines. A storm blew up, and flurries of rain and hail drove at him, and he shook with cold. He'd had a persistent cough for months and each time a paroxysm seized him, he came into perilous proximity to the barbed wire. By the time they were cut down, his teeth rattled in his head, but his forehead sweated, and inside his bones ice seemed to be impacted.

Next morning when he was let out to a pump to wash, Graham, the NCS activist, stood beside him and signalled with his eyes that he wanted to give him a message.

"They're going to make it tougher – off to Boulogne … field zone. They can shoot us there."

Many hours later they were unlocked and marched to the railway trucks that Bob had spotted on their arrival at Le Havre. Inside the trucks was dark and stifling. Kit-bags, provision boxes, rifles and all the belongings of the military escort were sandwiched in beside them. The candles used by the soldiers, when they loaded the train, soon flickered out, leaving them in total darkness much to Bob's relief. He could smell the resinous odour of the countryside and he heard night noises, owls, cows mooing, and they comforted him.

On reaching Rouen, they left the train. The town appeared to be under British control, and Bob saw crowds of men being herded into a huge shed by the railway station. Some waited to be sent to the trenches, others to go on leave to Blighty. Again, he had the impression of people being moved by a great mechanical force. They stood there, lacking any identity, exhausted and helpless.

As they approached Boulogne, Bob braced himself for the next stage. He knew the army would never give up, and they on the other hand had resolved to die rather than be conscripted. Hunger and weariness made it difficult to concentrate on any train of thought. Food obsessed him. For breakfast and tea the staple diet was doled out of a slice of bread with some sort of fat scraped over it. At dinner they might receive a small portion of bully beef and pounded-up biscuit made into a mush with hot water. The empty gurgling and griping of his insides pained him more than the rawness in his wrists and ankles during and after Field Punishment. He had two strategies for dealing with it: either he let himself dwell on the pictures of Mother's roast mutton and boiled potatoes, or Sunday teas with their jam tarts, tea-cakes, currant loaves, scones, until he could almost taste them; or he tried not to think of food at all, but concentrated on a poem or a passage from the Bible that he knew by heart.

On arrival at Boulogne there were more orders to drill, and Bob felt the familiar clenching of his stomach muscles as he refused, and waited for the repercussions. Off they were marched to the Field Punishment Barracks. A soldier sped off to inform the colonel, and a little while later this tallish man strode up. Bob took in his little black moustache ... but the thing that arrested him was the colonel's curiously light eyes that had the whitish green tone of pop bottles. The colonel fixed them all with his chilling gaze.

"Get the cuffs on them! And lock them in the cells."

Two hours' crucifixion was scheduled for the afternoon, and Bob resigned himself to what would come.

The cells turned out to be rough structures made of wooden planking that projected from the back wall of the prison.

After the first three days, they were kept in the cells, arms handcuffed behind them, and given a punishment diet of four biscuits and water. At night the handcuffs were fastened in front. Bob's stomach griped and gurgled in its now familiar way. Hunger made him tired, and a lot of the time he fell into a dream world where he seemed to be back at home in Sheffield and sometimes wandered in the Rivelin Valley with Elizabeth.

During one of the cell days when he'd been gripped by stomach cramps and a headache that sent squiggly lines and flashing lights down his right eye, he became aware of someone whispering through the planking.

"It's me, Rendel Watson."

"What!" He forgot his headache and the pains in his inside. "So you made it after all?" He could have jumped in the air, capered about, broken out in hysterical laughter. For no reason he could think of, the greyness had lifted.

Chapter Twenty

Two days after he had received his visit from Amy, Rendel had been shipped to France, and after continuing to refuse orders, he was sent to the front. Military police had forced him into uniform and put a box respirator on him. Then they had tried to make him carry a rifle and a bayonet.

"If you don't accept this, Private Watson, then it's your own funeral."

Rendel's reply had been to stick the bayonet into the ground. At that they had taken him behind the lines.

"Dig the ground for potatoes!" a sergeant ordered.

They'd left him with a spade and retreated. What disturbed him most had been the sounds. There'd been a constant whizzing and cracking as shells flew over and then the dull thunder of detonations, and worst of all, the screaming and groaning, more like the death agonies of a thousand animals rather than human cries. He remained there nevertheless in the centre of the field surrounded by flares and puffs of smoke and the scudding of earth as shells ploughed into it, hissing and exploding.

At night he'd slept in a tin shack and one night that had been hit. With the first impact the roof splintered. It had been then as though his flesh had turned to stone. He had wanted to act ... move, do anything, but he waited for the next shell to explode with his nerves straining, heart banging so fast he thought it would burst through his rib cage. Often several minutes went by before there was a renewed on-thrust.

The following day they left him to wander about at the front trenches. He saw heaps of bodies, some sitting upright, wedged against the trench walls, others lying in the field as they had fallen. The obscene sweet stench of necrosis filled his nostrils and made him vomit. Gigantic rats with sleek brown bodies burrowed amongst the corpses, undeterred by his presence.

When the firing began, shells rained down, causing a deluge of mud and fire to spray everywhere.

Rendel had stood quite still, aware that everywhere around him spat fire. Any movement could mean instant death. Nearby too was a munitions dump. If a shell were to hit it, the whole area would be blasted off the landscape. And yet at that moment the strangest sensation had come over him. Whereas the previous day digging, he had trembled at times with shock, now he felt calm, at peace even. Everywhere was bathed in a primrose-coloured light, where the clouds had parted to reveal a pale sun. A thought grew out of the sensation: *this is the land beyond grief and pain, it's total tranquillity ... harmony. This is what 'the peace that passeth all understanding' means.*

During a lull a soldier had been ordered to fetch him in. The sergeant had given him a strange look. "You must be insane. I have to admit, you are an extraordinary man. Why on earth didn't you come back?" Rendel's answer was only a smile.

People had been amazingly kind to him. During one of the periods of 'crucifixion', a violent storm had raged and the sergeant had found him and cut him down. Soldiers would offer him their coats and blankets when he shook with cold in the hut at night, and try to slip him oddments from their rations.

What a waste it was out there. Not a blade of grass grew. The earth was cratered for miles around. Some said a million men had died in those fields. Even at night the noise didn't subside. Guns vibrated the huts and the ground they stood on and the sky was suffused by a dull red glare. In the early morning, an hour before dawn, at four thirty or earlier, when the hour's 'stand to' took place and the soldiers mounted the fire-steps with their rifles ready, and stared across at the German lines, there was a brief respite. Often the sunrise seemed to Rendel to have a partic-ularly fragile beauty. Its pale pinks and mauves made the morass of the earth and the scorched, deadened trees appear the more blasted and devastated by comparison. The same ritual was performed at sunset, and Rendel, watching, saw it all as a hideous game, like some diabolical cricket match, where the wickets were human lives.

So there he had been, sharing the existence of the soldiers, lying in holes and trenches and waiting.

One day the padre arrived and Rendel heard him lecturing the soldiers on the glories the war would create. "When the battle has been fought and won, you will reap a rich reward ... freedom ... and with that newly-won freedom, you will build a new and finer world."

Rendel had listened to him holding forth until he could bear it no longer. "Do you really believe that all this devastation can be so quickly forgotten?"

The padre had looked at Rendel in some amazement and didn't deign to reply.

Perhaps it had been his remark to the padre that made the authorities nervous of having a CO at the front line, for shortly afterwards he found himself with the others in Boulogne. The whole interlude had been characterized by its cumbersome, bumbling lack of any sort of organization. He had been catapulted from one punishment to another, and none of them had weakened his resolve. *Why hadn't they realized by now*, he wondered, *that only death would stop him resisting?*

In the cells were ILP members whom he knew and one chap told him through the chinks in the planking that his neighbour was Bob Henderson. He thought of Little Bits. He hoped she'd got the letters he'd managed to send through a soldier who'd handed them in with the outgoing mail. Would he ever see her again? She was bound to get her heart's desire, simply because she was so determined ... she'd got spark. The new world would need a lot of people like Amy ... and it wouldn't be the padre's new world either. This would be the chance for the rise of socialism. He'd thought about it a lot in the solitude of cells and reminded himself of the revelation of discovering Tolstoy. If he survived, he'd be fighting for a different sort of freedom, where people weren't forced to spend their days toiling in dingy factories for a pittance and where the undeveloped countries weren't exploited by their colonial masters. But when his father had heard him expressing those sentiments on visits home from the East End, unpleasant scenes had erupted. *You're talking balderdash, Rendel, I expected to hear something more sensible from you ... you've become a fanatic.*

All right, perhaps he was a fanatic, but if change was going to come, you had to dedicate your life to bringing it about, strain every muscle and become like Sisyphus heaving the great stone up the hill. Papa was a decent enough chap, lived within the traditional framework of the squire and couldn't see outside it. You could love someone and yet have nothing at all in common with them, have diametrically opposing views ... only it hurt. Those painful scratchy areas had been exposed now by this constant feeling of being at the limit of what you might experience as a human being. You had seen the dying, the indescribable agony ... the heroism, the degradation ... what else could there be after that?

Through the planking he had whispered conversations with Bob, told him of Little Bits' visit and heard his laugh of disbelief.

"There's a dreadful colonel," Bob said, "I think he finds me a thorn in his flesh."

"What's he look like?"

"He's got peculiar light eyes."

"Fascinating!"

The time in the cells fastened in handcuffs and on punishment diet passed far quicker now they could talk to each other.

On Sunday they were let out of the cells to get washed and wash their clothes. They stood in a loose group cracking jokes, so glad were they to be out in the open air. Rendel tried to take part but his head whirled and he felt too weak to stand. A Scot had been frying bacon in his dixie on a primus beside him in the trench three days before and then there was a flash, a whining noise, the ground had shaken, earth had been spewed in their faces and the Scot had been left a mass of bleeding pulp, headless, whilst the bacon continued to fry. The pictures played over and over in his head. The man's family wouldn't know yet ... they never would learn the truth. It would be stated baldly 'killed in action', not blown to smithereens in a trench whilst cooking bacon, a fate at once mundane and horrific. He wanted to vomit and he shivered with cold in the sunshine.

He became vaguely aware of Bob asking him if he was feeling all right.

"Not exactly," he said. Bob seemed to be talking about fetching someone to see him. Overwhelmed by a wave of nausea, he couldn't answer. His head went hot and his body shook with the chill that seemed to be in his bones.

* * *

When Rendel fainted, Bob approached the sergeant standing nearby, picking his teeth with a matchstick. "What's the matter?" the sergeant said, obviously irritated at being interrupted.

"He's very ill," Bob said, "and needs medical treatment."

"He'll not get that ... there are chaps who really need it."

"Look, I want to see the colonel, please."

"You can see whoever you like, but they'll tell you the same thing. It's your own fault you're here like this. You've brought it on yourselves and you can't blame anyone else."

"Very well, but please allow me to see the colonel."

More from surprise than any other reason, and on account of Bob's wheedling, the sergeant gave way.

"You'll be in trouble for creating a nuisance."

When Bob saw those pale, mad eyes, he thought he had been a fool.

"What is it?" The eyes came up from the desk. The colonel was established in a dingy little makeshift office which nevertheless had some semblance of comforts.

Bob made his request. "You aren't serious!" the colonel came back.

Looking at him, Bob decided he was probably a relatively young man, except that the war must have aged him, like it had Freddie, who had gone out jaunty, a carroty-headed youth, and returned an old man with death in his face, and eyes like a dead cod's on the fish-monger's marble slab.

"I'm perfectly serious, Sir."

"How dare you come in here and waste my time asking for frivolities. Don't you realize there's a war on? Are you impervious to the death of your countrymen? Whatever doctors there are here, are dealing with the mortally wounded." He shot up from behind the desk, and Bob sensed he would probably strike him. Bob continued to stand where he was but rocked back on his heels as the other man caught him across the face with the flat of his hand. The escorts standing on either side of him seemed embarrassed, but they'd no doubt witnessed such scenes before. Bob's eyes watered and his nose began to bleed. The scarlet blots stained his tunic and splashed onto the concrete. At the sight of the blood the colonel seemed to come to himself.

"Take him away!"

"But he needs medical attention," Bob insisted.

"I said, take him away and don't bother me with such trifles." The colonel's face was whiter than paper and his eyes were two lemon moons.

Later that day they were led out into the courtyard to listen to the death sentence passed a few days previously on a soldier who had been found guilty of disobeying an order. Bob broke out in a cold sweat as he thought of the men he'd met in the guard-rooms throughout Britain, and their terror of being court-martialled and shot. *What a poor business it was; bullied into khaki,*

forced to keep on to a mindless death, so that you were processed like
factory goods passing along a conveyor belt.

Bob was glad that Rendel missed the event. He was too ill to
leave his cell, and Bob got the idea that even the sergeant was
beginning to show concern.

That evening whilst they were all exchanging messages
through the planking, Bob heard the approach of boots on the
flags outside. The others must have noticed too because everyone
fell silent. Rendel's door was unbolted and they could hear the
voices of the colonel and the sergeant.

"Is this the man?"

"Yes Sir."

There was a loaded silence. Bob strained to hear and was sure
all the others also had their ears glued to the chinks. Bob heard
Rendel say, "Well, is it possible?" and give a weak laugh, and the
colonel said, "You!"

* * *

Rendel gazed at his brother in amazement.

"Leave us!" The soldiers withdrew.

"This just had to happen," Rendel said, staring at Henry and
noticing with pain how changed he was. His face had grown
gaunt and fierce. He was no longer the elegant, rather conventional young man who had sat on white cane chairs sipping china
tea from wafer-thin cups. This was his older brother. The
awfulness of it made the tears constrict his throat.

"You ... you!" Henry's voice had risen but he was trying with
an effort to keep it under control. "You idiot ... medical treatment
... do you know, do you know I've seen battalions of fine young
men go over the top. I've had to order them to run into the face
of machine guns. Do you know that? Generals who thought it
was about cavalry charges ... dear God!"

Rendel could only watch him striding about the narrow cell,

his face muddy white, his eyes two chips of silvery lemon.

"Can you know what that's like? Generals sitting at headquarters feeding men like beef into a mincing machine. Christ in heaven, my contemporaries, my friends, bodies mutilated, limbs shot off ... oh, let's not forget the gas. By God the gas canisters blowing back and asphyxiating our men ..."

He looked down at Rendel for a moment, his face so contorted with hatred, that Rendel was shocked. "Oh, I could kill you," he hissed. "I could kill you for being alive, for having made those infamous speeches ... for having survived."

Rendel slumped sideways as Henry began to kick him. His boots caught him in the ribs, again and again. He heard his ribs crack. A blow to his head sent him sprawling. *He's going to kill me*, Rendel realized. And then the battering stopped. Henry marched to the door and was gone in the staccato clipping of his boots on the pavers.

"Are you all right?" he heard Bob whisper through the planking, but he felt too exhausted to reply.

* * *

June brought unbelievably beautiful summer days with the sky hard and blue. The mornings started with a light mist. Cockerels crowed and hens clucked as they laid their eggs. But you could also hear the boom of artillery as the heat came on. Rendel thought of the intricate network of trench lines not so far away, of the hours of intense boredom punctuated by sudden death: men eating from their dixies, talking, smoking and the next minute they were spread-eagled in the trench apparently unmarked, but quite dead. He had seen German prisoners of war, and they were young, blond boys, mere children. Then there had been the Australian CO whom they'd dragged along on his back across rutted fields so that his clothing tore and his bare flesh was ripped by pieces of shrapnel and sharp stones until it bled and became one mass of raw bleeding meat.

Bob and Graham and the others helped him by. They played guessing games and held debates, discussed the doctrines of Marx and Tolstoian philosophy and pondered on the virtues of vaccination. His fever subsided but he still coughed and his lungs hurt.

Most evenings one or the other of them was crucified. The military police got into the habit of trying to slip them an extra biscuit, sometimes pieces of bread and marge, or even a piece of cheese.

Rats were everywhere. They were like the ones Rendel had seen in the trenches, sleek and engorged with human flesh. They scurried to and fro, large as cats, drinking from the fire-buckets and sometimes during a meal, they would run over his back and shoulders.

He found himself dwelling on the scene with Henry; somehow he couldn't let it go. If he looked at it from Henry's point of view, he could see that watching all those young men being sent to be slaughtered, must make Henry find the CO's viewpoint inconceivable ... Could that have caused his fury ... or had war turned him crazy? The hate, that was what hurt; that look of loathing ... the desire to kill. He had seen it in Henry's face, felt it in the boots slamming into his ribs. There had been fights when they were boys. Henry had always got mad if any of his things were damaged, or even used by someone else ... they'd slugged it out the day Henry had accused him of scraping his cricket bat. Mama had intervened, he remembered. It had been a scorching day and she'd been resting. Preparations for a dinner party were underway in the kitchens and Mama had withdrawn from the scene with a migraine, but then she had heard the shouting in the gardens and had eventually come down in a wrap with her hand clamped to her forehead.

When he felt himself sinking, he thought of Keir Hardie, and heard his voice saying, 'Live for that better day.' He must hold onto to international socialism, and remember that across the pocked fields behind the German lines other men like himself, German comrades, would be facing firing squads. He centred on the faces of the comrades in the other cells; Bob, that little, handsome chap with his black hair and winning smile; Graham, a squat figure, blunt and honest; he'd tell you the truth, though maybe sometimes you didn't want to hear it. There were the quiet Quakers and the Seventh Day Adventist, who suffered with his teeth, and the Jehovah's Witness chap from Skegness. He let himself picture Amy on her visit, her wide grin, her sparkling dark eyes, and her enthusiasm. Organic Chemistry, she'd even had the book with her ... He saw her standing behind the counter of a chemist's shop, her face just poking above the counter, and he found himself laughing.

Chapter Twenty-One

All this time Bob was amazed by what he was learning. Rendel talked to him by the hour through planking about the Independent Labour Party, and what they must do when the war was over. Whoever survived must carry on the work. "More people are killed by poverty, over-work and dangerous working conditions, than by war ... we're only just starting, it's up to us!" Bob, listening, felt his head buzzing with ideas. Here was a challenge. He was so preoccupied in thinking about the creating of 'the kingdom', that he was almost surprised when they were warned that as they were now within the war zone, the military authorities had absolute control over them and disobedience could mean death.

He wrote to Amy and his parents, "Perhaps it won't be so bad. Try not to be down-hearted. I am very cheerful and feel proud that I have been given the chance to be amongst those who are defending the cause of peace. Rendel W. sends his love to Amy."

"You do send your love?" he asked.

"Oh indeed I do, and tell her to keep going at the Organic Chemistry. Perhaps next time I see her she'll be a chemist."

Life in Britain seemed remote at that point. Amy, a chemist; Bob wondered if he ever would see it. The fact that he might not didn't disturb him; he felt he had turned his face away from everything save that moment and its slow, inexorable grinding towards the climax. His earlier fears had melted before this state that he could only describe as contentment.

"What day is it?" Bob asked when the cell door banged open.

"Monday 9th and you'll get read out now," the sergeant growled.

In the courtyard, they found a military escort waiting. They climbed the hill overlooking the town and from there a panoramic view of the Channel spread out. Bob, realizing this would very likely be his last chance, kept on gazing across in the hope of seeing the white cliffs of Dover. That would be his farewell to them all.

When they walked into a vast military camp, many of the soldiers stared at them in amazement because they looked so cheerful. The day was very bright and everything about Bob played on his senses: the great open space of the parade ground, perhaps 150 yards, seagulls mewing and squawking, the sun warm on his cheeks. He was marched with the rest into the centre of the ground and stood there, handcuffed, waiting. A long time passed whilst the parade ground filled up with soldiers drawn up on three sides. Bob wondered why it took so long to execute people. *Why didn't they get on with it, instead of making such a performance of it?* He supposed they had to scare the troops and prevent them from getting any ideas ... A stillness fell on the ground, scratched by a gull's plaintive screeching. It was almost like the cry of a small child. Whitby and picnic hampers ... Mother telling them not to dirty their clothes and Matty and Joe and he longing to race off down the beach and plunge into the waves.

The Adjutant began to read out the sentences. He heard him say, "Private Robert Henderson, 075632 of the Second Eastern Company, tried by Field Court-Martial for disobedience whilst undergoing field punishment, sentenced to death by firing squad." There followed a pause. Bob didn't falter; that was it then, what they'd threatened all the time. But what about Father with his weak heart, what would this do to him? And dear Mother ... he saw her in her blue hat, wearing her Sunday dress and dangly glass earrings, her profile straight and enduring, at the church door, two years ago.

The Adjutant was speaking again. Bob gazed at the lines of soldiers, men like himself, only with slightly different ideas, perhaps they might come to believe in pacifism by witnessing this, but who could say ...? "...confirmed by General Sir Douglas

Haig." The Adjutant halted again and stared ahead of him. *Some superb actor*, Bob thought; army ritual in some ways resembled church ritual. " ... and commuted to ten years' penal servitude."

The same thing happened to each one of them as he stepped forward.

Bob met Rendel's eyes and then he was marched away, still trying to find his way back into life.

Chapter Twenty-Two

When the letter arrived from Bob, Lydia cried. William became very quiet. He continued to snip away in the shop and lay on lather with practised fingers but he didn't wield his cut-throat razor with his customary flourish. Familiar forms shambled in and sat in the chairs. Old Alec Ford subsided, sighing, under William's hands.

"'Ow's your lads, then?" he asked, looking up at William.

The barber hardly trusted himself to speak. "Our Bob's very like to be sentenced to death."

"What?"

"Aye, that's how it is, Alec." William put the towel round the foundry man's neck and fetched his shaving mug. He knew the bald places on his customers' heads, and watched how as the years passed, the hair would recede at the temples on some, or start falling out at the crown on others. It was his job to try to hide the depredations of age. People like Alec had never cared. With his rough joviality he bumbled through life, battered everywhere. It showed in his cracked thumbnails, horny hands and the deep, bold runnels across his coarse-grained skin.

"You don't think they'd do that?"

"Aye ... he's across in France ... and we've no idea. For all we know, he could be dead already."

"Dead!"

"Aye, shot. That's what he said in his letter."

"He's a brave lad, chip off of the old block."

William did not dare look at the other man, or make any rejoinder, otherwise he would have wept. He cut sure tracks down the snowy planes of Alec's cheeks. Alec seemed to understand.

* * *

Lydia threw herself into a flurry of housework. The basement kitchen steamed. Her reddened hands rubbed at towels in mountains of suds. How her back ached! She thought of Bob's smile, the way he would slide his arms round her and put his lips against her ear ... dear, charming Bob. Her son gunned down by a firing squad. The thought of it made her dizzy. She could see it ... her son, her baby. He had been quieter than the rest and full of some hidden passion. Shot in France. Bessie's Freddie had died in the trenches, 'killed in action' they said. Nobody ever asked, *What action?* Like a lot of war things, nobody enquired into their meaning. They never told Bessie how it had happened, they just handed her this vague expression. But the main thing was, Freddie was dead, and now Bob might very well be too. Tears wet her cheeks. All that morning and afternoon, she cried as she worked.

* * *

Amy arrived home from the chemist's shop and read Bob's letter. She took it upstairs into her room and sat there on the bed gazing absently up Spital Hill. It was a summer evening, summer 1916.

"Rendel W. sends his love," she read. And she thought of him in that little room, rising to greet her and then sitting opposite her at the table. At once the world seemed very wide, so that however much an individual might try, it would always be impossible to do more than scratch its surface, and yet the world, her world, was very small and restricted. In a few minutes Rendel had shown her another way of thinking, though perhaps she'd been moving in that direction herself. *Socialism is my religion, not Christianity, no.* In a flash she was back in those Sundays: *an eye for an eye, a tooth for a tooth ... if a man smite thee ...* Those formed the background to her youth. So who was this God; did it really matter?

And now she stared at the summer hill, where late evening

shadows lay in inky pools under the few scraggy trees, and the faces of shops and houses no longer had a friendly aspect but presented a forbidding aura. So now Rendel, that curiously buoyant figure, and Bob, dear Bob ... perhaps they were no more. She couldn't cry, she simply gazed at the hill and the occasional groups of women and oldish men and soldiers. What a monstrous injustice that they should be shot. It made her heart bang with fury. All the taunts and insults massed in her head – *pasty faces, shirkers, better dead* – the words of idiots.

Somewhere, she had lost her youth. She was nineteen and it had crept away as they'd waited for that day when the boys would be taken. The king, the government, what were these? How could people talk of dying for their king and country? Godfrey had chilled her with his mouthing of those phrases. At last she knew fully what they meant: they meant senseless carnage.

As she sat there with the thin brown envelope in her hand, she vowed that whatever happened, she would try never to be carried along on a wave of thoughtless emotion. Nor did she think she would ever feel part of that city again. *Hendersons were traitors* ... all right, she would be content with that.

Later they ate bread and dripping and drank sugarless cocoa in the parlour. Amy noticed that her father had put on his best suit. Nobody said anything but Amy knew they were all remembering Bob, and she thought too of Rendel. She felt her emotions shifting and sliding ... he had stirred her like no one else. At the sight of such courage she was speechless. She looked at the clock and the shiny black pyramids and the last family photograph and it was only then that she began to cry.

Chapter Twenty-Three

Joe hardly slept during the first night in prison. From sheer exhaustion his racing pulse slowed. His back and shoulders ached from contact with the bed boards. "You'll get a mattress after fourteen days," the warder had said as he slammed the door. The judder of that door still resounded. An odour of disinfectant rose from the wood and that set his thoughts off in another direction: what pestilences had it been used to eradicate? Lice and vermin – just the words made him itch. They must be crawling over his skin ... loathsome things; perhaps they would bite him, and then he would be covered in pustules such as he glimpsed on another prisoner at slopping-out time.

Next morning a bell clanged at 6.30. Joe jerked up from the boards and tried to focus. His eyes were crammed with grit. He'd been wrenched from a dream where he was at home in the bedroom he shared with Matty and Bob. But he wasn't there at all ... instead he saw dirty grey walls and the wooden table and stool, and he knew he'd be looking at those for a long time.

Whilst he was still finding his way back from the comfort of his dream, the door crashed open and the warder glared at him. "Slop out!" he bellowed. Joe had to take his slops from the last fourteen hours and empty them in the nearby urinal. The stench was sour and disgusting. He wanted to make an encouraging remark to the warder ... in his dad's shop he was used to chatting away to the customers, even the grumpiest, because the customers had to be cosied along. But here you weren't supposed to speak. Anyway, what on earth could he say ... *Nice day, good weather? Have you slept well?* He found himself grinning like a lunatic.

No sooner had he returned to his cell, than another warder brought a mailbag in. "Get sewing that!" he commanded. The massive door swung to and he heard the thump of heavy boots on flagged floors. Presently spasmodic tapping started on the pipes. This must be some sort of Morse code. Prisoners were talking to one another. At times someone would let out a high-pitched mewing, or bark like a dog, then the footsteps banged along in the corridor, followed by the unlocking of a door.

Joe's stomach gurgled and churned. He pictured Ma's sago and apple puddings; the round, transparent sago globules floating about the apples that had been cored and were sweet and mushy. Yellow custard coated the steaming bowl and set off the tartness of the apple ... oh for sago and apple! Or ham-bone stew with rings of carrot floating in it and the chunks of white potato ... food, food! Did they intend to starve him to death?

He struggled with the mailbag, hurting his fingers. Then, when he'd given up hope of ever seeing the warder again, the heavy tread sounded. He waited, ears straining. *Oh God let it be food* ... A pint pot of lukewarm porridge, a piece of bread and a mug of cold water were pushed through.

For an age he sewed on, often jabbing his fingers. Progress was very slow. The more he tried and the worse it looked.

When dinner came, it was a plate of potatoes and a mug of water.

At 4.30 the warder locked all the cells for the night. They would not be opened again for fourteen hours.

Joe realized that he had not uttered a word since entering the prison, nor had anything been said to him, apart from, "Empty slops" and once "All right?" When the warder had said, "All right?" he had been too surprised to do more than nod and grin. Afterwards he mulled over the two words obsessively. Why hadn't he replied, "Dreadful," "Impossible", "I can't bear it a minute longer"? He suspected that had he made any attempt to reply, he would have been unable to stop talking and would have whined and grovelled.

As soon as the 4.30 lock-up came, the tapping started on the pipes. Who were all these people and what were they saying?

The warder had said no letters for two months. Ma and Father and Amy would have no idea where he was. He was cut adrift ... it was as though he had dropped into an underworld, a subterranean kingdom from which there could be no return.

At times when he was lying on the plank-bed, his heart would toll like a death knell and a wave of suffocating heat would come over him, so that his whole body was drenched in sweat. *How do I know I'm alive?* he thought. Now he knew why that unknown man had screamed, *Somebody, somebody speak to me! Don't let me get so desperate that I show them all what a poor wretch I am,* he prayed. *Dear God, let me keep some self-control.*

Chapter Twenty-Four

Amy, as it was her Thursday half-day off from work, walked through the centre of Sheffield on her way home for lunch, and noticed how high the sky seemed and how there was a new coolness in the breeze. The leaves on the few sycamores had been frazzled at the edges and were slightly rusted.

Drawing near the Town Hall, she heard the sound of brass flaring and drums rolling, feet tramping. The City Battalion was lined up for its final parade. Women and children and old men stood waving, almost hysterical with excitement. Young boys wanted to race out into the road and join the soldiers. And yet the intoxication did not seem to be so total as that she'd witnessed at the entrance to the station in the summer of 1914. The sight of so many young men, some of whom she recognised, drawn up to attention during the solemn pomp of 'Land of Hope and Glory' and 'Rule Britannia', filled her with a sickening sadness. They made the sacrifice of Bob and Rendel Watson the more poignant. Sometimes she dreamt of Bob, Matty and Joe, but never of Rendel ... if only she could have dreamt of him too! In the morning it was always with an intense feeling of regret that she would wake to find that they were not there. Rendel was someone whom she scarcely knew and yet whom she would have wanted to know more deeply. At odd times she would think of the scene in the cell, and always with a sort of yearning because she would never see him again. On one level, though, she couldn't believe he was dead, for he had been so alive. *Socialism is my religion.* What would a man like that have done had he lived?

She kept resolutely on past the backs of the crowd. They sang "Land of hope and glory, mother of the free, how can we defend thee, who are born of thee ..." Tears rolled down the women's cheeks. Inside Amy a core of anger blazed. *You're being duped*, she thought, *duped*. She heard Rendel talking: *They are fighting to defend a freedom they have never possessed ... freedom can only come in another way.* It wasn't 'land of hope and glory'. She fumed her way back in the late summer day, hardly noticing the people in the streets or the shops and houses. That was unusual for her, because she had the greatest curiosity about people and wanted to know the workings of their minds. Ma considered this desire to know unseemly. *Why can't you let things be, Amy?* she'd say, her face bunched with irritation and a droop in her mouth's corners. Amy would notice the sag and think, *I'm not going to look like that. I'm going to have an adventure ... be it, do it.*

"Amy, there's been a letter." Amy met her mother on the doorstep and saw how her mother's usually pale face was pink with excitement. "Amy, he's alive!"

"What? Where? Quick, show me!"

"Sentenced to ten years' penal servitude, back in England in Wormwood Scrubs."

"Oh, Ma." They clung onto each other, crying. *What about the other*, she wondered, *Rendel, Rendel Watson?*

The letter was scribbled in pencil, just a brief note. "R. is here too, I think," she read.

She escaped into the yard with tears plopping onto her blouse, and stood by the wall, to gaze down over the grey stone city. They were alive ... alive, ten years' penal servitude. *Oh God, what would a man be like after that? But alive ...* She couldn't stop crying. Months and months of anxiety exploded as she leaned against the hot, jagged stones. A tabby cat rubbed against her ankles. She saw a swallow twirling and pirouetting above the sooty chimney pots and her gaze followed its smooth beauty and fearlessness. It knew freedom. Her imagination tried to follow her brothers and Rendel into the grim fortresses where they must pass so many years. Joy and horror alternated in her, as she forced herself to picture them.

* * *

A few days later they heard that the City Battalion was involved in the Battle of the Somme. What William didn't glean from the newspapers, he heard from his customers. Rumours went wild.

"Oh, they're going to finish the Boche ... break through their trenches ... if they don't the war'll never be over."

As the news of the casualties came in, there was hardly a single family William knew who hadn't sustained the loss of a son or a husband. The entire Sheffield Battalion had almost been wiped out in a single encounter, so it seemed.

Tales filtered back from the wounded, who told their fathers, who in turn poured it all out to William as they lay back in the barber's chair, being shaved and having their hair cut.

"The officer just said, *Over the top* ... and they went ... got their rum tot like and went ... and they were just gunned down ... oh yes, not a chance ... over the top and no chance."

* * *

It was at the beginning of August that Amy received a letter from Godfrey's father, saying that Godfrey was listed as *missing believed killed*. As she and Mr Dows and the new dispenser, Olive Little, counted tablets and made up medicines and sterilized bottles, Amy thought of Godfrey. She returned to the evening of the dinner and the marriage proposal. *I think you should marry me now, Amy.* And why hadn't she been able to? She hadn't really known at the time ... or had she? To have married him would have meant the surrender of too much. It came back to Rendel's 'freedom'. No, she hadn't known 'freedom' - not yet anyway. She wasn't even sure what it was about. It remained a muddle, and she was trying to urge some coherence upon it. How could she say she was free? She couldn't vote or take any active part in the work she did ... Dows was the chemist. He made the decisions, he must check everything she dispensed, he must hold the poison cupboard keys. And yet now she knew as much as he and was more efficient. They'd promised her three months at Manchester next year ... she wasn't going to give that up. But she'd been very fond of Godfrey, clever, languid Godfrey. It was painful to think that he was in all probability dead.

People threw away their lives for such strange reasons. Godfrey had been forced to die because his brother had been killed. Honour, duty, heroism – she was sick of those words, sick, impatient with them. She wrote the label for the *Mist Kaolin Sed*, licked its back, and stuck it squarely on the gleaming bottle of whitish yellow liquid. The routine went on: men gored one another to death, blew off each other's heads, but the country floundered along and tablets were counted and pestles ground in mortars just the same as before.

Most evenings Amy worked late, poring over her Maths, Physics and Chemistry. When she was busy with her studies, she could shut everything else out. They presented her with a challenge, which was what she loved ... but she hated the pressure of exams. If she could be left to her own devices, she succeeded. Somehow the idea of compulsion tended to throw her into a panic. She became all too aware of the magnitude of the venture and the consequences for her, if she should fail to carry it through.

"Amy, you work too hard," her mother said, almost irritably. Amy knew Ma couldn't see why she was so concerned with this idea of becoming a chemist. It would have pleased her had Amy married Godfrey, and the news of his probable death had upset her a great deal. "Such a fine young man," she'd murmur from time to time. Amy knew what that meant and found it disturbing. It touched her guilt and also hardened her opposition. She ought to have sunk gracefully into a decline, but she hadn't and wouldn't. There was always bubbling up in her a new set of plans – badness and hilarity, and a quite hard-headedness which she was beginning to cultivate and had done increasingly ever since her brothers had disappeared. She knew her mother considered her preoccupations unladylike: girls were mostly concerned with finding husbands and raising children, with cooking and sewing and running the domestic budget. Amy simply wasn't interested in such things. She dreamed of new horizons. She had found 'How I Came to Believe' by Leo Tolstoy in a second-hand bookshop one Thursday afternoon shortly after her visit to Rendel. She thought a lot about those sixty-four pages and would have liked to discuss them with him. Her intellect was starving, withering before it could ever develop; she saw it like a seed that couldn't sprout. She wanted to know everything, anything ...

"Oh Miss Henderson, you are so curious!" Mr Dows often exclaimed. "Never satisfied, always wanting to know."

And she did, oh she did ... and then there was another side to her, which she hid ... she too had yearnings.

"Dear Rendel," she wrote, "I never really could believe you were dead. I intend to come and visit you and Bob. If you are to be there for ten years, I shall no doubt pay many visits."

Useless, stupid things to say, but she went on. "I have been serving in the shop – *three pennyworth of liquorice, Miss* ... barley sugars, aspirins, Doan's Back and Kidney pills, Owbridge's Lung Tonic. Then I was darting about wrapping things up in neat packages and tying them with green string, whereas really I'm not here at all, it would be very handy to be a sea gull at the present time. I would fly down and hover over the exercise yard and watch you and Bob.

"Some people think that only upper class women should be enfranchised, for that at least would establish the principle of female suffrage. I don't. All or nothing. Yes, I think that very often. Half measures are a waste of time. My father says I am too much in earnest ... but then so is he, but he forgets."

She wanted to tell him lots of things. "I intend, above everything else, to earn my own living. It is surely very important for women to be financially independent of men – why, if they are not, they will always be kept in a subservient position."

It seemed to her that she could write in the confidence that he would be interested in her outpourings. He had a way of listening intently when a person was speaking and pondering with his head slightly on one side.

When Matty's letter arrived, saying that he and Joe had been given the opportunity of opting for a government scheme and had been transferred from prison to Princetown on Dartmoor, Amy's thoughts became set on journeys – she would first visit Bob and Rendel and then the other two. Ma would not be too happy about the idea, but whatever you thought, the war had changed things; lots of women living close by now worked in the munitions factory ... of course that was another ambiguous matter. The liberation of women ... she loved that expression ... was arriving through a very unpleasant means. Amy wished she could find a cause she could have supported unequivocally, but whatever she fixed upon, deepened her natural tendency to scepticism.

Chapter Twenty-Five

Matthew heaved as he struggled to urge the huge hand-roller forward. His neighbour, Edward Lawson, thin as a blade of grass, burst out in a paroxysm of coughing and had to pause. The others pushed on, groaning and sighing as the roller bumped along the hillocky field. "We'll never flatten this," Arthur, a solicitor said. "One man and a horse could have ploughed it in next to no time."

"That's the point," Matthew said, "they just want to demoralize us. If they shackle us to idiotic things, it'll wear down our morale."

"I'm sorry about this, chaps, I don't seem to have much puff." Edward stood back, still panting for breath.

"Just pretend," Matthew said. "If you walk along with your hand on the roller and your head down, nobody can see what you're doing."

Straining and shoving, Matthew kept on. His palms burned with friction and his arms and back ached. His body was slippery with sweat. From time to time he glanced up at the sky and then away, past the massive grey prison fortress to the moor. Even in summer it was bleak, unpredictable, terrifying and yet strangely haunting. Convicts never escaped from there, and those who'd attempted it had been caught later, wandering in circles in the mist, by tracker dogs, so a warder said. Perhaps the prison's usual occupants were glad to have been shifted to another prison so the 600 COs could take their place, Matthew mused. His head shot up when he heard a voice shouting his name. "Matty, Matty!" he heard again and saw, some way off, a working party manipulating a piece of machinery. Someone had broken away from this and hurtled towards him, stumbling over the bumps and ridges.

"Matty, I don't believe it!" Joe shouted.

Matthew let go of the roller and Joe fell into his arms. Tears blinded him.

"I never thought you'd be here," Joe said. "So you took the Scheme?"

"Yes," Matthew said, "couldn't hold out any longer ... it was finishing me. In a sense I've failed ... but I couldn't go on. I wanted to be an Absolutist, but in the end it defeated me."

"Same here. It was the silence and being starved ... and I thought I was going barmy," Joe said.

Back to the rolling, and Matthew took his place beside the other seven men, who grinned at him. On he went, straining and pushing, boots tramping the stony, uneven ground but he found himself smiling. He was back in Sheffield, seeing himself upbraiding Joe for being frivolous, doing handstands and reciting 'Song of a Shirt' in a loud grating voice; Joe giving him a trim and catching his ear ... *What a pompous creature I was*, he thought. But Joe was scrawny now, had lost his chubbiness, and that disturbed him. The bounciness had gone and lines shadowed his forehead.

Arthur had a clear tenor and he started them off with one of the old Labour Church Movement hymns, 'These things shall be a loftier race' and everyone else joined in. Matthew let himself go in the lift of their voices, drifting out over the compound.

* * *

One Sunday, not long after their arrival in Princetown, Matthew and Joe and two more COs decided to attend church in Walkhampton for the evening service. It was a long time since Matthew and Joe had been to church, and Matthew couldn't help wondering how they would be received. He sat at the back of the church, trying to concentrate, but his guts bubbled and he couldn't make much sense of the priest's sermon. After the service as they filtered out, ready for the walk back to the

Settlement, Joe touched his arm. "Heighup," he murmured, "give Arthur a nudge, something's up."

Matthew looked along the flagged path, down the yew arch and saw the group waiting for them at the church gate. He slipped his spectacles into his pocket, and they continued on their way.

"Swines, pasty faces!" somebody growled. With that, the man flew at Matthew, clouting him in the face. He gave Matthew a shove and sent him tumbling, whilst several others booted him in the ribs. Joe, Arthur and Edward staggered nearby. Blood spouted from Matthew's nose and splashed bright stars onto the stones. The sight of the gore-stained pavers seemed to halt the attack – they were also perhaps bored at receiving no resistance – and they made off down the road. Matthew stared after the dark Sunday-suited figures, and then watched the parson gentling the church door shut and disappearing into the interior.

"God bless the righteous," he said, dusting himself down and trying to staunch the bleeding with a rag. It was reminiscent of the attack outside the steelworks when Father had handed out The Labour Leader.

They limped back to the Settlement, all of them bruised and battered.

A few days later the local paper carried reports of 'Princetown's Pampered Pets', the 'coddled' men and the 'COs' cosy club'. The vicar of Walkhampton Church had made a resolution, at a gathering of fellow clergy in the area, which the meeting carried and was reported in the newspaper.

"This meeting desires to express its gratitude to the editor of The Western Morning News for the strong protest that is being made through the medium of his paper against the ridiculously lenient treatment that is accorded at Princetown prison to so-called COs, and guarantees its heartiest support in any steps that may be taken with a view to the introduction and enforcement of stricter methods of dealing with COs generally."

"A true man of God," Matthew said and cut out the newspaper report. "I think such things are real curiosities."

Following this, Matthew managed to come upon more outraged letters of complaint in the press. Protest meetings against the COs had been held in Plymouth. Princetown was bristling with bile at having COs in their neighbourhood.

After the press denunciation they were summoned to a meeting, over which the Governor presided.

"You are forbidden to enter any town, other than Princetown. Should you transgress, you will be transferred immediately to a closed prison. Your food supply will now be reduced – instead of twenty ounces of bread and two pints of porridge per day, you will henceforth receive eleven ounces of bread and one and a half pints of porridge."

On their way back to the cells, nobody spoke. Matthew remembered the awful silence of his former prison cell and swallowed his disgust. *You must play the sly fox, learn to be quiet, think your own thoughts and not give the powerful any reason to notice you.*

They held a meeting amongst themselves that evening, and Matthew had doubts as he listened to Walter Sands, the chairman of the Men's Committee, saying that somebody in authority must be fomenting trouble and they should all be on their guard and take care not to rise to provocation. He was uneasy with Walter Sands' loud voice and his need to dominate. *Why was it that Sands always managed to evade any trouble?*

Days passed in grinding labour, either out stone-breaking in the quarry, or making futile attempts at land reclamation. It was heavy back-breaking work, but Matthew listened to the conversations flowing around him. There were university men who talked about Goethe and Schiller in a way reminiscent of Dr Ziegelmann. They held lectures in the evenings for anybody who wanted to attend, and discussed Hegel, Kant, Marx, all names he had only heard of before. He'd return to his cell at night, head filled with a mosaic of new words and concepts he only half understood. Excited, amazed, he lay awake into the early hours hearing the tread of boots as the guards paced the corridors.

* * *

Now and then he'd look up from wherever he happened to be labouring, whether in the quarry or out in the fields, and the austere beauty of the place would touch him and he would shudder with awe and the realization that for him, an ordinary Sheffield lad who had left school at thirteen, this was the most extraordinary and vital experience.

"Look," Edward Lawson said to him one day, "if you really are interested, I'll set you a prose to translate. Do you want to have a go at this?"

Matthew spent hours in the evenings repeating lists of strong verbs to himself; searching his head for elusive nouns and genders, and learning which case was demanded by which preposition. Then there was the business of whether motion was involved – was the book lying on the table or being placed there. These questions chased out thoughts of anything else. Edward moved onto the subjunctive, clauses with 'wenn' and Matthew became intrigued and impressed by the symmetry of the language. "Well," he said, "perhaps someday I'll get to visit Germany and use the language."

Edward smiled. "I hope so," he said, "someday. If we ever leave here, you'll have to come and visit me in London. You'd be very welcome."

* * *

As the weeks turned into months they'd be out on the moor or in the fields whatever the weather and Matthew noticed how Edward's cough hacked away and he would be stopping to gasp for breath, with his chest wheezing and gurgling. After a particularly wild day when they'd had the wind slamming in their faces for seven hours as they pushed the roller, Edward took to his bed and didn't eat with the rest in the dining hall.

"No point in going to eat," he told Matthew. "I'm just not hungry and can't swallow the stuff. It sticks in my gullet."

"But you'll not recover if you don't eat." Matthew listened to himself and thought he sounded like Ma. Sweat beaded Edward's forehead and a hectic pink flowered on his cheek bones. "We've got to get you better," he said, feeling now how his stomach knotted with anxiety.

The next day the group went out into the fields with the warder tailing them as usual, but Matthew hung back so as to miss the working party. The warder hadn't noticed his absence, but he waited to make sure they'd all left, and then he set off, in what he hoped was a nonchalant stride, towards a farmhouse he'd observed when they'd been out crushing oats during the so called 'reclamation' work. It was the only house in the immediate area and Matthew wondered how on earth they could scrape a living where the earth was so stony and the weather unpredictable and the winters often cutting the moor off for months on end.

Any minute he expected to feel a hand grabbing his shoulder, or the dogs savaging his ankles. He sweated and listened to the drumming of his heart. You mustn't look furtive. It was important to appear confident. What if they summoned the warders? Set their dogs on him?

As he entered the yard, two bat-eyed collies ran at him. He stood still and let them bump their noses against his trouser legs, but he wouldn't have been surprised had they attacked his calves. After they'd nosed him for a while, they let him stroke their heads. Through the window he could see on the table what appeared to be a jug of milk. The door stood ajar and he called out. "Hello, hello, is anybody there?"

He was shocked when a figure in a man's jacket with the sleeves rolled back, and a cap, thrust the door wide. A young woman, and she'd got flour on her hands and smudges of flour on her cheeks, and strands of her mahogany-coloured hair had come adrift from under the cap and wafted against her cheek bones.

"Yes," she said, "what do you want?"

"I'm sorry to bother you but I wondered if you could let me have some milk for my friend. He's very ill and can't swallow the food they give us at the prison."

She didn't even flinch at the word 'prison', which surprised him. "Are you a prisoner?"

"You could call it that – I'm a conscientious objector."

"You'd better come in. I'm making bread. Sit there!"

He sat down in the armchair she'd indicated. A fire flared in the Yorkshire range and the room was warm and smelled of baking. Two striped cats snoozed in the hearth. The comfort of it stirred the longing in him, and he was back at home in Sheffield, watching Ma pounding a ball of dough. The woman worked away, thrusting her fingers into the white ball, kneading it, flipping it over so that it landed on the deal table with a *splop*. Next she cut it up and fitted it into greased tins, opened the door and slotted them in the oven.

"There," she said. "So, tell me, are you one of those who won't fight?"

"Yes."

"Why won't you?"

"Because I think it's wrong to kill."

"Why is your friend sick?"

"I expect it's the hard work out in all weathers, getting drenched ... he's got chilled again and again ... lots of things."

"You can wait for the bread, can't you? And I'll give you some milk."

"I'm very grateful."

"I've lost a husband and my brother in this war and a father who's died of a heart attack. There they are," she said, pointing to the family photograph on the dresser. "That's my husband. Was married a month."

"I'm very sorry," he said. She seemed compelled to talk, and as she did so, she looked straight into his face, fixing him with a level gaze that didn't waver, neither with embarrassment nor fear. She'd probably gone beyond that ... the times were doing this to people. He met her cinnamon-coloured eyes and did not feel uneasy. Her dead husband was wearing khaki and he smiled proudly at the onlooker. The sight of the unknown man's high spirits reminded Matthew of Cousin Freddie when he'd first come to see them in his uniform. By the time of his next visit he stared about with dead eyes and talked compulsively about rats and bodies rotting and the stench; war wasn't nice and clean and grandly heroic ... no, it was about decomposing bodies and evil smells.

"They all said they had to fight for their country."

"I see." He watched her tidying away the baking things and washing them in a bowl of water.

"I can boil some eggs hard for your friend."

"Thank you very much." He had noticed several Rhode Island Reds scratting about in the yard and supposed they must provide a good egg supply.

"Come back tomorrow if you can," she said, "then I'll give you some more. These are for you." She'd wrapped two currant buns in paper.

"On second thoughts, I'd better not take the milk because I can't conceal it. The guards would pounce on it straight away."

He managed to get back to the Settlement, hand the food over to Edward, who stared up from his sick bed in amazement, and reach the working party. He saw the warder looking at him and he mimed stomach ache and WC. The warder's face was still knotted with suspicion but a break-down in the roller diverted him from taking the matter any further. Matthew pushed and shoved at the roller, grunting and sweating to impress the warder with his industriousness. Even with the chill wind blasting in his face, his cheeks glowed. *How had he reached this point?* he wondered. He'd been such a stickler for the truth, with Father's words ringing in his ears: *Lying is a sin.* Only there might be a reason to lie. But it was dishonest, it meant your word couldn't be trusted. You might go beyond caring. From the day the police arrived and accused him of shooting Dr Ziegelmann, he'd changed. There he'd been, beside himself with sorrow and they'd accused him of murder. And the tribunal had made it worse. What did all these powerful fellows know? Seeing their sponginess, their lack of moral fibre, made you realize there was no higher authority than yourself, and that gave you an awesome responsibility.

For the rest of the day he kept returning over the meeting with the woman, his shock at her weirdness, the male jacket, the cap, her abruptness, and apparent lack of fear; he saw again her cinnamon-coloured eyes gazing at him, the thick arcs of her brows and the maroon of her lips. She was not pretty, no, but he could almost have called her beautiful as she kneaded the dough, tossed it down on the table and thumped it again. She had the face of women he had seen in Dutch paintings in the Graves Art gallery in Sheffield, composed, concentrating on whatever they were doing. The dead husband beamed from his frame on the dresser, and the family group, drawn up in their best clothes, carefully posed in a photographer's studio.

* * *

Several days passed, when Matthew didn't dare to pay the woman another visit. Once the warders' suspicions had been stirred, he would never be able to go there again. There were days of high winds and driving rain. Edward's health didn't improve. When Warder Hollings insisted that he join the working party, he collapsed out in the quarry and had to be carried back to his cell, where he lay panting and fighting for breath on his plank bed. It was after this incident that Matthew decided to make another visit to the farmhouse.

Again he waited until the working party had plodded out and then he stalked off, trying to appear confident, though all the while expecting to be seized. He gained the house, and was met by the dogs, who snarled and ran at him, but calmed down as before after he'd stood and stroked their heads. She opened the door at his knock.

"I thought maybe you were in trouble for coming here ..."

"No," he said, "they didn't find out, but I have to be very careful."

"How's your friend?"

"No better ... collapsed in the quarry."

She wore the same jacket and cap as before, and wires of mahogany hair wafted about her cheeks and he guessed she must have been out working. She saw the direction of his glance. "Had to see to the animals ... there's only me now and a young lad comes from the village to help. You'll have a cup of tea?" she said.

"That would be very nice."

"I've got some eggs and bread for your friend."

"He was astonished and so grateful for the food."

She handed him a cup of tea, and he took long swigs at it, delighting in the pleasure of a beverage he had last drunk at home in Sheffield. He found her watching him.

"You drink like a man who's thirsty," she said.

"I'd forgotten how marvellous it tastes. I dare not stay long or they'll miss me."

He realized he enjoyed sitting there in her kitchen where the cats snoozed and the fire spat, glowing scarlet and purple at its heart, and she got on with her daily tasks and the conversation wound between them like a skein of bright wool.

"Will you come back again?" she asked, when he said he must get back to the working party.

"I shall if you don't mind, and if I don't get caught." That was when she asked him his name and told him hers was Dora.

Dora, he loved that name, and he whispered it to himself, as he tramped on back to the fortress. What if they caught him? He wouldn't think about it. Instead he let himself centre on the moments in that kitchen with the wind-blown woman, who'd got lines of pain about her mouth. How must it be for her, living there in that remote place, totally alone now but for her animals? When the winter set in, she might not see anyone for months, he imagined, yet she had a dignity, a resignation, which he had to admire.

* * *

He made several more visits to the farm, always bringing back some food for Edward. He never told anyone about his trips, not even Joe, whom he didn't see often because he belonged to a different working party. The rest of the time he slogged away on the treadmill machine, which sixteen of them manipulated by hand instead of foot. All they produced after a day's labour were six bags of ground oats. Arthur, one of the working party, said the difference in value between the crushed and uncrushed oats was 6d a bag. They could congratulate themselves on adding three shillings to the wealth of the community; so much for the 'work of national importance' at Princetown.

Sometimes they worked breaking stones in the quarry. This was more difficult for Warder Hollings to supervise, and if Matthew saw his chance, he would grab a moment when the warder was watching one group of men, and slip away.

It was a day of autumnal weather, gloomy and cold, with lowering cloud. Edward had suffered a haemorrhage and couldn't leave his cell, despite the warder's growlings that he should bestir himself. An anxious, panicky feeling in his guts drove Matthew to make for the farm ... not that he didn't also want the opportunity of a few brief moments with Dora.

It took him about forty-five minutes to reach the farm from the quarry. All the way he felt the gnawing anxiety in his stomach: she might not be there, he might have made the journey for nothing. But he had to. The dogs didn't bark now, but ran to nose his hands. She must have seen him in the yard, for she stood in the doorway smiling in welcome.

"How's your friend?" she asked.

He told her and she shook her head. A paraffin lamp shed a marigold light in the twilit room where it already seemed to be evening although it was only early afternoon. The kettle steamed on the range and she made tea, and handed him a cup. The way she poured the tea from the brown pot was now familiar to him, as was the swell of her hips. She caught him looking again at the photograph of her dead husband.

"I talk to them all," she said. "You see, I forget at times that they're dead ... of course I didn't know Ben very well. I married him because he was going."

"I expect that's happened a lot," he said.

"Why wouldn't you fight?"

"I'd sooner die than kill somebody. But I have to tell you ... this whole situation has made me cunning. I've lost my innocence."

She was looking at him with that long straight glance, and he sensed she understood. "I know," he said, "that I should not be coming here ... and in the past I wouldn't have done it, but now ..."

"I'm glad you've come," she said.

"If I should fail to turn up again, Dora, it will mean that they've caught me."

"I hope they don't. I'm always looking for you and when I don't see you for a while, I wonder if the guard has stopped you."

He finished the tea, rose and placed the cup on the table. "Thank you so much for all those cups of tea and the food for Edward. You've been so generous, Dora. Look, I'd better be getting back." Only a few feet separated them.

"When you speak like that, Matthew, it sounds as though you don't expect to return. I can't bear another parting." She came up to him then and flung her arms round his neck. He felt the warmth and roundness of her breasts and her lips shocked him with their soft moistness. He had forgotten the otherness of women ... It pained him that she should have to touch his dusty clothes that were stained and ingrained with quarry lime and earth from the fields. But she didn't seem to mind. He didn't know how they got there, but they subsided onto the rag-rug before the range. Her hair had come loose and tangled about her shoulders. He found his way through the mysteries of her long skirts and undergarments and shivered as he touched the surprise of her flesh.

The weight of anxiety in his guts at the thought of Edward and the gore on his handkerchief and his ever-weakening frame was all mixed with the sweetness of Dora's body. He felt her flesh but did not see it. Her face was dappled with the shine from the lamp. *We're both driving out the pain,* he thought as he shuddered into her.

He seemed to come round a long time later and noticed that outside the window he could not see sky, only a thick, swirling greyness.

"Oh goodness, the mist's come down," she said, "you'll never find your way back."

"I have to," he said. "I don't want them coming here."

"It's too dangerous to go out there," she said.

"They'll have discovered I'm missing by now ..." He didn't want to leave her, was still buoyed up by those moments on the rag rug, felt light and euphoric, and the miracle of that afternoon lifted him above the constant gnawing anxiety that gripped him when he thought of Edward. For a brief moment, he pressed her against him and then he left.

Stepping out into the greyness was like plunging into a bath of icy water. The leaden damp seemed to penetrate his bones, working its way into his tissues and ligaments. He stumbled along, hearing nothing but the muffled scrunch of his feet. He hoped he was heading in the direction of the prison but he couldn't be sure. This was what it must be like for convicts trying to escape. The stories had it that they walked round and round, unable to get away from the moor, and then when exhaustion brought them to their knees, the bloodhounds found them and they were carted back to the prison. But he wasn't trying to make off, he merely wanted to return. Those whom the dogs didn't locate died of exposure out there. The moor didn't let people go. On he tramped, seeing nothing but the swirling fog. Perhaps he never would find the prison, perhaps he would die out there ...

Worn-out, he'd been trudging down what he thought might be a track for a long time, when he heard dogs panting and barking, and vague figures loomed up. Two creatures bounded at him and he felt their teeth gnashing through his trousers and grazing his skin. He was skewered by them, caught in a pincer grip but he made no move to tear himself loose.

"Henderson, what's this you're playing at?" It was Warder Hollings, accompanied by two other warders. They carried hurricane lamps, which they held up to Matthew's face. The dogs kept snarling and the one with his teeth locked onto Matthew's trousers shook his head to and fro as though trying to worry a captured animal. "You know they never escape from here."

"I'm not trying to escape," Matthew said, wishing the bloodhound would stop pincering his leg.

"You're captured now. What's that you've got?" They wrenched the food parcel intended for Edward out of his hands.

"Where'd you get this?" Warder Billings said.

"Someone gave it to me."

"A likely story – you've pinched it, haven't you?"

"No, I most certainly didn't."

"Then who give it to you?"

"I can't say. I just wanted the food for Edward."

"Well he won't want it now 'cause he's dead."

"What?" Matthew thought he would vomit. "What are you telling me?"

"Come on, march now ... can't be dilly dallying about here all night!"

"I don't understand," Matthew said. "What's happened?"

"He's dead. That's all there is to it ... and you're going to be reported for this."

"He can't be dead."

"I'm telling you, he is; is that so difficult to understand?"

They blundered forward in the ashy night, accompanied by the panting dogs, who padded along beside Matthew. He had a pain in his chest. A picture of Edward slid into his head and wouldn't fade: Edward coughing his guts out and trying to hide the terrifying scarlet of his handkerchief. Matthew wanted to rage at Billings, remind him of the many times he'd begged Hollings to fetch a doctor to see Edward. Hollings' only reply was, *He's shamming, what he needs is a bit of hard work. You lot are just layabouts – thought you'd escape being men.* But he choked down his fury, and stumbled along between the dogs and the warders, following the hurricane lamps' orange glow.

* * *

Two days later Matthew was brought before the Governor, who sat behind a boardroom desk which disappeared into the distance. He drilled Matthew with a chilly gaze. His nose was a wood pigeon's beak and caused Matthew to stare.

"Henderson, as you have disobeyed prison rules, you will be returned forthwith to an ordinary closed prison."

* * *

The next day during the dinner-hour the guards arrived to arrest Matthew. The prison yard was full of COs and they all waited, watching the guards. Matthew held out his wrists for the handcuffs. At that moment Walter Sands shouted, "Let's stone 'em!" and he hurled a chunk of stone, striking one of the guards in the chest. There was an awful stillness. Nobody moved. *This is temptation*, Matthew realized. The tension wound ever tighter. He felt proud of them all for refusing to be provoked. Then they were on their way to the station. It wasn't until he arrived there, that he saw a long procession of COs following Edward's coffin, which would be travelling by the same train as himself. They sang 'Lead Kindly Light' and the words drifted out into the bleached afternoon. Matthew stood facing the railway tracks, tears blinding him. He'd lost a friend and teacher, and he was leaving behind Dora in her man's jacket and cap, Dora who had pressed herself against him, sucked him in, pleasured him ... And the back-drop to all this was that wild, temperamental moor and the grey walled fortress with its arched gateway where the big bell hung. Outside and beyond that world the war still raged and men died, were maimed and sent crazy.

Just as he was about to mount the steps into the train, he turned and saw Joe, who waved to him. Joe was crying too. Before he could leave, Joe ran up to him and embraced him, though Matthew, handcuffed, could only stand within his brother's arms, smiling through his tears.

Chapter Twenty-Six

Back in England again and Bob could scarcely believe it. He sat and stood in trains crowded with exhausted soldiers on their way home. He looked about him, seeing nothing he knew, and aching for Sheffield and its well-known landmarks: the red-brick corn-exchange, the narrow grimy streets by the steel works, the rusty River Don flowing beside clanking yards, the familiar lines of grey stone houses. Sheffield had its own smell, its own atmosphere. On winter nights you'd catch the smoky, sooty aroma of the works' chimneys, and the sky would be stained with a frantic orange glow – they'd be teeming in the Bessemer furnaces. Just beyond the stone terraces lay the Rivelin Valley where the river tumbled and gushed over shiny brown stones and the sunlight trembled through larch trees. He'd spent holidays there with Matty and Joe and Amy, strolling by the river and stopping to eat their potted meat sandwiches, and drink hot lemonade from heavy green bottles. He could almost hear the explosion as the tops were pulled out, and feel the prickly, sneezy sensation in his nose after taking a great gulp.

It was annoying, he reflected, how even at the most dramatic times of his life, he seemed to be separated from events by a web of exhaustion. This was a long way from Rivelin Valley, from Derbyshire and the moors. How he loved the sweep of the hills. Their grandeur had made him feel as he used to do in church, before the schism – the fall – he could smile at it now, almost. Perhaps that was how it went with most things; in the end you could be detached.

They had all speculated a great deal about the fact that they had not been shot. Rendel had heard rumours that Asquith had saved them, as he had learnt of their plight through the note thrown out of the railway carriage window, which had found its way to the No Conscription Fellowship headquarters and from there to him. It was still amazing to be alive. Bob found himself having to adjust his thoughts to life, whereas he had prepared himself and been utterly ready for death. The reversal had cost him energy and now he felt tired out.

Wormwood Scrubs had on the outside something of the college about it, with its arched cloisters, green lawn, and Gothic chapel, but inside it followed the usual pattern. It was like being in the belly of a whale or a Roman Amphitheatre. Bob felt his spirits plummeting. What new trial was in store?

* * *

Rendel caught sight of Bob in the exercise yard, where they had to walk round concrete circles, and remain five yards apart from one another. Guards were planted at intervals to make sure nobody spoke. Bob, Rendel decided, looked dispirited. His shoulders drooped forward and he seemed very slight, thinner even than before. He hated to see the little Yorkshireman so cast down, but at the same time, he kept experiencing the same heady exhilaration that he had in France at the sight of all the other COs, far more here of course, close on six hundred, all trudging round the exercise yard. When he looked at them, he thought, *we'll make it, we really will … we'll eradicate poverty and despair and we'll build the New Jerusalem.*

Once Rendel had tried to make a sign to Bob and had turned his head but the movement had been intercepted by the warder. "C6741, you'll be for the Governor tomorrow." That of course would mean bread and water and possibly the loss of a day's remission.

The mail bag sewing took ages at first, but Rendel struck up a friendship with one of the warders. He was a slow, garrulous chap with a sense of humour. One morning he stood watching Rendel battling with his large needle, trying to press it through the canvas. The lead knob of the skewer was strapped to the palm of his hand and it was irritating the flesh, causing a painful indentation. "I'll never manage seventy feet at this rate," Rendel said, grinning. "It'll take me seventy years to do it."

"Do it like this!" The warder took the needle and showed Rendel how he could do three stitches at one pull of thread. After that, he zipped along with the work. As he sewed he let his thoughts drift. Miriam came into his head, Miriam, that strange, tough, unpredictable girl whom he had loved. She had been intent on trying him, he supposed. The needle probed the canvas, and he could bring back her face, the pale, rather heavy features, full lips and wide nostrils. In an act of defiance she'd had her hair cut short like a boy's and it curled about her head in blonde waves and twirls. *Women must be freed from servitude. Why shall I be regarded as a lesser person than you?*

She'd chained herself to railings, becoming increasingly militant. Then there had been the prison sentences. They'd let her out under the 'Cat and Mouse' scheme and he'd fetched her from the prison gates. She was so emaciated, she could scarcely stand and she looked at him with her big challenging blue eyes.

Well, Rendel?

He'd taken care of her, helped her back to health, ready for the next term of imprisonment.

Women with ideas and strivings were always attractive to him. He had no time for languid beauties like Lucy.

As Miriam had grown progressively more war-like, he had needed to distance himself from her. Her last violent act, an attempt on the life of Lloyd George, had finally severed the tie, and yet he could still admire her. She was not 'living for that better day' though; she was an iconoclast, ramming herself against the present moment.

His thoughts flitted away to Henry ... all that had happened in France was some horrific nightmare. He was not even sure that it had taken place, but now and then something about the stale, unwholesome odour of the cell would recall the sweet stench hanging about the trenches, and he felt his gorge rising and had to struggle with an overwhelming urge to vomit. At such times he found himself trembling, caught up in a fever. His pulse raced and his skin felt cold though his palms sweated. He staggered about near the ammunition dump with the shells hissing and exploding about him ... now, he didn't dare to recall that intense sense of peace, the inner illumination which had sustained him through it.

One day Rendel received a letter from his mother. It was as though she were talking to him, kind and concerned, but governed by totally different considerations from the one which influenced him. She had her place in society and couldn't imagine why he had taken his particular course. Naturally his father thought the whole business of conscientious objection disgraceful and his renunciation of the family property and its obligations a betrayal ... but that was an old story. It was only now that he thought he saw his relationship with his parents quite realistically. For years it had been an inflamed area, which could not heal. He had hoped for changes, but he had learned gradually that those wouldn't happen. You could not overcome a man's conviction about the rightness of his own beliefs.

"You will be delighted to hear that your dear brother has been mentioned in despatches and is to be decorated. You can imagine how we live here, constantly wondering what has happened to him and fearful lest anything should harm him."

He read on, "... I am sure you believe that what you are doing is right, but I cannot hide from you the fact that I wish you had chosen a different path."

* * *

Amy wrote to him.

"Dear Rendel,

"I keep wondering how you are spending your days there. It

is difficult to imagine being so cut off from everyday life. I try to picture the sensation of it … at least you are still alive! For ages I thought you and Bob were no more.

"Here we seem to be pretty busy as usual. I shall be going to Manchester for three months in October. Now that the chance has come, I am a bit twitchy. I am to lodge with two other ladies whom I have yet to meet. Fancy being away from home for the first time! It will be an adventure. You and Bob and Matty and Joe inspire me. You know I am a fairly timorous creature. Women are never taught to be fearless and adventurous, I fear, whereas for boys these attributes are much praised.

"What about the Revolution, then? I could imagine how exultant you were. Wouldn't it be a fine thing if one country at least could lead the way?

"I shall come to visit Bob. May I visit you too?

"Until we meet,

"Your friend, Amy."

He smiled as he looked at the small curly handwriting. *It looked like alyssum,* he thought, the bubbly clumps, which the gardeners used to plant beside lobelia at the edge of formal flowerbeds at the top of the drive at Heyford. *Indomitable writing, Little Bits!* He could see her facing him across the table. There was an honesty in her and a naturalness, which at times made him laugh and at others commanded his admiration. She wouldn't suffer fools, nor would she be impressed by externals – no, she was reaching out for the truth. In times like these every-thing became far more immediate than ever before.

* * *

Amy did visit him. This was the only visit allowed during his sentence, he had told her. They were each standing in a cubicle and had to speak through a wire mesh, which was thick and dirty. A warder stood behind Rendel and Amy could see how he listened in to what was being said. She knew he was not to speak about prison conditions.

"Hello," he said, and the sweetness of his expression brought the colour to Amy's cheeks.

"I can't believe it ..." She couldn't stop smiling.

"Oh, I love your crinkly smile, Amy, and what a hat!" He was smiling too. "This isn't ideal," he said, indicating their surroundings.

"No ..." Now Amy struggled to keep tears back. She had seen Bob already and was horrified at what imprisonment had done to both men. Rendel had an unnatural pallor and his cheek-bones, two gristly bumps under the skin, were emphasized by the transparency of the flesh. She wanted to ask him what it had been like, but kept a watchful eye on the navy-blue uniform looming behind him, and didn't dare.

"I didn't know this was what happened when you visited people in ..." She touched the mesh.

"Oh yes."

"It sort of makes you forget what to say. I'd got a list of things I'd had in mind to ask you, can't think of a thing now." Amy grinned at him. She felt wildly, stupidly excited and her emotions veered to and fro from moment to moment.

"We'll have to leave the profundities for another time. I tell you what, in here you become out of practice at speaking."

"It must be dreadful."

"Tell me about your work."

"I'm still concocting poisonous brews. I say, I've read 'How I Came to Believe'."

"And?" Rendel was smiling.

"I'd like to talk about it with you ... I mean it makes me want to *do* something ... perhaps I've lived in a sort of community, you know ..." Amy was determined to tell him, she had waited months for this, but at the same time she felt ridiculous declaiming to the thick mesh and having to speak loudly so that

Rendel could hear. The warder, like a stuffed tailor's dummy, glowered at the back but all Amy could see was an array of silver buttons appearing behind Rendel.

"You shall, you shall, Little Bits."

The warder tapped on Rendel's shoulder, telling him that their time was up. Amy saw him turn round and then he looked back at her. The hopelessness of it came at her, caught her in the guts. They would take him away and that would be that, and he would be gone out of the world, securely locked into that other one. Her skin went cold with shock. Tears filled her eyes. She saw the pain reflected in Rendel's face.

"It's au revoir," he said. "Write to me about Tolstoy."

"Yes, yes," she mumbled as the tears splashed onto her hands.

All the way back in the train she sat in a dream. The meeting with Bob and Rendel churned round and round in her head. She replayed chunks of dialogue, heard their voices, was back again in those cubby holes, shouting through dirty mesh. Both men had seemed remarkably cheerful and quite without anger. She felt angry on their behalf. When her rage had passed, she fell into a dreamy mood and let herself luxuriate in that feeling of heightened life which Rendel generated. After seeing him for a while, she had noticed that she felt re-charged, everyday objects took on a firmer outline ...

There was the greasy demoralizing mesh and on the other side of it, Rendel ... and he was smiling; still the same straight jaw and resolute, sparkling eyes, laughing behind his glasses.

I'll remember him always, she thought, *always* ... she saw him addressing the crowds, telling them about freedom, about their rights, about taking hold of their own destiny. Sentiments like those could make you thrill with their enormity: they were the big and yet simple truths underpinning life. *Oh*, she thought, *if only I could spend a few hours with him* ...

And it was in this mood that she got off the train in Sheffield, caught the last tram home and entered her parents' home.

* * *

Lydia had been sitting up, knitting, waiting for Amy's return. The whole day she had felt uneasy at the thought of Amy travelling so far on her own. Young women didn't behave like that ... it might be misconstrued.

She looked up from her knitting when the door banged. "Oh there you are, thank goodness ..." She was struck by the after-glow in Amy's face. Lydia knew how to recognize passion, she had seen it too frequently in William's eyes not to miss it.

Now she looked and wondered and felt afraid.

Chapter Twenty-Seven

Amy crying ... and he couldn't put his arms round her and hug her, but must stand behind the mesh and then have to turn away and leave her. She had unsettled him, and he thought of them both, the brother and the sister, and he felt an easy warmth towards them with their sincerity and earnestness. Bob was the solemn little chap whose eyes twinkled. Amy giggled. Her face would screw up with fun, rage, impetuosity. She was in a hurry to live, so much he could see already.

The mail bag lay across his knees and his fingers plied the needle without his really noticing it. He smiled to himself, acknowledging his newly acquired skill ... he imagined after several years of mail bag sewing he would be able to zip through his seventy feet in a couple of hours. Nowadays his fingers very rarely hurt.

* * *

As the months passed, he involved himself increasingly in the secret life of the prison. They were supposed not to have any writing materials or communicate with one another in any way. What happened in practice was quite different.

The NCF saw to it that each CO had both a packet of leads and one of court plasters, so that he had a means of communicating with the outside world whilst in prison. Using the leads Rendel wrote articles on sheets of toilet paper. The publication became a major challenge. He managed to produce forty closely filled sheets of news. The cleaner acted as postman. News filtered through by degrees, for they were not supposed to hear what was happening in Britain or beyond. The news of the Russian Revolution was tapped in via the heating pipes. Rendel, on receiving it, had found it hard to sit still ... he wanted to be out in the streets rejoicing. In a fever of excitement he continued to speculate on the possibility of a British revolution. Perhaps the workers would rise. The Glasgow poor could spark off such a revolution ... he was jubilant, joyous, floating out on a wave of euphoria. It all found its way into the newspaper, just like the news that women over thirty and all adult males were to be enfranchised. He toiled away at the microscopic letters, setting out the marvellous news.

When cleaner Smithy looked through Rendel's half-open cell door – they were allowed to sit sewing with their doors open but must not speak – he threw Rendel a particularly concentrated glance, and Rendel nodded, so that the other man knew the newspaper was ready. It was then put in the lavatory, where readers could install themselves on Tuesdays and Thursdays for a lengthy session. They were charged, as subscription to the paper, several sheets of lavatory paper from their personal supply.

On Sundays there was a chapel service. When the hymn-singing got underway, they chanted messages to one another. Once a warder bellowed at Rendel, "C6741, you're for the Governor." Rendel took no notice but continued to look across at Bob, as though he hadn't heard. The voice came again and finally the warder climbed down from the high look-out stool and strode to Rendel's side.

"Oh, are you addressing me?"

"Answer to your number."

"I'm sorry but I only reply when I'm addressed by name."

"You're for the Governor."

The second lesson that day was, "Woe unto ye, Scribes, Pharisees, hypocrites for ye devour widows' houses, and for a pretence make long prayers." Rendel thought how appropriate it was – of course the difficulty was that the Scribes and Pharisees might not recognize themselves.

A hymn followed and all manner of refrains interwove in the

growling sing-song, but heads remained motionless, steadfastly turned to the front. Shoulders didn't shake, though Rendel found his lips twitching.

The parson moved surely into, "Do as Christ bids you: never mind your conscience." Rendel decided the old boy was getting a bit mixed up. He couldn't ever remember being told before to dismiss the voice of his conscience. Quite an innovation, he supposed.

After "Forth in thy name oh Lord we go" the service was concluded. The Governor climbed onto his rostrum. He was of military bearing and had a little bristly moustache, and his shiny hair was plastered flat to the sides of his head. In a droning voice he read out the week's war news. "I'm sure you will all rejoice to know that the enemy losses have been very heavy." At that he surveyed them with bright, unblinking lizard's eyes. The organ began to rumble, a sign that they must rise for the National Anthem. They did get up but stood with folded arms and didn't sing. A thin discordant chant arose from the other prisoners, who were the only ones left to sing. The Governor's mouth drew into a dangerous slit as he beaconed at the lines of silent COs, but he made no comment and they filed out of the chapel one behind the other.

As a result of the chapel incident Rendel was called up before the Governor.

"C6741, you are up for disobedience in the chapel."

Rendel pretended not to have heard and stared about the big office with studied carelessness.

"I am speaking to you, man."

"Hah, Governor ... no offence, I'd no idea you were addressing me, as you didn't use my name. May I introduce myself. I'm Rendel Watson, pleased to meet you."

"Stop fooling around. You know what the rules are here, Watson. I don't expect this from a chap like you."

"That does not mean that one should not try to change them,

Governor ... where there is inhumanity ..."

"Oh, very well, Watson. Anyway, it's six days' punishment diet."

The following days passed in a blur. Rendel had hours to gaze at the heavily barred windows through which only a meagre spray of light entered. The sole furniture in the cell was a stool. He examined every angle of the stool and then turned his attention to the chamber pot and the Bible. These must have been seen as basic needs. He tried to link them. The Bible was obviously supposed to reform one's criminal nature, it couldn't be to punish, could it? Anyway, it contained lots of interesting stories. The chamber pot punished. Fourteen hours and more of stench in your close proximity could hardly reform.

The silence was broken once daily when the warder brought in his pound of bread. On the first day Rendel had an overwhelming desire to attack the loaf, and he dug his fingers into it, dragging off chunks. After a few seconds, sense prevailed. The strategy was to divide the bread into three portions to make it spin out.

By the second day he had become so weak, he could no longer sit on the stool and he was incapable of concentrating long enough to read the Bible. At the end of the six days he felt oddly light-headed. It wasn't the relief he had expected, because he had gone beyond the point where it would have made a difference to him. Weakness was like a drug, it took away fear and appre-hension. It also removed pleasure and joyful anticipation.

After being returned to the normal routine for a few days, Rendel began to ponder increasingly about how the prison routine could be changed. They had often discussed it amongst themselves and it seemed that only all-out disobedience could have any effect in improving the lot of the ordinary prisoner.

Little things would strike him, like the fact that the prisoner in the cell opposite sat there hour after hour, if he happened not to be sewing mail bags, staring straight in front of him. He never read, not even the books allowed. Rendel would glance across at him often and see his rather handsome but deeply cratered face, fixed in some sort of inner concentration, and yet it had a certain vacancy about it. As time went on, he managed to have a series of disjointed conversations with his neighbour, and discovered he'd been sentenced to twelve years in prison for theft, and that he could neither read nor write. Rendel wrote letters for him to his wife, and Ernest, being very skilled at deception, transferred letters back and forth without the warders ever catching him.

He thought a lot about Ernest ... there he was, quite a clever chap, but lacking basic literacy skills, and when he was released from prison, he'd continue with his petty theft career. Imprisonment would never change his life. What a waste it all was ... Had he never experienced prison life personally, Rendel knew he would have had no idea of its brutality. It was intended to break a man's spirit ... and the dreadful thing was that if you kept on protesting about conditions, it usually did. Punishment diet and total silence for months on end and the lack of all creative stimuli wore you down and made you passive and comatose.

They were all beginning to get tougher, which was in a sense inevitable: you must either resist or succumb. He was reminded of the struggle going on in India – Gandhi's anti-colonial movement – when he thought of that, he forgot the rigours of imprisonment ... they were dedicated to living their ideals. If he held to their example, it would inspire him to keep resisting to the end ...he needed it, because at times he had felt himself slackening with despair.

Chapter Twenty-Eight

Amy moved into the digs in Manchester, which she was to share, for the duration of her course, with Miss Mary Pringle and Miss Eliza Stanley. They had already been studying Pharmacy for a year and were about to embark on their second year of study. They had a preoccupied, knowy manner and it daunted Amy at first. She was all too conscious of her lack of knowledge. Miss Pringle's father and grandfather had been pharmacists. Miss Stanley's family had pharmacy connections too. Their conversation was often anecdotal and Amy felt excluded. Another profound difference between her and them was a financial one: Amy had to count every penny she spent, while they enjoyed a pleasant affluence. They could pop off to a tea shop when they had the whim and buy themselves tomato and cucumber sandwiches and have a choice of iced buns on doily-covered cake-stands. They spent a while discussing the relative merits of one tea shop over another. Amy was amazed that even though sugar was so scarce and so expensive, it was still possible to enjoy such things. She made do with bread and margarine and a tray of tea in her room, if the landlady was feeling well-disposed.

For the rest, it was concentrated slog, a three-month crammer's course.

When Amy had any spare moments, she wrote home. Her mother and father had looked oddly deserted the day they'd gone with her to the Sheffield Midland Station to wave her off. For years they had been a family of six and now all of a sudden the two founder members were alone, as in the beginning.

The boys and Rendel were allowed only one letter a month, so she couldn't expect to pour out her heart to them as she would have wanted, instead she must think carefully about what each would like to hear, and say it as briefly as she could.

"Miss Henderson, you're always writing letters," Miss Pringle remarked in the first few weeks. "I can't imagine what you find to say."

"Oh, that's never a problem." Amy grinned. "My only problem is not being able to stop."

Manchester reminded her in many respects of her home town; it had the same grey-stone buildings and Doric columns in the city centre, the press of factories, and lines of shops, the war posters, the bill boards proclaiming 'British Advance ... Huns beaten back! Victory within sight!' The same headlines had been blazoned abroad for three years and more. That certainly made you begin to wonder ...

The school of pharmacy had a cool forbidding interior, and yet at the same time it thrilled Amy: here she was learning, this was where the mysteries would finally be revealed. It awed her. She had wanted this moment for almost as long as she could remember. Some people said that one of the most dreadful experiences was to get what you desired – no, she couldn't agree with that. It was a pity, though, that she couldn't immerse herself completely in the moment, but kept worrying about Rendel and the boys. And then there was the loneliness ... each day the routine was: off to lectures, then back to the room or the library and study. No talk, no jokes, just breathy library silence and the rustle of pages turning, or a chilly room, where she sat up in bed swathed in her dressing gown and wearing a pair of Ma's bed-socks.

Sometimes at night when she couldn't sleep, she wondered about Godfrey, 'missing believed killed'. Nothing more had been heard since. His mother would never give up hoping. Perhaps you did cherish fond hopes if death threatened your children. 'Missing believed killed' – it had been like that when she had mourned Rendel and Bob, whilst they were still alive.

* * *

When she'd been in Manchester two months, she received a letter from Rendel, asking if there was any possibility of her coming down to meet him one weekend. As he had served his initial prison sentence, he would be released and then rearrested and given a further prison sentence. It all seemed rather confusing. Amy only took in the word 'released'. *Released, released!* She wanted to leap in the air, hurtle about the room. Instead, she flung herself down on the bed, bumped up and down so that the springs creaked and wheezed. Then she reread the letter.

"I shall have to travel to Chester Castle where they will re-arrest me – it will probably mean two years' hard – I wonder what they'll do about the ten years' penal servitude? Ah well, at least we might manage to discuss all those many topics, some at any rate? Eh now, what do you say, Little Bits?"

What did she say? She was excited, ecstatic, wary, too happy to think coherently.

That day she found her attention wandering during lectures. Miss Pringle and Miss Stanley debated whether it should be Crawfords or Fields for afternoon tea.

Amy hurried home to write a letter. Of course she would go to meet him, but she wouldn't let anyone know her intention. The Misses P.S. would think she was homesick and had slipped off to Sheffield. This was a new line of thinking for Amy, who was essentially straight-forward. The little deceit made her heart beat faster ... *what if, what if?*

She wrote back – *yes, she would be there.* Now came the doubts: she hardly knew him. She had written to him, oh yes, pages and pages and seen him through wire-mesh, but she didn't know whether he took sugar in his tea, whether he was a joker like Joe, or a basically serious person like Bob, or whether he was a Matty, a precise, cool type with an accountant's mind. She tried to think what he was: like Father, he carried the aura of enthusiasm with him ... perhaps that was it, like Father. Only such people wore you out. They took you with them, snared you in their forward-drive for the better world. But what if they failed? What if idealism foundered? *Don't let emotion overwhelm you,* she heard in her head. She thought of the first heady days of war, the way people moved under a spell, and she shuddered. Rendel had spoken to her of the brotherhood of man ... when had she first heard about it? The brotherhood of man could take your breath away. Through their own efforts they could create a better world. He'd said, *if we come through this war we've got to be doubly good because we're still alive and all those millions have died.* Oh yes, she would meet him, but she felt almost sick with apprehension. Something was bound to spoil it ... or the meeting wouldn't take place at all. *Please God,* she thought, *let me see it through.* Somehow it must happen. Would she survive it? Such a lot of things in life seemed to play on her with an extraordinary intensity to the point where they became almost unbearable: the boys' going ... the whole dreadful war, her inability to marry Godfrey, and the reproach of his probable death. Often she wished she could grow some sort of impregnable skin to shield her from the impact of life's happenings.

It was a cold day with rain streaming down the windows and she sat in a chair watching it, with the letter lying on her knees and she traced the excitement passing over her in waves. What would she think in the years to come, when the meeting was merely a memory? One of her tricks for bearing the present was to ask herself how she would view events in the future.

She sensed dimly that to believe in the brotherhood of man might destroy the weak but enrich the strong ... but could even the strong survive? Rendel would dazzle her, show her a vision, but then ... Could she take on that struggle for ever and ever? She didn't know, but whether she liked it or not, she was under his spell.

Chapter Twenty-Nine

Amy was barraged with questions by the Misses P.S. who seemed to sense that secret plans were afoot.

"Are you homesick then, Miss Henderson?"

"Oh, I wouldn't say that." Lying came hard to her. She knew she tended to be honest in a brutal way.

"Can you afford the time?"

She shifted, slid, tried to be deaf and involved in travel preparations. "I shall have to, shan't I," she answered, hearing the defiance in her own voice. *Why wouldn't people let her be?*

* * *

At last she was on her way. Trains had a drama for her. She loved their different rhythms. They beat with the pulse of the unknown. Off to London. She had thrilled like that when she left Sheffield for Manchester. Trains contained dreams.

They were to meet at King's Cross. Trains, stations, all were packed with soldiers and sorrowing relatives. Amy looked about her, catching the atmosphere. Emotion charged the day. Men and women embraced, whether at parting or meeting wasn't at first evident, for they were there for a split second and then the train passed and they slipped from view and their drama was suspended in mid-air.

She saw him at the barrier as she walked down the platform, wedged in the crush of soldiers and their relatives and lovers. Between the spread of ladies' hats, men's shoulders, faces turned in grief or flushed with anticipation, he remained staring at her. He was gaunt now and that made him appear even taller.

"Well, Amy!" He held out his hand.

Instinctively she would have wanted to fling her arms round his neck, but she stood there, smiling up at him, her hand in his.

"It's all a bit overpowering."

"Yes," he said, "it is ... I can't get used to the noise and the people after ..."

"Yes of course."

"And the smells ... and all the corners and the traffic and the sky ... let's take a walk, shall we?"

So they started out, wandering through the heart of London. On the Embankment the wind came whipping up from the Thames, smelling of open spaces and watery dankness, and brushed their faces. Amy was amazed at the vastness of everything. Here was sophistication, glamour, places she had only read about in books and newspapers. It all had a different flavour from the north. *It's now,* she kept telling herself, *this is me in London, and I'm with* him.

He kept on coughing and she was harrowed by his exhausted manner, but he still could smile at her in the way she remembered.

"You've got to bear with me a while, do you know that? I've lost the habit of speaking, Amy."

She went cold with a flash of insight. Days and nights of total silence still surrounded him.

"Let's find a tea shop somewhere."

He sat opposite her at a small table and they gazed at each other, trying to prise away the unfamiliarity and strangeness ... and yet there was also a fascination in it. Amy thought they seemed like people trapped in the present moment, like two strangers who had not lost the edge of their first impression to the blurring of familiarity. His hands rested on the table cloth. She kept hers on her lap. She was waiting for him to break through to her. He continued to look at her.

Cucumber sandwiches appeared and a walnut cake on a cake-stand with bubbles in the base, and then what Joe called 'sawdust cake' buns on a three tier cake-stand.

"What a feast! You can get obsessed with the idea of food ... I never thought I would, but ... hot tea ... oh, this is good! Hot tea, the ambrosia of the gods! Refreshing tea and hot baths, that's what you miss ... life's little trimmings ... but Amy, when you finally get them ..." He gave her a wide mischievous smile.

They drank their tea but Amy still continued to feel oppressed by the momentousness of the day; it was so crammed with emotion as to be bare of it.

"I suppose you'll not know how Bob is?"

"My only contact is when we're exercising ... but of course we can't speak."

"Tell me what it's really like." Amy's eyes challenged him across the table.

"It's infuriating and degrading ... and now I know what ordinary prisoners have to suffer. You know, Amy, since this whole thing started, I've learnt so much ..." He paused, seeming to search for words. She looked at his long humorous face, the fan of laughter lines about the eyes, the square jaw, a face you could never forget.

"...as though the world opened up for me." He stopped there.

She tried to guess at all those secret things, the moments of revelation that he couldn't talk about. In her own restricted life, she had seen hints of mysteries. There was a dream she experienced recurrently, a dream of houses with many rooms. One contained a scream. It was a room with jaundiced wallpaper hanging in tatters. The scream echoed and re-echoed through the vaults of her skull. She was always looking for an undisclosed object in those houses ... rather she dared not look and their contents remained hidden, but their menace persisted.

"Perhaps," he said, and his eyes took on the old enthusiastic gleam, "perhaps afterwards we'll have the revolution ... but people have to take freedom for themselves, you can't give it to them."

"No," she said, "I don't suppose you can ... then it's patronage, isn't it?"

"Yes ... I say, do you like the sandwiches?"

"Mm."

"So do I, enormously. They're the best things I have ever tasted ... prison makes you appreciate everything with so much more appetite."

They lingered in the café a long time. Now and then Amy intercepted curious glances from fellow patrons. They focused on Rendel. He was deathly pale and terrifyingly gaunt which accentuated his aura of wildness. A strange man and not in khaki.

When they went out into the streets once more, they continued their spasmodic talk. In the silences Amy listened to the sound of their feet on pavements and waited.

"Bits, you hear such stories ... my head's full of them. One chap I met in a guard-room once, he'd been a soldier and then gone over the top and been wounded and left in No-Man's-Land and he couldn't crawl back ..."

Amy, listening, wondered at it all, phrases she didn't know, meant to convey experiences totally beyond her ken.

"... and when it got dark, he realized there was somebody else, not a corpse but another chap still alive like himself. He started talking to him and then he discovered the other chap was a German. Can you imagine, Amy, there they were, they talked and talked about their families and their lives before the war. Of course the next day the British soldier managed to crawl back behind the British lines, and the German went the other way. The effect on the chap was tremendous. He became a CO overnight, meeting with the other fellow out there, he'd suddenly felt that shooting Germans wasn't an abstraction."

They continued on for a while in silence. Amy imagined the two soldiers out in the thing called No-Man's-Land and her nerves thrilled with pity and wonder. To change your mind on such a vital subject at the very battle front must indeed be like a miracle.

"Shall you come back with me to my room?" he asked her. "Tomorrow I'll have to take the train to Chester."

"Yes," she said, feeling terrified. *I believe in free-love,* she heard herself saying to Godfrey in the back kitchen at the shop. *Oh yes, absolutely. Don't see any point in marriage ... for women it's bondage, slavery ... freedom ... free-love ...*words she liked to say, special words, part of her theories for the life of a liberated woman.

She argued it back and forth as they walked in the wind. And then she thought of one of Father's favourite sayings: *'Whatever thy hand findeth to do, do it with all thy might.'* Absolutist Father. She was an extremist too, she supposed. When she made up her mind to act in a certain way, she must explore all possibilities to the very end.

He was striding along beside her with his head thrown back. She glanced at him sideways, seeing the buoyancy in his face but also the sadness. Now he appeared much older than in the beginning, on that day in Sheffield when she had seen him addressing the crowd. She thought of all that he had been through, the death sentence, the months, now years of imprisonment, and she knew she had taken the decision. She wanted it, would have it. Even as the precious minutes slid by, she wanted to halt them, know them, examine the texture, the feel of each. She noted foreign tenements with rain-silvered facades. Of course he would have to have lived in such a place. One day it would be spring ... but that wasn't now. She would take this moment, like some juicy peach and suck out the juice, lingering as it ran down her chin.

He paused before a tenement block and stared up at it. "Fancy the old place ... home," he said and laughed. "I shall carry you over the threshold, Little Bits!" And he did. She caught a glimpse of curious faces, but she didn't care.

"I can't quite believe it ... not quite."

For a while they stood together in the room, looking round it.

"I never thought of you being here," Amy whispered.

"I haven't been for a long, long time ... and sometimes I've thought I'd never see it again. Take your coat and hat off ... nobody will stop me talking with you."

Rendel gave a great bark of laughter, caught her round the waist and swirled her about the room. "I expect a guard to grab my shoulder and pull me away from you. No talking! You're for the Governor! Oh God, I don't care, not a jot." He pressed her against his chest and laughed, and she could feel the throbbing of his heart.

Fear trembled inside her. She thought of her parents' horror, the consternation of the Misses P.S., Mr Dows' amazement and Olive Little's incredulity – *What, Miss Henderson, no I don't believe it!* She didn't care either. That morning, early, before dressing and taking the train, she had stood naked, looking at herself in the bathroom mirror, seeing her paleness stippled with the damp patches on the mirror, where the silvering had worn away, and she had enjoyed a voluptuous fantasy. 'Love's Coming of Age' ... she would find out; whatever it cost, it must be with him. *My lover*, she had said, *my lover.* Nobody was going to rob her of the wonders of the flesh.

"I feel there's so much I wanted to tell you," Amy said again as she sat down on the old sofa and looked across at Rendel, who seemed bemused, half amused, half sad, "only then I think to myself, if we talk about this or that, the time will have passed and it will be too late and the clock seems to ..." She smiled at him. "'You're always in too much of a hurry, Bits,' that's what Father always says."

"Would I like your father?"

"Oh yes, he's rather like you."

"Good or bad?"

"Good but can have drastic results."

"Oh yes ...?"

"Don't ask me why!"

He sat by her but didn't touch her. Even that threw her into a fever of restlessness. It was as though her body glowed with heat. All of her was acutely aware of him, spell-bound. Outside the traffic rumbled. The sense of voluptuous suspense was so great that she could have lain on the bed and cried. She hadn't known she could feel like this.

"Amy," he said, and she looked at him. "Amy, the things I've seen ... human suffering and courage and endurance beyond anything a man might believe ... if I could tell you."

She listened, knowing terror and awe. He had seen the dreadful things at the centre of life, what Freddie and the boys had refused to describe for her. She understood without ever having experienced them herself – they were things in dreams, half sensed, half known.

"Tell me, Rendel."

His voice was low and it became monotonous and at times almost inaudible. He told about the living dead, the piles and piles of skeletons and corpses and the huge sleek rats and the stench of decomposition; the pits of dead and the mud and the shell craters, the false hopes, the insane confidence, the callousness of those who ordered wave upon wave of young men forward to slaughter and be slaughtered.

"Amy, I wouldn't want to forget, do you understand ... I wouldn't want to lose the memory ever. It's a goad. If I live a short life or a long one, I must keep on looking at it ... Amy ..."

He leaned back against the horse-hair sofa and she watched him take off his spectacles and the tears came. He sat with the tears glistening on his cheeks. She was appalled and stirred to her very roots and she put out her hand and took his and held it between hers and stroked its back and pressed it wordlessly.

"Amy ... thank you."

After a while his mood of deep seriousness seemed to pass. They listened to the patter of rain on the windows and the flurries of wind. It was mid-afternoon and already growing twilight. They had not bothered to light the gas. Amy had no clear idea of the room because what Rendel was saying left no energy in her to attend to anything else. Whilst they were still recovering from the revelation, Amy heard heavy steps on the stairs.

"Who is it?" she whispered.

He looked shocked and put on his spectacles. "I've no idea."

Someone rapped on the door. Rendel rose and Amy had a premonition that the day was over.

"Rendel Watson?"

"Yes."

"We have a warrant out to arrest you as a deserter."

Amy clenched her fists and bit her lips. Tears filled her eyes ... *all, all for this. Oh I can't bear it,* she thought, *I can't bear it ...*

He turned back into the room. "Amy," he said, quite controlled, "it seems they've already come for me."

Amy had stood up and she went towards him. She couldn't speak. He got her hand and squeezed it and then, for the first and only time, he kissed her on the lips.

"I'll come with you to the station," she said, putting on her coat and hat.

And so they parted at the station, he for Chester and she for Manchester. As the train bore him and his military escort away, she stood on the platform looking up at him. He leaned out of the carriage, and for a brief while their fingers held together entwined.

"I would have loved you ... I would have eaten you with love," he murmured, so that she only half-heard the words. The guard blew the whistle and Rendel's voice was shredded in the wind.

I've been cheated, she thought, *cheated.*

As Amy went back to the booking-office to enquire about a train for Manchester, she heard a sudden peal of bells. It sounded as though all the bells in London were clanging and clappering and she asked a middle-aged woman standing just in front of her why they were ringing.

"Didn't you know, there's been a great victory," the woman said, tears in her eyes. "Our tanks have crossed the German lines, been a big British advance at Cambrai ... after so long ... perhaps there'll be a total victory."

People standing nearby joined in. "Oh yes, in the end we'll finish the Hun ... I've always said, it was just a matter of time."

Amy moved away, she didn't want to hear anymore.

Chapter Thirty

Bob had long since grown used to the grinding routine of being awakened at 5.30, marched to the urinals to empty the slop bucket and wash. Afterwards he had to scrub his cell and all the furniture: bed-board, stool, table, shelf. The cutlery and the food containers had to be cleaned and laid out according to a certain pattern. If any item was out of line, the warder awarded a punishment.

Breakfast, the pint pot of porridge, arrived at six. Bob could force down the glutinous mass, which was made with water and not milk, without thinking about it, and had ceased to feel revulsion. Following breakfast came the forty-five minute plod round the yard. He looked forward to that, because it was the time when messages were passed. People bumped into one another in corridors. Anything could happen. Looks flashed back and forth. The sight of familiar faces caused his spirits to rise ... there were the lads from France, and Rendel and Graham. It was never half as bad when you thought of the rest, all sitting behind their doors, thinking similar thoughts and suffering similar doubts and depressions.

Mail-bag-sewing took them to lunch-time and the usual half pound of potatoes, six ounces of bread, ten ounces of beans and two ounces of fat bacon. Then work dragged until four fifteen.

During the spells of sewing Bob often brooded over his past life. It occurred to him that his own resistance to the accepted order of things had started early in his youth.

His first job had been office-boy at 'Bessemer's'. He'd been thirteen, a scrawny little lad. Jobs had been very hard to come by and he'd landed the Bessemer job through one of his friends, Sam Broady. Amy had written to say that Sam had fallen at Passchendaele. Sam had worked in Bessemer's foundry and had somehow heard rumours of the office job. But what a job! Five or six neatly dressed chaps, not much older than himself, strutted about the office in their white starched collars. They'd come in at nine and finish at five whereas his hours had stretched from six to six. For some reason he'd found himself assigned to the boss, Colonel Sir Archibald Waring, a short, peppery fellow with a meaty face and a nose threaded with purple veins.

Evidently endless messages must be conveyed to the Colonel. He'd lived in a very select area outside Sheffield, where massive stone houses lurked at the top of long drives and there were rhododendron bushes with hard glossy leaves and cedar and pine trees. No children played in the streets and there were no yapping dogs. Silence reigned and it was a well-bred silence. Bob remembered how tired he'd felt after two tram rides and a lengthy walk, because of course such houses were well away from tram-tracks. The cook would meet him at the back door and invite him into the kitchen, and give him whatever she'd got to eat. It might have been a slice of apple-pie, swimming in cream, or a piece of iced cake left over from some ample afternoon tea-party, and there would be lemonade to cool him down. She'd watch him eating and say, *Now then, that's better, you want feeding up, my lad.* He'd eye her busy arms, that were red and freckled and with the flesh jellying as she pounded dough or rubbed in flour and fat. He'd felt a particular bond with her. They used to wink at each other when they'd hear the Colonel yelling, Bob would say cheerio and set off back to Bessemer's.

One of his regular jobs had been to clean up the boardroom table after meetings. Heavy cut-glasses with half an inch and more of yellow liquor still in them were abandoned, and ash trays crammed with cigarette ends and the stubs of cigars. Forbidden objects. Pubs were places of disrepute, which you would never enter. He'd sipped the stuff from the glasses and it had cauterized his throat and burned all the way down to his stomach and made him feel sick. Next he'd puffed on a cigar and choked. *You look really poorly,* Ma had said, when he couldn't eat and had to go straight to bed. That had been a lesson, and he never tried it again.

Other occasions scraped his nerves. He could smile at them now. He'd often had to take a hansom out to the golf-course to book a game for the Colonel. One day he arrived back at the works and announced that he'd run his errand, and the Colonel had turned on him, his face working and eyes glaring like Amy's pot doll's. *You're a damned young fool!* he'd spat at Bob, and Bob had thought the Colonel would strike him. When he was angry he hissed snakelike and the saliva frothed over his glistening lower lip. Bob watched fascinated and repelled. He never did know what crime he was supposed to have committed. Perhaps it had been totally unconnected with him. Masters and servants ... Of course he'd kept his place, but he'd looked and wondered and questioned why there should be colonels living in huge villas and messengers who must book games of golf for them and lug golf bags out to cars. He'd seen the same question in the cook's eyes, or suspected he had.

Rendel always said, that the war had simply postponed the day of reckoning, which would come.

The pot of porridge and half pound of bread interrupted the long-running sequences of his thoughts for a short time. He had learned to make an event of meal times by eating very slowly.

The cells, being poorly ventilated, were stiflingly hot in Summer. One morning when the warder unlocked the cell opposite, Bob saw that the other CO was lying unconscious on the floor. He broke out in a rash of sweat and thought the man must be dead. Before he could do anything, the warder bellowed, "D412 slop out!" and hurried along the landing. Then Bob heard him shouting, "Come on, get up! Out you go!"

"But he might be dead," Bob said.

"No talking!" the warder screeched and continued shoving the prisoner with his foot.

Later in the day the other man sat again on his stool as before, and Bob realized that he must have fainted with the heat.

In winter they suffered for the opposite reason: it was intensely cold. The heating pipes didn't work and damp seeped through the stone floor. Bob noticed shiny red bumps on his toes and heels. Chilblains appeared on his fingers too and they kept him awake at night with their itching and smarting. But these were minor afflictions compared to the tooth-ache, which gnawed and drilled immediately they went out on exercise in the cold air. Once it started, it persisted the whole day, and Bob could think of nothing else. His jaw burned and throbbed, and there was no way of getting respite from it.

The awful monotony was broken up at times by still more dire events: they hanged men periodically. The whole prison was sealed with a deathly hush. Bob knew they all listened for the condemned cell to open and for the man's footsteps as he walked to the gallows. They waited for the striking of the clocks and later the tolling of a bell signifying that the sentence had been carried out. Bob wept in his cell and tried to pray for the unknown prisoner. How horrible to be walking towards that drop and falling with the noose strangling you! And what about the chap who'd have to carry it out? Suppose the man had been innocent ... poor wretch. The parade ground had been like that when they shot the lad who'd deserted ... For days the same doomed feeling lingered in the prison. They were all degraded by it.

The carrying out of the death sentence made you question still further the world in which you'd grown up. People like Colonel Sir Archibald Waring were the important ones in the town – just like Sir Reginald Northwich, the chairman of the Tribunal. They only had to snap their fingers and the minions leapt up and came running. Leaving Bessemer's had given Bob a lot of satisfaction. By the end he would have preferred to starve rather than continue as the Colonel's lackey.

Things filtered through to them. The mood of the COs was growing more militant. They were beginning to refuse to work in prison because they said they were being forced to engage in Work of National Importance, which had been given to those who had opted for the Government Scheme. They had rejected the Scheme and had chosen to remain in prison. Bob could sense the mounting tension and waited to see what would happen. About this time he noticed that Rendel had disappeared and he learnt from someone that he'd been released, re-arrested and sentenced again. This was a process which some men had already endured three or even four times. Joe was still at Princetown and Matty in Lincoln Prison. *When would it all end?* he wondered. At times he couldn't remember why he was there, or what he was doing. He'd forgotten the cause. Perhaps he would die there and be buried in the grave-yard together with those poor bastards they'd hanged ... so be it. Let them have their war and their power and glory ... 'For thine is the kingdom, the power and the glory'. Such words were even in the Lord's Prayer. The discovery horrified him for a whole day and a night. These were words he had repeated over and over at least once daily for as long as he could remember and now they appeared primitive to him. Power was synonymous with might, and glory was self-aggrandisement – words used by conquerors. And he knew that there could be no winning and losing: they were the same thing. Christ would not have had anything to do with power and glory. He came back to his old favourite, St Francis of Assisi, 'It is in dying that we are born to eternal life', a different message, different values. Give up all and at the end, you might, just by chance, glimpse grace. *Nothing ever is as you think it will be*, he mused one afternoon. He could hear children over the thirty foot high wall. Perhaps it was a school, who could say? But hearing the clear, young voices made him think of freedom ... and it came to him that he was helping in some very minor way to extend freedom to them. They were as yet untouched by the world's corruption. He was struggling to let them hold their own beliefs and think for themselves. At that, a wonderful sense of comfort stole over him. He paused with the needle in his hand: he was happy.

Chapter Thirty-One

He puzzled as to why Amy's face could move between the two extremes of plainness and beauty. As the train gathered momentum and the vault of the station began to dither and flash with speed, he was left with an impression of mysterious loveliness. A small figure in a pale-blue coat and skirt and high-necked white blouse, she had been standing alone, gazing after the train. Then she was sitting on the horse-hair sofa, holding his hands. That day had passed in the twinkling of an eye, whereas the weeks and months of solitary confinement seemed not to move. It was as though he had ceased to exist. And then he thought, *why should I complain? We've had this day, we took it, we lived it.*

He was able to smile and chat with his escort and hide the day's preciousness, along with his memories of Keir Hardie and the moments in France. They were not for everyday remembering.

It was the same old thing: two years' hard labour and the reading out before three thousand soldiers.

"Thank you," he said, on hearing the pronouncement of the sentence, "it will be an honour to do it."

By now the wrongness of the silence rule had begun to prey on Rendel, and he decided to protest against it. He talked openly to the CO in the cell opposite, and he was immediately brought before the Governor and sentenced to bread and water and solitary confinement.

"I'm afraid, Governor," Rendel said, looking across at him, "that I'm no longer prepared to obey the no-speaking rule, because I believe it to be inhumane. It can send people mad."

The previous day, he had managed to smuggle a letter to the press, taped under someone's foot, describing what was happening and what he intended to do. News spread like wildfire through the heating pipes and men bumped into one another in corridors. Soon everyone was talking. They were marched into the hall normally reserved for remand prisoners and put in the punishment cells, but mass-resistance grew. Rendel watched the excitement igniting the prison and smiled.

The following day, without explanation, they were returned to their normal quarters. Rendel guessed the authorities were afraid. Nevertheless the talking continued, and they formed committees and regulated their times of silence and their times of communication. Men sang, there were poetry recitals, debates – amazing bursts of sound burst out. Voices called, shouted whispered. It took a while for the first crazy uproar to die down. It lasted two whole days, and then early on the next morning Rendel was taken away, handcuffed, to Liverpool prison and placed in solitary confinement on bread and water.

It was getting to him now and he lay on the floor coughing until he vomited. His chest hurt and he sweated. It was a return to the old fever he'd known in France. Time stopped again and he felt light-headed and didn't know where he was. Henry and he were playing in the nursery. They argued over a wooden train. *It's mine! No it isn't. Yes it is. You break my things.* Henry's eyes were crystalline and their glitter came at him like a snake. *Darling, do please stop!* Mother found it tedious. *Where was nurse?* The clock chimed. No, he was alone in his room under the eaves where the swifts and swallows built in summer. The grooms' voices blurred below in the yard. Horses' hooves rang on cobbles. Down in the water-meadows it was extraordinarily peaceful. Dusty-white meadow-sweet swam above the long straight grass stems and jade dragon-flies hovered over the trout stream. Summer days lying on the bank, peering into the weedy water, watching darting minnows. Oh what joy! Now they will tell you ... he was addressing a crowd somewhere. He aimed to change the gloomy distrust on their faces, to touch them and draw out hope and enthusiasm. It could be done, each man contained ... oh, he had brushed shoulders so long with the Quakers ... contained 'that of God' ... that of God. His head ached. *Oh, Amy*, he thought, *you'll be cross and sad and lovely.*

What year is it? he wondered fretfully, as a renewed spasm of coughing caught him. He froze and burned. It seemed impossible to keep warm, and even wearing all his clothes, his teeth still chattered, and his limbs shook until they ached.

At times he became aware of a warder looking down at him, but he was a long way away and his eyes wouldn't focus. He was probably being commanded to get up and exercise but he couldn't, nor could he even speak.

One night he was again dimly conscious of two figures in the door-way. Somebody said, "Relatives ought to be informed, we don't want any trouble." "No need; might not make it."

He wondered why that would be and what it would make. None of it mattered. He didn't care anymore. He seemed to be back in that moment near the ammunition dump, with the shells exploding round about him and the earth hissing and raining down ... it was the face of bliss, total capitulation: a land of no more striving, where a man might laugh at his petty struggles and blunders ... even his greatest triumphs faded before that awesome simplicity.

Chapter Thirty-Two

Amy swotted. She worked with despairing intensity. Rendel, being at the start of a new sentence, could receive no letters or visits for two months, so communication between them was completely dead. Or was it? She had begun to dream about him. She returned to that room in the tenement and heard the rain lashing the windows. He was always just about to tell her some vital piece of information, when somebody entered. On other nights she was back in that house whose rooms she dared not fully investigate. Sometimes she tried a locked door, rattling it repeatedly, but always gripped by the horror that it would open.

At the end of the three months' tuition in Manchester, she travelled back to London to take her pharmacy exams. That proved an awful disappointment. She passed in all but two papers and she had to re-take these. As there was no further time for tuition, she had to return to Mr Dows and the shop in Sheffield. She would have to re-sit the two papers in a further three months, whilst she was working.

Instead of a joyful home-coming, hers was a sombre event.

* * *

Lydia prepared to congratulate Amy as she stood in the doorway. "Amy, love, so you're back. We've missed you so much ..."

"Yes, Ma, I'm back. Work tomorrow."

Things had obviously not gone well. Amy had grown thin and her complexion, always colourless, now looked sallow. She had an air of defeat about her. Lydia went on folding towels, smoothing out creases and tweaking edges straight. How irritating children were and how much simpler life would have been, had Amy stayed at home and married Godfrey – but then Godfrey, it seemed, was dead. A sharp rheumatic pain caught her between the shoulder blades and took her breath away. The other day she had suddenly examined her hands, noticing how the joints had become arthritic and the backs already freckled with age. She'd been proud of her looks and this admission of age hurt. Her jetty hair was now brindled – as a girl, she remembered, it had been blue-black and its shimmer had entranced William, when after kidding her, he had pulled out her hair-pins and let it cascade down her back. They'd both been young then and he'd been handsome and very lively with his quick-silver moods. She hadn't known how his enthusiasms devoured him though and made him blind to her physical discomfort. Oh, he'd always been a good father, but he put his beliefs first. She had gone with him, because she was a loyal wife, but deep in her heart discontent nagged. Sometimes she had let herself dream a little ... she would have loved a touch of luxury: a feather boa, a string of creamy pearls, to be taken to a dance, where she would glide over glassy parquet and there would be emerald palms swaying gently and couples sitting at small tables whilst the band played, a world where you didn't have to make bread with coarse brown flour, or try to eke out meagre amounts of sugar to bake buns and cakes, which would nevertheless taste appetising – and not the eternal rub, scrub, pound in the cold cellar kitchen, and then the food queues. She'd stood hours in queues for sugar, butter, meat, just to be told they were sold out.

Amy had turned away, her face closed and all Lydia's frustrations and resentments sounded in her voice as she said, "Well, Amy, I must say, after all this time, I did expect you to be a bit happy to see us – instead there's just growls and moans and groans. Why can't we have a bit of pleasantness? I wish you'd never taken on the studying. I really do. It's been nothing but bother."

"Yes," Amy said and Lydia was surprised at the violence in her tone. "Yes, you would."

"You'd have done better settling down and getting married."

Amy didn't respond, but turned on her heel and went out into the yard.

* * *

Amy stood leaning on the wall. It was a cold day, the air smelling sooty from the many smoking chimneys, and a pall hung over the city. Home, and she was back, but she felt restless and depressed. She would have to start swotting again, but she felt she had lost the impetus. How the war was dragging on. She remembered hearing the bells ringing on that November day and the people rejoicing over the victory which they supposed to be within reach. About a week later everything had changed and they trembled before the German advance. It was the usual infernal ping-pong.

Just before Christmas, Amy received a letter from Bob, saying that concessions had at last been granted them. They could now talk during exercise and were allowed to walk in groups of two and three, and instead of the single exercise period, they were being given two outdoor breaks per day. But most marvellous of all, they were to be allowed four books at a time; *would she please send him his German grammar and a copy of The Tale of Two Cities, which were both in his bedroom, or should be?*

Only a matter of days after receiving his letter, Amy came home from work, feeling feverish. Her head ached, her legs were leaden and she was shaking with cold. Lydia stared at her.

"You've got flu," she pronounced. People were dying of flu. Auntie Bessie had been at death's door and a four year old two doors away had died of it. People were growing panicky.

Amy was sent to bed immediately with a stone hot water bottle wrapped in a piece of blanket. Lydia piled blankets on her. "You've got to sweat it out of you," she said, handing her a glass of lemon barley water.

For several days, she didn't know where she was and she

didn't much care. She was aware of her mother sponging her down, but the dampness and sweating persisted. Everything seemed to reek of dankness and her head ached.

From time to time her father came into the room and stood at the foot of the bed smiling at her. "Now Bits, how are you?"

"All right, Father, thank you," she always said, but she felt far from all right.

After about a week and a half she could get up but she felt too weak and dizzy to walk about, and she sat in an armchair, swathed in rugs. She was sitting like that one morning, when her father came with the newspaper in his hand.

"Bits," he said, and his face had fallen into folds of the utmost seriousness, "I've debated with myself, dear, but I think you ought to see this."

Amy understood from his tone and the set of his face, that she wasn't going to like what she would see. Her heart fluttered in her chest and she felt sick. He handed her the newspaper and she looked at the obituary column. At the top she saw Rendel E. Watson. She read it and put it down.

"He's dead, Father," she said, "Father, he's dead." Then she began to cry. Through her tears she saw the smudged jet pyramid with its sparkling mother-of-pearl birds and magic signs. The white faced clock ticked on.

"There, there." Her father stood beside her, stroking her hair back from her forehead.

* * *

Amy was off work for a month and when she was finally able to return, her skirts and blouses hung on her and her skin had a dull, yellowish gleam. The old zest had gone. She saw how her parents watched her at odd times. She didn't cry again, not after that first out-burst, but became very quiet and secretive. All her energies went into the work for her examinations. Even Mr Dows noticed she was different, and she was aware of him studying her too. She was glad that he was too nervous to ask her what was the matter – it would have hurt too much to explain, and she knew, if she once tried to speak of it, she would cry.

To and from work and all the time she served customers, Rendel was never far away. She walked with him along the Embankment and searched her memory for any nuances she might have missed. He carried her over the threshold. She sat facing him on the sofa and then he cried and she held his hand ... if only they could have had that night together ... why hadn't it happened? Fear and guilt had chivvied her throughout those hours, but somehow she had set them aside. How dreadful to have a potential for experiencing something quite wonderful and yet be so afraid that you did not live at all. Dows had not lived. And she? She had been trembling with terror but she had gone on. And now he was dead. She returned over that first period of mourning, when she had thought him shot in France. If only this time too, he were not really dead. She tormented herself endlessly with the idea. One evening she found herself leafing through the Bible in search of miracles. *I want a miracle. I must have a miracle. Please God, do let a miracle happen. Why were things set on an immutable course? Why, oh why?*

She was glad of the necessity for study, because that prevented her from following along the same obsessive track. Inside she was dead, quite dead. She went through the routine of dressing and brushing her hair, pinning it up, setting out for work, but it all happened to someone else.

When she walked through the city centre, past the Town Hall, she remembered the frenzy of the crowds, the lines of young men drilling, so much pomp and doomed innocence. She would try to recall the smell of Rendel's skin, the angle of his jaw, his gestures. He was in danger of hitting his head on lintels, and seemed to fold up when he sat down. His long legs were cramped unless he could spread out. When he sprawled, he seemed to be gaining energy for the next onslaught on some new project.

Where could he be? So he'd never made it, never left prison at all. Perhaps that wasn't necessary, perhaps he was free already. 'Live for that better day', he said, quoting Keir Hardie. *If we should come through ...*

Chapter Thirty-Three

Bob received regular letters from Amy. She had told him of Rendel's death, but he knew of it already as word had come through on the heating pipes and someone had seen the obituary in The Times. Somehow he couldn't shake off the despair which swept over him at the news. He thought of France, of the scene in the cells and hearing the Colonel, Rendel's brother, screaming with fury and the dull thump of flesh being pounded. He had been afraid for Rendel then, but he had thought ... what had he thought? He hadn't dared to think past the present moment. What would Rendel have done, had he lived? 1918 and still the war dragged on. Sometimes short letters came from his mother, and she didn't find writing easy.

"My dear son,

"We do miss you so much, as we do Matty and Joe. I wonder when we will see you again. Things are difficult now they are rationing sugar, butter and meat. But at least that cuts down the queues. Still can't grumble. Amy has been very poorly with the influenza, also Aunty Bessie. D.V. she will pull through.

"Hope you are well. I remain as always, your loving Mother."

The rain deluged and didn't stop for sixty hours. The cell was shrouded in perpetual twilight. Bob's nerves were troubled by the continual trickling of water in the pipes. He knew it was fatal to start noticing small things like that, the locking of doors, the warders trailing their keys, chink, chink, along the outer walls, the scrape of boots. They could drive a person into a complete frenzy.

Older men were being conscripted now, even the forty to fifty age-group were called up for the first time. He wondered at the disorganization this would cause in the men's families. Most would be fathers, who had perhaps already seen their sons die. Now the wives and daughters would face the loss of the breadwinner. It grieved him to think of it. They must be very short of young men by this time – all dead or maimed, a whole generation wiped out.

* * *

Months passed. Bob hardly noticed them slipping by. And then it was May and the cell became very hot and that filled him with a new restlessness. When he wasn't sewing mail-bags, he would pace up and down. The chap in the cell opposite went mad one evening when they were locked up and smashed every article of furniture in his cell. Bob heard the raving and the cracking and banging and the man's screams as the warders manhandled him down into the punishment cells where they would thrust him into a strait jacket.

He watched a full moon through his cell window, saw it float above a bank of cloud and rest there, bathed in a bluish-gold phosphorescence. The sight of it calmed him. The rising tide of bitterness and despair receded. He continued to sit on his stool, gazing up at the brilliant constellation spangling the webby mountain. There was peace, a mysterious, sounding void, it remained untouched alike by man's animosities or his joys.

* * *

The summer passed. The Germans were said to be within fifty-six miles of Paris. The Governor's war news was a jumble of offensives and counter offensives. They heard about President Wilson's fourteen-point peace plan. Bob pondered on what he had learnt, but he had the fear that the very peace treaties could contain the seeds of future wars: a wise man did not insist on the total humiliation of his adversary.

Autumn dragged on. Amy wrote to say she would be travelling down to re-take her exams. Then he heard she had passed one of the previous subjects but had still failed the other. He imagined her disappointment. She had once come to see him since Rendel's death and her thinness had shocked him. She'd had her long hair cut and shingled and she looked different – not the old Amy at all. He hadn't known how fond she and Rendel had been of each other, but he suspected the relationship had gone far deeper than he had ever imagined.

Afterwards he remembered that the date was November 22nd ... at the time, it had been just another November day. He was stitching in his cell when the maroons were fired. He didn't know what it could possibly mean. Eleven am and so gloomy it might have been late afternoon. He rang the emergency bell, and after a while the warder's heavy steps stomped down the corridor.

"Whatever is it?" Bob asked.

"The war's over."

For a second Bob sat speechless on the stool, his needle suspended, and then he felt the goose-pimples prickle on his back and forearms. *The end of the war! Dear God ... the end ...* He was glad when the warder slammed the cell door shut and blundered off. Four horrendous years later, the war was over. He thought of the millions of dead and the folly of it all, and he continued stitching, refusing to be moved in any way by what he had heard.

That evening the moon swam clear again. It was in the first quarter. He heard the clocks round about chiming the hours. They continued throughout the night after having been silent for four years.

Chapter Thirty-Four

On the Monday when the Armistice was announced, Amy had gone to work as usual and then the town's sirens began to howl. Everybody in the shops and offices around converged on the street. Strangers rushed up to one another and embraced. Amy saw a man and woman kiss. They were all caught up in the same ecstasy as they had been in 1914. *They haven't learnt anything*, she thought, watching the wild laughter and singing about her. *No, it's just the same as before, they're gone with the moment, possessed by it.* She turned on her heel and went back into the shop.

"Miss Henderson, aren't you pleased? The war's over, the war's over!" Olive Little clamoured.

"Well now, look at that!" Mr Dows even allowed himself to smile. "After all this time ..."

"Yes," Amy said, "the war's over."

Nobody worked any more that day. Amy, on her way up the hill, going home, met a neighbour, whose youngest child had died in the flu epidemic. "Look at them," she said, staring about her, "on Saturday I heard our Percy had been killed ... what have I to rejoice over? Let 'em have their Armistice ... it's nothing for folks such as us."

She, Amy recollected, had been scathing about the Henderson family at the beginning of the war ... so had most of the neighbours come to that, but now ...

* * *

It was perhaps a fortnight following the Armistice, in mid-December, that Amy received a letter from Godfrey's mother.

"Dear Amy,

"It is a long time since I was in touch with you, but I felt I must share our great joy with you. Godfrey is alive! We have received notification from the War Office that he is now in a military hospital in the London area. We are to go to see him today. Sadly it seems he has been blinded as a result of a head wound, but is otherwise well. I will be in touch with you again once he comes home.

"Yours ever,

"Marion Campbell."

Amy had thought she would never be able to experience surprise or pleasure again, for she had swung so often from joy to despair, that she could react no more. Nevertheless the news did delight her. Alive after all that length of time! She imagined his parents' complete wonderment ... it would still no doubt be too fantastic for them to grasp – Godfrey alive!

She showed the letter to her mother.

"Alive! May the Lord be praised – well, I never thought to hear that – but blind, poor boy, blind."

* * *

Six months after the Armistice, Bob, Matty and Joe arrived home separately. The first to come was Joe who had been in Princetown for two and a half years. Matty travelled from Lincoln one afternoon in the same week. Last of all was Bob. It was April 1919.

On an early May evening they all gathered in the parlour, together again after the passage of more than three years. Lydia looked at her sons and had to blink back her tears. William, work over for the day, put his arms around their shoulders. His eyes too were damp.

Only Amy was missing. She was re-sitting her pharmacy exams again in London.

"I always imagined this," Bob said, looking at Matty and Joe, and then at his mother. Her hair had whitened over those years, he noticed with regret, and his father's head was a little sunken and he lacked the bubbling good humour and bounce that Bob remembered. All of them were thinner. Joe's complexion was grainy and weather-beaten, his hands coarsened and nails broken from hard labour in summer and winter on the Moor. Matty had acquired a prison-pallor like his own.

To avoid the strain of having to speak, Bob escaped into the yard almost overcome by an uneasy feeling in his guts. He wasn't used to being with other people, and was quite content to lean on the wall, gazing down over the city. The taste of those days in 1914 came back to him ... he'd stood at that wall in a dream of Elizabeth Stanley, watching the lights come on in the houses and wondering what she might be doing. It was like half a life time ago. How could you consider that brief dalliance with her as anything other than a childhood incident? If you set it against friendship, a life-line in despair and suffering, it was just an embarrassing infatuation. Encountering death, not once but many times, gave you a greater reverence for all things sentient. He was amazed by the beauty of the spring evening, by the pattern of houses lying below and the navy-blue sky with its lone star. If he stretched out his arms, he could feel the air and no restraining walls. He could walk down that hill, feeling the darkness washing over his face. Then he thought of Rendel ... perhaps he was around too ... he must be.

He jumped with shock at the sensation of someone standing behind him. "Oh it's you!"

"Yes," Matthew said. "It's been a long time. Many's the time I thought I'd never make it."

"We're only just starting," Bob said, remembering Rendel. "That was all just a run in for it, preliminary training you could say. There's no time to lose."

Matthew didn't answer. He had taken up a position, with his hands resting on the uneven stones of the wall and was also gazing out over the city.

"You wonder about a lot of things, don't you," he said, turning to look into Bob's face. "At the time when they rushed you off to France – it was the Easter Uprising you remember – I was in Pentonville in July. There was just this little high barred window … you know how it is … I wanted to look out. I was suffering from one of my attacks of claustrophobia. I got up on the stool. It was evening. I could see the prison garden and some flower beds. There was a big chap walking there, swarthy, very arresting. You'd have called him a fine-looking man. Bob, he was gazing at the setting sun. I got a close look at his features. I've never seen a face like it, so noble, so calm. I got the idea he was at peace, ready for his fate."

"Who was it?" Bob asked, intrigued. It struck him that Matthew was different now from how he'd been before the war; then he'd been a rather pompous, annoying older brother. Joe always considered him a 'tight blighter'.

"Sir Roger Casement."

"Goodness!"

"They executed him of course, but you know, Bob, ever after, whenever I thought I couldn't bear it, I remembered that man's face in the setting sun. Yes, they executed him as a traitor, but I couldn't judge him for that … what's a traitor, what's a hero?"

"No," Bob mused. "I think we've all seen too much ever to want to pass judgment."

"Come on, we'd best go in to the others."

They went in together. The gas had been lit and Joe was telling Father about the Princetown routine. Ma came in with a tray of cocoa mugs and one of her miracles, almost fatless cakes.

"I've saved sugar for this," she said.

"Did Amy tell you, she heard from Godfrey's mother that he's still alive after all, but blinded?"

"Yes," Bob said. "Has she seen him?"

"No, not yet, when he comes back from his convalescence I expect she will."

It might have been just like old times before the war, Bob reflected, but it wasn't, and never could be again.

Chapter Thirty-Five

I've passed, she registered, *I've passed!* She'd thought if the day ever came when she'd be a fully qualified pharmaceutical chemist, she'd be leaping in the air and crowing with delight. And it did come to her pleasantly enough, and yet not with keen joy.

She'd spent the previous night in a hotel bedroom, suffering a bilious attack, as was her wont before exams. Now she was conscious of tentative hunger pangs. The examiner's cryptic words still rang in her ears. *Well,* Miss Henderson, *not brilliant, but a pass. I think I must pass you this time for a change.*

Before retiring to the station buffet, she sent a telegram home. 'Have passed,' it read, 'love Bits.'

After a tomato sandwich and a cup of tea, she caught the Sheffield train. She had letter from Godfrey's mother in her handbag and she re-read it.

"Dear Amy,

"Godfrey is back from Bournemouth and we hope you will come to tea. He has asked after you a number of times and I have told him you are busy with your examinations. However I would be delighted if you could visit us next Thursday – I know that is your half-day off. Please come at 3pm. Unless I hear to the contrary, I shall expect you.

"Yours ever,

"Marion Campbell"

The prospect of seeing Godfrey daunted her. They were all changed, totally changed – but would the alterations be so great as to prove insurmountable? She had written a note to say she would go.

At home they all embraced one another and wept. Amy lingered longest over Bob, because he had known Rendel.

"Congratulations, Bits!" they chanted.

Lydia had managed to whip up another cake. "You'll have no sugar for your cocoa for months after this," she said, surveying her handiwork.

"Ma, the war's over," Joe reminded her.

"That doesn't mean food can come flooding in. There isn't the man-power, love."

"So you're a chemist at last!" William said, an arm round his daughter's waist.

"Yes, Father, I've done it. I admit I've wondered whether I ever would."

"You're a stout lass, and I'm proud of you."

They toasted her in lemonade. "To Amy!" they said, standing round the parlour table. She saw their heads and backs reflected in the big over-mantel mirror, together with the black marble pyramids and the clock with its Doric columns. Those objects had been there as long as she could remember but now they were imbued with strange vibrations from the past, as though they had soaked up wave upon wave of emotion: love, despair, sorrow, anger, loneliness. They had become more than pyramids and a clock.

"Thank you," she said, smiling. "And can I make another toast, to the dead!"

Bob, standing beside her chair, took her right hand and squeezed it. Amy felt her tears brimming over.

Chapter Thirty-Six

It was a detached house in a well-to-do neighbourhood and it took Amy two tram-rides to reach it. The day was very warm but over-cast. She wore a pale-grey costume and lilac blouse and some lilac satin shoes. Colour always dazzled her but in those months since Rendel's death, she had been unable to bring herself to think about matching clothes or attractive window displays. Now, for some reason, she fell back on her old love of colour for support. She had dressed with great care, even though Godfrey couldn't see her.

She went up the drive between the pale mauve and pink rhododendron billows. Bees hummed over the blossom. The previous night's dream returned to her. Again she entered that now familiar house with its locked doors and its scream, but this time she passed from room to room, finding them all empty. She had woken with a curious feeling of gladness.

Mrs Campbell answered her ring.

"How very nice, do come in."

Amy took a deep breath. She had an impression of tall, willowy graciousness, which matched the interior of the house, where rugs and carpets were pale and water-colours adorned the walls and there were big armchairs and deep sofas covered with chintz. Roses crowded silver rose-bowls and smudgy-blue scabious inclined gracefully from a slender glass vase.

"He's in the garden," she said, "would you rather go down by yourself?"

"If you don't mind, Mrs Campbell, I think I will."

"Just down there!" She pointed out through some French windows beyond a shrubbery.

Amy tried to make sure her approach was audible. He was sitting in a basket-chair with his back to her.

"It's all right," he said, "I've heard you."

"Oh good."

"Don't be scared."

"I'll try not to be."

She went round his chair and sat down in a striped deck-chair beside it. "Mm, that's nice. What a marvellous garden."

"Glad you like it."

"It's a lovely area, this."

"Yes, I suppose so."

"So quiet – no trams, no barking dogs – just beautiful gardens and long drives."

"And snooty people."

"Now then …"

"Come on, you were different in the old days, weren't you?"

"Was I?"

"You know, you were – have you forgotten all those back-kitchen discussions – dare I say 'arguments'?"

She let herself look at him properly then. His clever eyes, often probing and mocking in their expression, wandered vacantly. A deep red scar like an Indian ink scrawl scored his right temple and travelled across the bridge of his nose.

"No, of course I haven't."

"Do I look very bad?"

"No."

"No need to lie. We were frank with each other before."

"I've told you the truth."

"No, you haven't. What do you look like, Amy? Have you changed?"

"I've got short hair now. Yes, I suppose I'm older."

"I wish I could see you. I've got so much to learn. It's like going back to early childhood."

"I can imagine."

"I don't know what I intend to do yet. By the way, heartiest congratulations! Mother tells me you're a fully-fledged chemist now."

"Thank you."

"You were determined. Does it feel good?"

"I've not started yet, have I? I'm going to save until I can open my own business. It's what I've always said, isn't it?"

"I was grateful for your writing to me all those months and months."

A lull fell on them. Amy listened to the humming of the bees and every now and then a cricket chirred dryly. Blackbirds sang and she saw swallows swooping above the house.

"What are you thinking?"

Amy jumped with shock and couldn't answer at first. "I was thinking how peaceful it all seemed compared with …"

"Yes, I never expected to come back … no …and then, oh it doesn't matter … Tell me what you've been doing, tell me about you."

She found things to say, trivialities. Bits of news about Dows and the shop and its day to day running and the exam questions, but never about her terrible loss, or the grinding emptiness, the feeling of despair. For him she pretended those had not happened.

Afternoon tea was served out there under the trees. Mrs Campbell poured mint tea from a silver tea-pot and the china was so delicate Amy feared lest she break something. Occasionally a reference would crop up to John, the son who had been killed.

Godfrey concentrated on discovering the whereabouts of his cup and managing to replace it on the saucer. Amy guessed at the strain and frustration of trying to locate objects and estimate their approximate distance from one another.

At the end of tea Amy said she ought to be going.

"I wish you wouldn't," he said, "you've only been here five minutes."

She stayed until eight and saw that he still didn't want her to leave, although he looked exhausted. He walked down the drive with her and stood by the gate.

"I'm glad your brothers got back safely," he said. "They are very brave men."

"Thank you," was all she could manage.

"I would like to keep in touch, Amy, if you should have time now and then ... I appreciate ..." his voice tailed off. Amy's eyes filled with tears.

"Don't ..." she said. He'd noticed the change in her voice, for he groped to find her hand, and held it.

Chapter Thirty-Seven

Matthew, much to his surprise, found a job almost immediately. A relative of Dr Ziegelmann, who had been interned on the Isle of Man for the duration of the war, had been released and had returned to his directorship of a steelworks. He took Matthew on to head his foreign section. But Matthew, now spruce in his navy suit and tie, sitting before his typewriter, drafting letters to European countries re-building after the war, found his concentration slipping away, he was in the grip of a longing so intense it felt like a burning ache in his chest. He saw the woman in her man's jacket and cap, dark bronze hair blowing across her cheeks as she stood in the yard looking across at him. She moved about that twilit kitchen where a fire always burned in the range and two jungle-striped cats and sometimes dogs sprottled on the hearth. And he watched the sway of her haunches, saw how their lovely roundedness called out to be caressed. There she was marooned in her isolation on that moor ... a place of dreams. Curlews and peewits called overhead in summer and the gorse shone yellow as egg yolks and the heather and ling blazed pink and maroon ... and then the winters raged and the mist bowled in. He hated it in his guts but he longed for it, and for Dora, the fae woman ... *What a fool he was, he didn't even know her postal address ... couldn't write to her.* Things like letter-writing had been remote from their minds. They hadn't been able to imagine a world when the war would be over.

When this mood came on him, he was almost overpowered by restlessness, saw himself back in his convict days, working in the quarry, with the white dust flying about him and the sun burning down on the bleached stone, and ochre ragwort flourishing in the gullies. *Why was it,* he wondered, *that a painful experience could hold you in its thrall so that you might long for it?*

On his way home in the evenings he stared about him at the

smutted buildings. The factories resounded with clanking and screeching and dust jigged along the tram tracks, where the rails gleamed like blades of sprung stainless steel. The works never closed, day and night the blast furnaces blazed. He set all that, his home town, against the unfettered wildness of the moor, and he was tormented by a longing to be away from the confining city. But he knew he must bide his time ...

* * *

Joe, back in his father's shop, found his hands clumsy on the scissors and wielding the cut-throat razor. The white coats and towels, the prissy tidying and brushing down, settling of cloths round customers' necks, all seemed alien to him. He didn't remember it as being like this. He missed the working parties and the jokes, but then he'd find himself back in his cell with the endless silence and the voices screeching for mercy, and he was relieved to be cutting hair, and pretending to his father that he knew what he was doing. Sometimes though he'd notice how his father watched him, almost as though he'd realized how it was with him.

* * *

For Bob, things were far harder. He could find nobody to employ him. Matty, he guessed, could maybe have helped him secure a post, but he didn't want that. As a former CO he was a marked man. Lots of COs suffered the same fate, he knew. Former teachers and lecturers were regarded as social pariahs and not reinstated.

Through a letter from Graham, Bob learnt that the NCF was to hold a Concluding Convention at Friends House, Bishop Gate in London, from the 19th to the 20th of November, and he decided to attend.

It was a strange and moving moment to be amongst hundreds of men who had all known similar experiences. He saw faces he recognized from Wormwood Scrubs and those from France. Rendel was brought painfully close, so that he could have wept for him and all the others, the seventy or so dead COs and the millions of young soldiers who had not survived. He looked about, seeing his contemporaries, all prematurely aged. There they stood, a handful of representatives of that missing generation.

At the end he listened to Clifford Allen, once so striking, now a cadaverous, wasted figure, broken in health.

"We have discovered in our prison cells that very notion, which is today challenging the old world order ... the notion that men will only feel obliged to serve the community, of which they are part, when they come to respect each other's liberty."

He went on to conclude, "We were in prison. Today we are free, but the world is still in prison. It can be released by the spirit of unconquerable love. 'Ye that have escaped the sword, stand not still!'"

And it was as though Bob felt Rendel's hand touching his shoulder. He knew he would return to Sheffield and in some way, how he didn't yet know, work for that better world, and he would not forget.

**TOP HAT
BOOKS**

Historical fiction that lives.

We publish fiction that captures the contrasts, the achievements, the optimism and the radicalism of ordinary and extraordinary times across the world.

We're open to all time periods and we strive to go beyond the narrow, foggy slums of Victorian London. Where are the tales of the people of fifteenth century Australasia? The stories of eighth century India? The voices from Africa, Arabia, cities and forests, deserts and towns? Our books thrill, excite, delight and inspire.

The genres will be broad but clear. Whether we're publishing romance, thrillers, crime, or something else entirely, the unifying themes are timescale and enthusiasm. These books will be a celebration of the chaotic power of the human spirit in difficult times. The reader, when they finish, will snap the book closed with a satisfied smile.